Routine Matters

Routine Matters

Published by The Conrad Press Ltd. in the United Kingdom 2023

Tel: +44(0)1227 472 874

www.theconradpress.com

info@theconradpress.com

ISBN 978-1-915494-54-2

Typesetting and Cover Design by: Charlotte Mouncey, www.bookstyle.co.uk

The Conrad Press logo was designed by Maria Priestley.

Printed and bound in Great Britain by Clays Ltd, Elcograf S.p.A.

Routine Matters

Neil Deane

An unused memory gets lost, ceases to exist,
dissolves into nothing – an alarming thought.
The faculty to remember must be developed.
Before your inner eye, ghostly arms emerge,
groping around in a dense fog, aimlessly.

Christa Wolf, from: 'Kindheitsmuster' (1976)

This book is dedicated to three Liverpool legends
who passed away before, during and after
the writing of this book: Bert Deane,
Eric Wheeler and Sylvia Deane.

1

Nat Wilson's unruly past was repeating on him again and in a form he knew only too well: the dreaded dream, this one packed with a disturbing mixture of beauty and pain. Odd bedfellows indeed, as they joined him in an unholy threesome, making the struggle through another balmy night in Greece without air conditioning and female company that bit harder. The woman in the dream fitted the bill with a vengeance: natural, overripe, with an understated but inviting smile and full lips that beckoned him to move his close to hers and kiss them. This was the beautiful bit, but something was preventing him from doing just that, and he realized that she could neither see him nor feel him. The sole purpose of her presence was to reawaken all the old desires without fulfilment. That was the pain bit.

There was an additional edge of sadness throughout the dream sequence which ensured a sweat-drenched pillow when he finally awoke: there was a matter-of-fact message circulating inside his brain, like a public announcement endlessly repeated at an airport or railway station, conveying to him that the loss of the dream woman meant that he would never again find the slightest crumb of happiness for the remaining years of life on Planet Earth.

He was now on the edge of sleep, just on the waking side, and it was frightening stuff. Only Kafka's oversized beetle was scarier in the story of Gregor Samsa waking up to find himself transformed into an insect; but at least *his* agony was of relatively short duration when his traumatized but unfeeling family quickly gave him the coup de grace a few days later, not allowing his insect life to drag on for too long. Kafka's other non-hero, Franz K., the man plagued by guilt after being arrested in his bed for no apparent reason, was also put out of his misery after a few short weeks of confused meanderings. But the message in Nat's dream had a harrowing ring of eternal damnation about it.

Nat's panic ebbed a few seconds after he opened his eyes: he realized that he was neither a beetle nor was he about to be arrested. He rapidly distanced himself from the infernal nature of the dream and normal service resumed almost instantaneously.

As he shook off the emotional torment the dream had been trying to create, he began to appreciate that it had, aesthetically speaking, much to commend it. The images of the long-lost woman were wonderfully idealized. As he lay there pondering, he felt slightly peeved that there had not been more bare flesh to enjoy – the closest it came to raunchiness was a shot of the girl in a short, white summer dress from behind as she gracefully disappeared up a narrow Mediterranean alleyway.

Many years before, at the height of his broken heart anguish, such dreams made an almost nightly appearance and he would dread going to bed for fear of fiendish images haunting him through the night. Recovery times took up half his days and it was at least a year before the dreams started to go away. By the end of the second year of suffering, they were only happening once a month, and after three years, they came and went, amounting to an average of half a dozen per year. Their intensity never weakened but they began to bounce off him more quickly, as this rare nocturnal Grecian jolt just had. The 'time heals all wounds' cliché, like all clichés, was boring, but annoyingly true. Recovery eventually came and he was able to turn in without the constant fear of hellish nights.

He had the time to ponder on this particular dream, philosophize and develop his thoughts on its contents because he was, as usual, not in any hurry, not being subjected to the normal rigours of working life. He had decided to live on a Greek island during the winter months. He would return to another island off the North West coast of Europe, called Great Britain, when spring returned and stay there until the summer equinox, before returning to his exiled home, Germany for the final months of summer.

A solid comprehensive school education, caring, hard-working parents and on-the-same wavelength friends who shared his love of music and football contributed to Nat growing to become a stable, thoughtful, likeable sort of lad in his home town of Liverpool. Unspectacular, modest post-war prosperity meant that he wasn't spoilt but, as an only child, he never wanted, either. Memories of his parents' way of coping in a world of low pay, no connections and strictly limited opportunities always kept his feet firmly on the ground and his gratitude swelled as the years went by. Not leaving school at the first opportunity to contribute to the family budget was still not the norm in such strands of society during his teens but his mother's belief and desire that he should get "an education that we didn't get" prevailed.

On 22 June, the anniversary of Hitler's first big mistake in his Second World War project, the invasion of the Soviet Union in 1941, Nat was planning to return to the place which caused all that trouble for his parents' generation: Berlin. He had left the strike-plagued, divided, underproductive battlefield of Britain at the end of the seventies and happily embraced the serious, no-nonsense, full-on prosperity of Germany. For thirty years, Germany gave him something he always doubted Britain could: the chance to make a good living in a society that grasped the fact that social justice and stability had a price worth paying. Thatcher was for him the beginning of the end for those sorts of aspirations and as he observed the direction of travel his country had taken in the subsequent thirty years or so, he realised that leaving was one of his better decisions.

As the eighties got underway, it seemed that his hometown was almost suffering as much damage as a result of Thatcher's monetarist policies as it had suffered under the wartime bombs dropped by his new host country. He was happy to be out of it; Liverpool had been the only reason for his feeling any sort of pride in his roots despite the overpowering sense of gloom enveloping every aspect of life there when he finally left. He felt a dull pain when he gently tore himself from those roots but his sense of owing a debt to Germany for providing a safe haven was now stronger.

Nat's crumb from Germany's economic miracle cake came in the form of the flat he had been able to purchase in Berlin towards the end of his working life and the few rainy-day pennies he had in the bank. He had made the flat his base during the summer months until 3 September, another sinister date in the history of Anglo-German relations. He had booked his flight to Greece for that day, restarting his annual cycle just as the locals were getting ready for the final batches of late summer tourists.

This freewheeling, semi-nomad lifestyle was possible thanks to a lottery windfall that had come his way a few years previously. It was not an amount that would allow him to buy yachts, private jets and uninhabited islands in the Caribbean, but he soon discovered, after a brief but intense look at the maths, life expectancy tables and projected inflation and property value figures for the next dozen years or so, that he could just manage a financially care-free life with the occasional dose of hedonistic madness and casual spending thrown in. Moreover, he wouldn't have to work another day in his life.

This comfortable life could go on, according to these calculations, until his sixty-sixth birthday, by which time the money for occasional luxuries would dry up, although financial security would then be assured thanks to two pensions accrued from thirty years of uninterrupted employment with slightly above-average earnings. This final security blanket would kick in on the aforementioned birthday. He would then also have enough money to pay off the mortgage he had taken out on a spacious cottage in North Wales. He would sell up in Germany, to add an extra layer of financial security, and devote himself largely to what he believed, perhaps mistakenly, to be his true vocation: writing.

He figured that the North Wales cottage plan would be the ideal environment for a budding writer like himself: cool, damp weather, peace and quiet and fuck-all else to do with your time. He also reckoned that by the time he reached his mid-sixties, he probably wouldn't be up to doing much more with his life than writing a thousand words a day, going for a daily gentle stroll and having the occasional quiet pint. He was already bracing himself for a vaguely anti-English feeling down at the local pub but felt sure he could cope. Surely that age of nasty Welsh nationalism, when the English regularly returned to their holiday homes in North Wales to find them vandalised, daubed with insulting graffiti or even burnt to the ground was over? Anyway, it wouldn't be a holiday home, but his home full stop, so why should that rile even the most extreme Plaid Cymru member?

He didn't feel English anyway; he was a Scouser, a breed the Welsh might see as a fellow sufferer under the oppressive boot of a London-based English establishment. And the Welsh of North Wales were used to Scousers, those people who flocked to their less than sunny beaches, filled their B&Bs on bank holidays and generally cheered the place up with their raw gay wit and repartee and their endless thirst for ale. Anyway, that's what he hoped, although he was aware that sometimes his socio-romantic naivety raised his hopes too high: the locals may well start talking Welsh the moment he entered the lounge. So what? They might have an exiled German barmaid with whom he could speak German and get his own back.

There was a further important reason for North Wales figuring in Nat's endgame plans: at the time of his Lotto windfall, he received an email from Liverpool Football Club informing him that it was "possible" that his application for a season ticket would bear fruits in the year of his sixty-sixth birthday. With the improvement of rail services on the North Wales coast allowing him to be at Anfield within sixty minutes, Nat romantically believed these developments to be a joint sign from God and his deceased father – they were telling him to visit his beloved hometown every second weekend to demonstrate his unshakable faith in their beloved football team. Amen.

An Anglo-Italian colleague from one of his previous lives in Liverpool once told him that when he woke up in the morning he didn't get into any long-winded prayer rituals, but just said, to God presumably, "Give me one more day." This seemed to him to be a pragmatic and no-nonsense way of maintaining some sort of regular communication with whoever had decided to give him a shot at life. It also neatly echoed the only line of the Lord's prayer that Nat knew by heart and which he muttered daily: "Give us this day, our daily bread". Nat had further refined his daily communication with God by saying thanks as he closed his eyes at the end of each day, rounding off his daily prayers with the minimum of effort and fuss.

Nat, therefore, liked to believe that he had his life "sorted". Up to this point in the proceedings, he reckoned he had had good luck and bad luck in fairly equal proportions. He had been brought up to believe "there's always somebody worse off than yourself" - a favourite saying of his mother's - and this blindingly obvious truism had often given him comfort when he found himself short of luck. If this bad luck/good luck cycle continued in a similar fashion until the final whistle, he believed he had the experience, common sense and, perhaps most importantly, the money, to see his modest plans through and shuffle off his mortal coil while thanking his lucky stars for a largely varied and fulfilled life. And the most important details of that life would be available for everybody to read when the final whistle did blow. Nothing ever turned out the way you imagined it would, of course, and he was painfully aware that his nomadic search for the truth through writing could be derailed at any time. He was already preparing himself once again for that eternal discrepancy between his feverish expectations and future reality.

Despite this sobering admission, he was pleased with himself for actually thinking about the future again: after turning fifty and letting in the customary demons that often accompany such milestones, he had spent unhealthy chunks of his waking hours mulling over the past, and it had been affecting his mental health. Neither did his obsession with the past make him popular with friends and acquaintances. In fact, he had gradually become a crashing bore, especially for those who had heard the long-winded stories of his previous life experiences many times before. In an embarrassing attempt to lighten up the proceedings, he would introduce most stories by starting to sing the Smiths' song *Stop me if you think you've heard this one before*. This annoyed people even more. He kept noticing that he was annoying more and more people, more and more often. This exacerbated Nat's mid-life crisis further and alienated him from his unappreciative audiences. He was in grave danger of becoming the classic grumpy old fart.

His last job before early-retirement, at a university in Germany, at least assured him a captive audience, his students listening patiently as he recycled his endless "when I was your age" monologues. He believed, naively perhaps, that part of his remit was to prepare young people for later life. What most of them really wanted was to muddle through their studies at a leisurely pace, become teachers (and civil servants to boot) and lead a comfortable life which would enable them to include trips around the world, including out-of-this-world adventures in funky Southern Hemisphere regions. When they were well into their thirties, their parents would dutifully offer them financial and property inducements to finally settle down properly and provide them with grandchildren, the only thing missing in their otherwise satiated, cosy post-war West German lives. These grandchildren would then one day become the next generation of materialistic pleasure-seekers, obsessed with social media, their thousand friends on Instagram and becoming specialists in getting what they wanted.

Nat had attempted down the years, largely in vain, to imbue these young folk with his incoherent, homespun Scouse Socialist Republic ideology, which he thought might change their thinking on the world and its manifold injustices. Ultimately, he was destined to be disappointed by the apparent lack of enthusiasm the world showed towards his well-meant ideas. Perhaps his former students were heeding his words after all, he thought, they just wouldn't admit it at the time. He assumed that young people would find their own solutions while old men would find theirs. Nat wanted out before any further generations depressed him into submission; the Lotto win had come just at the right time. He rarely missed anything about university life, apart from, perhaps, those captive audiences, even though most of his patient listeners were clearly ignoring his rallying calls.

Retired at fifty-two, the last few months had brought him distance and closure to help him to recover from his failure to change the world by influencing young people in what he thought was a positive and helpful way. He needed new priorities and decided that one of them should be to do something about his health, a challenge many men of his age attempted to face up to before the final remnants of sprightly youth and rising sap disappeared altogether. He would lose weight, take regular exercise, reduce alcohol consumption and organise a more sensible diet. He accepted that he couldn't change the world, so he would change himself; well, at least certain parts of himself, particularly his body, which was in need of an extensive overhaul after years of general neglect. Living on a Greek island, he argued to himself, would be the ideal place to maintain and develop a healthier way forward.

As he approached his fifty-fifth birthday, he reminded himself of another reason for cutting down on the bad life: his mother had died at that age and he breathed a sigh of relief when he got past that sad anniversary; he wanted to assuage the lurking fear of not making it. Not that his parents were ever able to indulge in anything vaguely resembling an excessive lifestyle; attending a weekly dancing course, an occasional drink in the local pub and a once-in-a-blue-moon trip to a steak house was as close as they ever got to pushing the boat out. And neither did a healthy diet and weight reduction necessarily stop you from getting cancer, the dreaded disease which finished his mum off; but at least he was doing something to ward off other debilitating and unpleasant malaises for as long as possible.

But as he continued to ponder about reaching the spooky fifty-five-year mark and his plans to write a book, he felt a number of important questions vying for his attention. Bearing in mind John Lennon's obvious but accurate quote about life being something that got in the way while you were making other plans, he asked himself the equally obvious question: was there any guarantee that he was going to reach sixty-six? And other equally urgent questions started bugging him: what was stopping him from starting his book now? Why did North Wales have to be the only location to write in? Couldn't you write anywhere? Weren't fifty-five years of material enough?

Were the next twelve years – if his Creator was going to grant him those years – so crucial for inclusion in this planned work? He already knew the answers to all these questions so he decided to make a start on a book immediately.

By bringing forward the starting date, he had also stumbled on a solution to a problem he had permanently struggled with since his Lotto win: the tricky challenge of filling the day with meaningful activities when you weren't in full-time employment. He would start writing that day and every day. The empty spaces in the next twelve years would be beautifully filled up with profound thoughts and creative ponderings, resulting in a work of mature brilliance. A new Nat, in rude health and feeling twenty years younger, would go out on a high.

He was enjoying his own self-deceiving pep talk until he remembered what his euphemistic "going out" actually meant, at which point his fear of dying alone in a house on a Greek island returned. He had collected all sorts of emergency numbers when he moved in, but he experienced a brief cold sweat whenever he wondered how long he would have to wait in the event of an emergency. He was never able to pluck up the courage to ask any of these emergency services this question, but common sense told him that, if the worse came to the worst, his isolated location could mean the difference between life and death. And death probably had a better chance than life. He pulled himself together and forced himself to focus on his major plan: writing a book. With that to occupy him and the positive effects of choosing good, healthy food, less booze and regular exercise kicking in, he should be around for a few more years yet.

He already had numerous bright ideas for his book, most of them not even half-baked. Not having attempted something like this before, he had no idea how to plan, start, organise and complete such a project. Did you plan your book or just make it up as you go along? Why didn't he just transcribe the contents of his dreams? There were certainly enough of them to fill a book. Kafka did that a lot, and *he* got away with it. This morning's dream would read well in print, he thought. Not much of a storyline, though. Did a novel have to have a storyline? Well, James Joyce's major works didn't. He quickly reminded himself that he was neither Kafka nor Joyce and attempting to copy, let alone emulate them, would be a sure-fire road to disaster. And (how) would he get it published? Did he want to get it published or just sell it or give it to anybody interested in reading it?

Writing a book was not as easy as it sounded. He considered taking a writing course - a distance learning course would be just the job. But then he remembered reading an article by Hanif Kureshi, a writer he respected and enjoyed, who trashed such courses as a waste of money. He had recently read Richard Ellmann's much-heralded biography on James Joyce in which he claimed Joyce believed that you found something to write about by writing. Sounded like a good, simple idea he could work with. He thought about it, eased himself out of his seat, got up, splashed water on his face, put the kettle on and contemplated another day on his Greek island.

Looking west, heading east

In the very beginning was love, endless love, long before Greece or Germany was on any horizon in Nat's field of vision. Anne hopes that in the end there will always be love. One day Nat would find out for himself.

He shivered as his mum washed his puny legs in the kitchen sink. From where he was standing, he could peek above the rotting double-hung sash window frame and look out into the backyard. Such was his high vantage point that he could see over and beyond all the backyards walls of the whole street; on summer nights, the western sun was just visible in the narrow band of sky to the left of the public house on the adjacent main road at the bottom of their street. Nat on high, with an imperfect but promising window to the world and the western horizon; his mum grounded, dealing with the practicalities of keeping a four-year-old lad clean in a world without a bathroom.

For over twenty years of Liverpool suburban life, the kitchen had doubled, tripled and quadrupled as a bathroom, meeting point, a place for food and endless cups of tea and as a place of refuge at the height of the May Blitz in 1941. The storage room under the stairs at the edge of the kitchen - known as a 'cooey' in Liverpool - served as a makeshift but ultimately useless shelter for four trembling little sisters and a hysterical mother during that frightening month of nightly air raids.

Anne wrapped him in a fluffy towel and heaved him out of the sink. 'God, you're getting heavy,' she sighed. The past also weighed heavy on her as she dried him off: she operated largely in two-time zones known as grim past and uncertain future.

Nat sensed that there was something for him out there, beyond the backyard walls; she hoped and prayed that there was. Time zone "now" kicked in and love took over: both revelled in cuddles and giggles as Nat squirmed around the kitchen floor. 'Are you ticklish, Nat? Are you ticklish?' she whispered gently in his ear as he squealed and wriggled in her arms. Anne wanted this to be forever; she knew it wouldn't be. All little Nat felt was a place that was safe and warm; later he learnt that other places offered something very similar from time to time, but never forever.

2

Despite his love of Greece and her people and his attempts to integrate into the Greek way of life, an early morning cuppa was a simple ritual from home that he could never shake off. None of this mind-blowing Greek coffee stuff first thing in the morning: that could come later in the day when tiredness set in, normally after a late lunch. This slavish adherence to the quaint British insistence on having a good and proper cup of tea before attempting anything first thing in the morning served to remind him that he was still a Brit, albeit a watered-down one. Nat had followed Leonard Cohen's advice from the outset about living in Greece as a non-Greek: remain a tourist. Well, a culturally-aware tourist.

With one hand gripped around the handle of his hot mug of strong tea, he sat on his balcony in the warmer months and enjoyed the view, the silence and the sea. He would rock softly on his chair, trapped in some sort of trance. The rocking soothed his vulnerability, helping him to forget that he was an awful long way from home. Sometimes a cat joined him on the balcony, which added further comfort and reassurance.

After gathering himself sufficiently, he continued his morning ritual with a strange German-Greek breakfast: German rye bread lovingly plastered with an odd concoction of feta cheese, olives, olive oil, and topped generously with freshly chopped garlic. Occasionally, he would open a tin of sardines and chop some onions and garlic onto that. The one constant was the presence of garlic; sometimes he would just have a slice of bread with garlic and a sprinkle of olive oil. (Over the years, his Internet research on the healthiest things to eat consistently revealed that nobody ever had a bad word to say about garlic and, apparently, you could eat as much of it as you wanted without any harmful side effects). He let himself down once a week with bacon and eggs: dangerously unhealthy and no garlic. Otherwise, it was a truly eccentric multi-cultural breakfast routine which sprang from his belief that you should take the best from whichever culture you come into contact with and disregard the bad bits. He believed that his breakfast habits neatly reflected this philosophy.

Since his break with the world of work at the age of fifty-three, Nat had spent a year in Liverpool after his dad's death and had been living half of the time since then in Greece. He lived in a spacious rented apartment on a small island in the South Aegean Sea. He moved in in September for the last four weeks of the tourist season and paid the same tourist rates throughout the winter in exchange for a piping hot daily meal of his choice from a local *taverna*, delivered to him every day at 4 p.m., a weekly change of bedding, and all his clothes washed and ironed. An Albanian cleaning lady gave the place a thorough once over every Friday morning between nine and twelve.

He felt a sudden attack of self-revulsion for wondering one day, as she bent over to dust behind his stereo system, whether she offered any additional services. Somebody at the agency that employed her must have been reading his dirty mind when the office manager, Kosta, hinted during his last visit there that he could send round a more versatile lady if Nat fancied the idea. Kosta didn't use such euphemistic and elegant language; it was rather a sordid offer, awkwardly intimated to him in his

Kosta's quirky English as they shared their customary Ouzo one Friday afternoon. He laughed off the offer, displaying fake indignation. But Kosta must have thought there was a reasonable chance of Nat considering the idea favourably and Nat was indignant that Kosta had guessed that it had crossed his mind, too. He was determined not to be enmeshed in any such sordid business arrangements, fully aware of the dangers lurking in starting that sort of life and those sorts of sex tourist relationships. Self-loathing would surely follow with a vengeance if he went down that road, he thought.

He was equally wary of becoming hooked on the demon drink; he frequented a local bar every second day, limiting himself to two small beers and having a knockabout chat with some of the local lads, young and old. Sometimes he would just sit there and read a book. He would treat himself to an Ouzo at the weekend and on feast days but drank only sparkling water with his late afternoon meal. When it was too cold to swim but still acceptably mild, he would walk through the hills for at least an hour a day. He watched what he ate and tried to limit himself to his substantial Anglo/German/Greek breakfast and the afternoon meal, never eating meat more than three times a week and always attempting to hit the suggested five daily portions of fruit and veg. He could watch live Premier League games at an "open-all-year" sports bar in town and the Internet provided any other information and entertainment he needed, but consciously fought the temptation of making social media his constant companion.

He got through two books in English a week and one book in French and German respectively per month. He could play any music he liked on his stereo system at any volume he wanted at any time of the day and night and nobody ever complained (There was nobody to complain, as the next living soul lived at least half a mile away). And he never went to bed any later than ten-thirty p.m. and rarely got up after seven a.m. He realized that for many people this sort of life might appear stifling and ridiculously over-structured. He justified it to himself by believing that a doctor would probably be in favour of this sort of regime, especially for a man of his age. If he cut out the alcohol completely, doctors would probably be citing it as the near-perfect one for a man approaching his mid-fifties.

He always remembered a comment made by a teacher at his secondary school back in Liverpool. Every Thursday, before the day's regular classes, he and his classmates were rounded up in the gym by a teacher with the mysterious nickname of M.B, who would talk about anything that he deemed beneficial for lads at the difficult age of fourteen and fifteen. There was little subtlety in his messages or communication style, warning them, for example, that shagging girls behind the bike sheds was not advisable. Girls who shagged behind bike sheds, he argued, were likely to be trouble.

Much of MB's advice was either not understood or ignored, but Nat laid great store by one of his utterances: 'You should never despise routine.' This piece of advice became more and more useful and relevant as the years went by and as Nat lumbered through his late forties, he turned the truism on its head and changed it to "You should always love routine". He used routine to keep nasty surprises at bay, improve the speed of daily task completion and compartmentalise his life. Yes, it was rather robotic, but robots are efficient and the need for economic efficiency was hard to ignore, especially at his age. Johann Wolfgang von Goethe, the highly esteemed German writer, poet and anthropologist, when asked for his philosophy on life, replied: 'To complete the tasks of the day.' Not a very spectacular reply, but the pithiness and truth of it were hard to deny. Woody Allen's statement, 'Living is 80% turning up' echoed Goethe's statement a couple of hundred years later.

At certain times in his life, Nat felt his overloaded head would explode as he tried to process all the advice and pearls of wisdom he avidly listened to from well-meaning older people and teachers down the years. He had also collected thousands of quotes from books, which he felt might help him to understand life. He figured that all this information would help to avoid later catastrophes, which, presumably, had already befallen the people giving the advice in the first place. His desire to pick up as many tips as he could along the way, and from as many sources as possible, probably had its origins in his father's reluctance to give him any. His grandmother's favourite saying remained strong and true: "The school of experience charges the highest fees."

He felt that his present life in three countries solution suited him for the time being but it could clearly not go on forever. There were sad bastard moments in the Greek slice of his year. The first week or two after the last tourists started leaving at the beginning of October was always a difficult transitional period. During September, he would invariably get chatting to tourists from Germany, Italy, Austria or Scandinavia. He missed them when they were gone.

He had devised his own outrageously judgmental guide to the different nationalities he met on the island. The Italians kept to themselves; the younger couples revelling in their own youthful beauty and sexiness, the older ones chatting non-stop, almost exclusively to fellow Italians, knee-deep in the seawater, but very rarely swimming. If they had children with them, they were spellbound in their presence and catered for their every whim and need. The Austrians were outwardly formal, consuming impressive amounts of beer and wine every day but available for a chat if you made the effort. You could spot the Scandinavians a mile off: subdued, but elegant and eloquent when you got talking to them. They took everything with a pinch of salt, commonsensical without being boring.

It was still hot in September and after one o'clock uncomfortably so. Nat became accustomed to the physical torture of this part of the day but fared worse with the dark and sinister mental torture chambers the heat vindictively pushed him into. This was the real challenge of the daily roasting hours during which every topic guaranteed to put the fear of God into him and breathe new life into any phobias, nasty hang-ups, painful memories he had or once had, lined up in his over-heated brain, licking their lips in readiness to inflict maximum pain and panic. His favourite music blasting through his headphones only served to intensify these nightmarish scenarios, particularly as many of the songs brought back vivid memories, not all of them good. This was also the reason why he invariably skipped the late afternoon siesta; he never slept without dreaming and the dreams were an unwelcome encore after the midday roasting session.

The heat gave every thought an unwelcome fuzziness; it was the enemy of clarity and rational thinking. The positive thoughts rolled around in a sweaty paste of fantastic unreality, negative ones drained him of strength and purpose, pushing him towards a frightening form of madness. Every form of physical movement was to be avoided between one and five o'clock unless he was in the sea or an air-conditioned room. And this was September when the fierce July and August temperatures touching forty degrees centigrade had receded. Nat had abandoned any plans of ever taking up residence on the island earlier in the year and all the locals had backed him in his decision.

Nat saw little evidence of his fellow tourists in the beach bar going through the same suffering as him in the September heat. Probably an age thing. They were, almost without exception, at least a quarter of a century younger than him and carrying far fewer kilos; their physical burdens were lighter and tortured memories of misspent youth and mistakes from the past had not yet found anything like a firm footing in their mental software.

Islands like these were ultimately reserved for the younger set, flown in from various northern European cities which produced beautiful Aryan specimens but which lacked beautiful weather to provide those specimens with the tanned finish their otherwise perfect bodies deserved. If Europe had suffered total defeat at the hands of the Germans in the war, these would be the citizens receiving all sorts of financial incentives to churn out as many offspring as possible to ensure that the "Master Race" enjoyed supreme power over any lesser races who dared to question that supremacy. The dream of racial purity would be an all-conquering reality in Northern and Western Europe and these folk would be shouting it from every rooftop and appearing on the front page of every Fascist periodical dedicated to personal health and Aryan well-being.

Nat was in little doubt that all the owners of the perfect bodies cavorting in front of him every day were getting plenty of practice in the bedroom in case they ever got the call to mass reproduce for the New Fascist Order; he was also certain, however, that they were taking all the right precautions in every one of their lengthy Tantra-sex sessions to ensure that potential offspring would not be slowing up their never-ending pursuit of pleasure and fun in the neo-liberal democratic order within which they were currently successfully operating.

Nat felt uncomfortable amongst so many young and beautiful people. He was well aware of the ravages of time on his middle-aged body and had accepted it as inevitable and natural, but the direct comparison with the perfect bodies regularly congregating within his immediate vicinity did occasionally weigh heavily upon him. He almost wanted to apologize for spoiling the view.

All these images troubled Nat as they invariably sparked off his regular, age-old contemplations on the transient nature of existence; as always, he knew such contemplations would lead him nowhere. He found some crumb of comfort in the fact that most of these beautiful people - the men, of course - might end up looking something similar to himself one day. He considered sharing this particularly sad gem of wisdom with one or two of them, perhaps after a couple of drinks. However, as all the men were, without exception, permanently and firmly physically attached to their delicious female companions, Nat saw little chance of gaining their attention to spread the bad news.

It wasn't an out-and-out party island and most of those he managed to make contact with were thirty plus, reasonably intelligent and generally charming. There were virtually no Brits on the island, which evoked mixed feelings in him: British banter with witty individuals could be world-class entertainment, but there was sometimes a goodly proportion of parochial bores. And if you got arguing with a rabid nationalist, for example, you were in big trouble.

He avoided talking to any woman who appeared to be alone: the thought of a quick "shufty" with anybody before they headed back to their home shores didn't appeal to him; in fact, it filled him with a certain degree of revulsion. He also found it hard to believe that women could take any great delight from such holiday hanky-panky. Sometimes, Nat would just stare across the bay, which might have put him into the creepy category with some women. He tried his damned best not to stare but sometimes failed miserably, thus relegating him to the worst possible category of male: the dirty old man.

Things got considerably tougher in the second half of November when night descended by five-thirty p.m., chilly temperatures ruled out any evening time activities and the wind sometimes howled all night. In this first year on the island, Nat descended into a mild depression. When December kicked in and Christmas approached, he shivered a lot, felt thoroughly isolated and started questioning his own sanity. He also noticed that in this period he was having more than just two beers every other day and his duty-free Scotch had disappeared by early December. Going to bed was a shivering, spooky experience. He momentarily reconsidered Costa's seedy offer, but realised, quite simply, that he was missing somebody to talk to.

January was the final mountain to climb, and when the worst of winter was over in February, he pulled himself together, reduced the booze intake and redoubled his exercise routine.

When the first Greek island winter was over, he realised he might have to consider an alternative, less miserable option for the following winter. He thought of booking an eight-week package deal in Morocco, or anywhere where there were sociable people and clement weather conditions in the winter months.

The first September of that first winter campaign did, however, throw up what might be called an interesting intermezzo. Reneging on his principle, he shared a couple of evening meals with a very attractive late-thirties Italian divorcee, Yvette. Everything was going fine until the third 'date', when she started opening up on her dastardly ex-husband. The details were starting to depress Nat and she insisted on his correcting and embellishing her English in order to express the profound horror of the final phase of their wrecked marriage.

'Ow you say, Nat, he was very, very, very....'

Nat proffered a few suggestions: 'Nasty?' 'Cruel?' 'Vindictive?'

'Oh, I don't know vindeective. What is meaning vindeective? How you spell that, Nat?'

Nat felt like he was back in the classroom, working very hard for his money with a very demanding client when all he really wanted to do was spend some quality time in harmless but tantalising flirting with Yvette as the Grecian sun disappeared into the calm Aegean Sea. As he normally footed the bill at the end of their pleasant but platonic evenings anyway, their arrangement had, in his opinion, all the characteristics of a bum deal.

But it got worse; a lot worse. A tear trickled down both her cheeks, quickly followed by a mild panting which developed into loud sobbing and much groaning. Her body began to rock from side to side. The other taverna guests were rightly disturbed, staring at this trembling mass of Italian womanhood. Nat wanted to point out to all the spectators witnessing this dramatic event that it had nothing to do with him but didn't know how. He grabbed a packet of tissues, quickly manoeuvred himself round to her side of the table and put his arms around her. The sobbing got worse. If Nat had subconsciously planned to get physical with Yvette, this was not the sort of physicality he had envisaged. Her face was a mess, red and puffy and smeared in make-up. Nat had seen many women crying before, but this was supernatural. And definitely not sexy.

The volcano slowly subsided, apologies profuse, but their evening was over and Nat knew with 100% certainty that their evening meal relationship had also come to an undignified end.

'So sorry, Nat, so sorry, Nat, I pay tomorrow, promeese,' she stammered as they said goodnight.

But Nat was determined that there would be no tomorrow and he spent the next four days in hiding, ignoring text messages, relieved when he spied her boarding a coach with a bunch of compatriots heading for the airport. He was a coward; he knew that. He also knew that he would have behaved differently a few years earlier. Now he just felt a sad sense of relief. The male instinct and desire were still there, the love of a beautiful woman still strong, but the choice was between exciting stress and emotional control, as it had also been so many times in the past; he now chose the second, healthier option. He had a beautiful Smartphone picture of Yvette and the two evenings before the meltdown were enchanting memories he could compartmentalise and bring out on cold, damp Welsh evenings.

His self-questioning regarding writing continued. Did he want to write literature? He thought yes. What was literature? Who decided which written works could be considered thus? Were the characters in books real people or figments of authors' imaginations? Nat found it hard to believe that characters weren't based on people that the author knew. And what about the events? Real or imaginary? Well, Yvette was real. Couldn't he make up something about her; a fantastic sequel to their final evening of tears and drama? He was drawing blanks and struggling to find a breakthrough.

He had often thought that high-quality pop and rock lyrics must have germinated from reality and been developed into fantasy. Take "A day in the life" by The Beatles: childhood memories from McCartney and adult flashbacks from Lennon. They stitched them together and made a work of art. Nat would try and do the same with his writing, but he would not have the help of The Beatles' music to elevate it to the giddy heights of lasting artistic achievement. Well, at least the challenge would keep him out of the pub and distract him from the other challenges thrown up by the advancing years.

He had often wondered whether booze inspired some of the great works of art. When you attempt to read Joyce's *Finnegan's wake*, it was hard to imagine him being anything other than paralytic when writing it. Was Dylan Thomas ever sober? Or F. Scott Fitzgerald? Hemingway?

On the one hand, the idea appealed to Nat for the image it threw up of the crazed, Romantic artist creating mysterious chunks of genius in a constant drunken haze; but on the other hand, common sense told him to fear the long-term consequences for his health which he had been lovingly coaxing back to an acceptable standard; it would be tragic to develop a serious drink problem for the sake of his art. He then hastily developed the half-baked idea of having one four-hour drunken session of extreme brainstorming twice a week, and then, on the other five sober days, he would bring the alcohol-inspired chunks of story into a clear coherent form. This idea disturbed him too: a sort of binge drinking way of life to enable the creation of literature.

The "How?" was one thing, but the overwhelming question remained the "What?" He didn't have an answer. He never read crime novels, hated thrillers and science fiction and found love stories wanky. He only had one surviving aunt and he knew what her first question would be. 'Is it a love story?' His answer would probably be, 'Well, it's about love.' This might confuse her but it seemed obvious to him that everything was about love, but not just about the sort of love his auntie was thinking of. He liked books that covered everything; if the book was about life, it had to be about everything that happened in a life and that included love. This all sounded extremely vague and he suddenly felt overwhelmed by the thought of writing about anything.

Nat was enjoying the intellectual gymnastics involved in the act of writing a book but was also aware that sooner or later he would just simply have to start - somewhere, some-how, with some grains from his experience of life that he could mould into a narrative and, hopefully, literature. He decided on the Joyce policy of finding inspiration for writing by writing: he would have to find inspiration because it more than likely wasn't going to find him. Well, it certainly hadn't made itself known in the previous fifty years or so. So, one cool late February evening, after a particularly tasty portion of grilled Calamari, and feeling reasonably fit and totally sober, he sat down and started writing.

3

Surviving his first winter on the island had been a close thing and there were moments when he had questioned his sanity. What was he trying to achieve or prove by living like a hermit for most of the time during the winter months on a remote Greek island? He only half-heartedly rejected his friends' claims that he was playing at being an aged hippy who was just dropping out. There was some truth in those claims. He *had* become sick of dehumanizing mass consumerism, weak-minded round-the clock media bombardments and people having everything they wanted, while remaining deeply unhappy. He felt rather vulnerable when other friends hinted that he was a failure, proof being that he hadn't managed to settle down with the proverbial nice girl and produce equally nice children. They had a point there, too, he supposed.

He cringed most of all when he heard himself answering the question as to why he had gone into exile for at least one half of the year: he wanted to find himself, find some sort of meaning to life and detox from the excesses of western civilization while determining to avoid the many mistakes he had made in life when he was controlled by lust, booze and irresponsible madness. How wanky did that sound? Very, he thought. Wanky it may be, but it was as close to the truth as he could ever come up with. Anyway, it was only a plan for three years, when he reckoned something would turn up which would push him into a new direction, answering all the questions he set himself at the beginning of the three-year sojourn.

It was always reassuring to have somebody or something to blame, so he blamed the Lotto win, that remarkable stroke of luck that forced him to decide what to do with the tidy sum he had won.

The winter had given him ample time to think about anything and everything that had happened in his life thus far. He always organised his thinking chronologically, starting with his earliest possible memories and moving forward in time. Bedtime seemed to be the best time to attempt this mammoth task but it turned out to be a bad idea as he never got much further than his sixteenth birthday before tiredness got the better of him. This went on for about half a dozen nights until he became a specialist in the first sixteen years of Nat Wilson, but the rest of his life was wiped out by sleep.

He shifted the activity to the waking hours and made more progress. It also meant he could make notes, useful material for his book. He had always wanted to try and remember everything he had done in his fifty-odd years of existence, inspired by a book title (which he still deemed to be the best book title ever): *In Search of Lost Time* by Marcel Proust. He found the exercise pleasurable and painful in equal proportions.

He spent many hours thinking of all the characters he could introduce to his reading public and many of them represented an era the modern reader might not be able to get their head around. Nat's Liverpool of the sixties and seventies was a mixture of grey grimness, heady idealism and ignorance which begot blissful innocence. But innocence faded away after his first twenty years when everything gradually became under-pinned by the realisation that those at the bottom would only ever be able to escape through education, good fortune and coincidence, or voluntary exile. In a moment of rare epiphany, he realized that his book should be spraying his readers with the gory details. Why not? Stories of happy lives made boring reading.

On the darkest nights on the island, he feared he was taking the concept of dropping out one step too far. He was starting to dread returning to North Western Europe, where, presumably, people would want to know what he had been doing during the winter months. Anything he said would sound affected and artificial; the words of an ideologue who had joined up to some wacky new cult. He realised that when he got back to Liverpool and Berlin anybody caring to listen to his Grecian tales would be giving him some seriously sceptical looks.

As March crept in and reviving warmth and longer days were starting to cheer everybody up, Nat was presented with temptation and it came from an unexpected source. It was Friday afternoon at Kosta's agency and he was paying his February bill. Kosta's generosity usually only stretched to one Ouzo on the rocks: today he was reaching for the bottle for the third time. Nat sensed Kosta had some new dodgy project in mind. Nat was not altogether wrong, but this time it was a family matter where Kosta believed that Nat could be of assistance.

'Do you know my sister, Nat?' Kosta asked in a slightly doleful tone.

'Don't think so, Kosta' was Nat's disinterested but polite reply.

'I think you should meet her sometime,' Kosta continued.

Before Nat could ascertain for what purpose, Kosta had already given him the reason.

'You see, she is also lonely, like you.'

Nat wasn't sure whether "lonely" was the right word, but before he could assemble his defence forces, Kosta was already launching into his charm offensive.

'I have told her a lot about you. Told her what a nice man you were. I mean a good man.' Nat was still trying to work out what the difference might be in Kosta's mind between "nice" and "good" when Kosta made the decisive move.

'Are you doing anything tonight, Nat?'

'Nothing planned, Kosta.' Nat didn't have the strength to lie.

He was fixing himself up with a date with a lonely woman he didn't know, had never cast eyes on and who was coming between Nat and his Friday night session with the greatest rock acts of all time and generous portions of Greek beer in the safe haven of his living room with the window wide open. Tonight he would probably be sipping Retsina, making polite conversation with Kosta's sister in the Cozy Corner on the edge of the village (the only place open at this time of the year) and desperately hoping it would be a short, painless evening at the end of which he could make up some infantile and embarrassing excuse for not seeing her again. This was assuming, of course, that she had enough English to talk about more than the weather and her favourite Elton John songs.

'I'll send a taxi at eight, Nat.' Kosta smiled triumphantly as he dropped him off back home.

Nat entered the living room and continued drinking; Kosta's generous helpings of Ouzo had nudged him into the dangerous "it's Friday-night-what-the-fuck" zone. He had been tricked by Kosta and was in the mood for taking revenge by ruining his sister's evening by being half-sloshed. *What a cheek! Lonely am I? No, I am enjoying some time alone, you impertinent, interfering*

Greek fucker! Nat was drinking steadily and losing control. Everything was fine until people started interfering, he thought. He was getting angry, mostly with himself; why couldn't he find the courage to politely refuse? He pulled open another beer.

He forced himself to get a grip and try to see things positively. What was wrong with some female company? It depended on the female company, of course. Maybe she was a cracker. Kosta wasn't a bad-looking bloke, so there was a fair chance that his sister might be the female equivalent. Nat hadn't even had a chance to ask how old she was. Kosta must have been touching forty, so if Nat was lucky, she might still only be in her mid-thirties. A widow? Left on the shelf? Just plain ugly? *No, Kosta wouldn't do that to me.*

He wondered why Kosta had done this at all. Knowing what he did know about Greek family life, he probably just felt plain sorry for Nat. Greeks who saw people alone without family automatically assumed they were unhappy. Or there could be the age-old problem of women being left alone without a suitable marriage partner; Costa was obliged, perhaps, as the eldest brother - if he was the eldest brother - to try and get the last remaining daughter off the family shelf.

Perhaps Nat's refusal to be tempted by Kosta's offer of a cleaning lady with extra services impressed Costa; he could at least rest assured that he wasn't handing over his sister to a dirty sex maniac. These were all the half-baked meanderings of a confused middle-aged Scouser, half-cut and out of his depth and slowly starting not to care any more about Kosta's intentions. He determined to have one very last beer and pull himself together. It was Friday night and he had a date. So what was the fuckin' problem? He put Pink Floyd's "The Dark Side of the Moon" on dangerously loud, slurped a freshly-opened can of beer and slumped back into the sofa's inviting cushions.

He heard a doorbell. It wasn't a Pink Floyd bell. It wasn't a dream bell. He had been woken up by his own doorbell and he realised that Pink Floyd had signed off with that sonorous heartbeat on the end of side two at least half an hour before. It was his taxi. He grabbed his wallet and keys, slipped on the empty beer can on the floor and fell over, his head narrowly missing the edge of the coffee table. He convinced himself that this was a good omen. It was the first time he had felt genuinely positive about his date, although the way he looked in the mirror as he staggered to the front door had probably drastically reduced his chances of impressing any female with even a modicum of taste.

The taxi journey was like most taxi journeys on any Greek island and it started with the usual question, an opening gambit taxi drivers probably used a thousand times when a non-Greek got in: 'Where you from?' The lack of grammatical structure in the question suggested that the five-minute conversation would be a limited one. Nat tried to keep upbeat by convincing himself that the small talk would be good practice, tuning him into the forthcoming discourse with Kosta's sister (he suddenly realised that he didn't even know her name). So he reeled off the usual short life history. He then had to endure the impene-trable accent of the rough-as-hell driver who was relating some garbled tale of visiting a cousin in Luton. 'Orrible place,' he kept shouting at Nat. Nat smiled and nodded and pointed at Cozy Corner, which they were fast approaching.

There was a gruesome beer stain on his pullover. He yanked it off and threw it at the taxi driver who gave him an incredulous look. 'Can you give it back to me later?' was Nat's puzzling parting shot to the Luton-hater and before a confusing conversation had a chance to develop, he paid, tipped generously and wobbled towards the entrance, wishing, with the deepest of convictions, that he was somewhere else. He didn't even know how he was supposed to recognise his blind date. He assumed she would be the only woman sitting alone.

The only woman sitting alone was at the bar, with her back to him. It couldn't be her, he thought. He had seen women like that in the centre of town at the beginning of the previous summer; they were very classy - and presumably very expensive - women of the night who had been appearing in ever-increasing numbers in the tourist season to cater for the demand of the modest sex tourism which had been developing since the Russians had started investing in the place. But the tourist season had come to an end. She turned towards him and said, without the slightest trace of an accent and with a look and a smile to write home about in a twelve-hundred-page letter:

'You must be Nat. I am delighted to meet you. I'm Maria.'

Nat felt weak; probably weaker than he had ever felt in his whole life, a weakness brought on by the almighty power of sensual female beauty. The generous helpings of alcohol were causing further havoc with his sensory and cognitive apparatus. The mere thought of spending the next couple of hours in the presence of this woman was removing any ounce of free will he had in his already weakened and intoxicated body.

'You're Kosta's sister?' he slurred. Both of them knew that this was a ludicrous question but it was the best Nat could muster at this moment as the delicious reality was just starting to sink in. He shook her hand, which seemed a ridiculous thing to do, as if he was greeting his bank manager. She confidently beckoned to somebody behind the bar and they were led to a table for two in a corner by the window.

In an instant, Nat decided that his drink for the rest of the evening could only be mineral water: if there was the remotest chance of becoming in any way physically intimate with this most divine of creatures, he would like to be as sober as possible for the unlikely event. And even if the evening produced nothing approaching romantic value, he at least wanted to be able to focus properly on one of God's best female creations for as long as the evening was going to last.

She had long, thick, dark hair, dancing brown eyes and a face that revealed only natural beauty; he was desperately trying to find something about her that didn't stimulate his whole shell-shocked body and mind. He couldn't. With a supreme effort, he developed some sort of strategy: if he could somehow drain out the mixture of Ouzo and Mythos beer from his body quickly enough, he might be able to start functioning again as the intelligent and interesting individual he sincerely believed himself to be. With a supreme effort he might even be able to impress her with some decent insights and conversation. And, more importantly, disguise the fact that he was pissed.

So the beginning of the evening belonged to Maria; her English was staggeringly good, the content of her thoughts coherent and cohesive, her accent perfect, yet loaded with powerfully charged seductive pellets. Even if Nat had not been under the influence and confused, he would have been disarmed and helpless. He shivered inwardly every time she moved her near-perfect body towards him. And her penetrating brown eyes were softly piercing his soul.

Before the first course arrived, he ordered a double Greek coffee, which he knocked back in one; unorthodox etiquette at the beginning of a romantic meal, but an important first step on the road to sobriety. He was slurping out of the bottle of mineral water like a man possessed and quickly ordered a second one, hoping Maria wasn't taken too aback by his continual longing for ever more mineral water. He assumed, or rather prayed, that the water would start diluting the alcohol. He was hydrating at record speed and his mind was clearing, which encouraged him to participate in the discourse which had up till then been dominated by Maria as she talked of study abroad placements in New York and London and the fascinating cultural experiences she had had there.

Nat was slowly catching up and he noticed she looked relieved that he was finally able to string sentences together that made some sort of sense. She seemed amused by his tales from Liverpool as she admitted how hard it was to hold back the tears when she heard the Kop singing "You'll never walk alone". She also seemed to be impressed by Nat's knowledge of the origins of the song and seemed noticeably touched when he talked about how he fell in love with the team when his dad took him to his first game shortly after "Sergeant Pepper's Lonely Hearts Club Band" had come out in 1967.

The conversation flowed with no room for even the shortest embarrassing pauses. Nat had little idea what he was eating; he simply asked Maria what she recommended and it all hit the spot. In the space of two hours, he had transformed from a grumpy, world-weary, half-pissed slob into a vibrant, sparkling, early fifties go-getter armed with erudite, witty anecdotes. He realised that the clichéd, cheesy, romantic dross "I don't want the evening to end", deserved to exist because it was the only truth in his world as the clock approached midnight. His transformation was so complete that he conveyed this sentiment to Maria, prompting her to say: 'Nat, the evening doesn't have to end.'

Before he was able to utter the classic 'But we've only just met,' Maria was already beckoning to the bar staff, which presumably meant that a taxi was about to arrive. His newly attained sobriety allowed him a confident swagger towards the taxi waiting outside, where he picked up his pullover from the driver, now smirking like a Greek version of Benny Hill. The driver knew where they were going.

That night, and the next three weeks leading up to his departure from the island for his north west Europe campaign, passed in a haze of sexual oblivion inside a seemingly endless cocoon protecting him from any of the usual worries and cares average mortal beings have. Maria had moved in, or rather had never moved out since that first evening in Cozy Corner. She had organised food, drink and every form of leisure activity a pleasure-seeking man could have wanted: she was totally in control and no matter how many times he told himself that this state of affairs couldn't and shouldn't last, he brushed aside such reservations with the confidence of a sleepwalker. He was a man who had had every element of resistance and will squeezed out of him from the moment Maria had turned around and spoken to him at the Cozy Corner and he knew that this was going to be the case until some external, higher force decided otherwise.

Despite being a delighted prisoner behind the bars of a cage of love, lust and never-ending desire for everything Maria was able to offer him and being in a place where reasonable reflections seemed an impossibility, Nat managed to find just enough mental strength to finally murmur a vital question on day twenty-one of his voluntary captivity: he wanted to ascertain who Maria was. Nat had known by the time they had finished their starters on that first date that Maria was not Kosta's sister and despite the fantasy world he was living in, something deep down in Nat's otherwise non-functioning mind demanded that he found out who she actually was. There was no way that she and Kosta could ever be related and he hadn't been mentioned in any conversation they had had. Nat wasn't even sure that Maria knew Kosta particularly well.

Everything about Nat's situation was surreal; the hermit-style life he had been leading in the first third of his three-year project also had unnatural elements to it, but it was at least underpinned by good, noble intentions within the bubble of a largely moderate and orderly structure. Maria had blown away that structure in a three-week blitzkrieg during which Nat had been defenceless as all men are when lust and love – in that order – take over. A woman was in complete control of a man; she had turned his Spartan lifestyle into a Roman orgy of mind-blowing physical and spiritual pleasure, a sensual feast of Babylonian proportions which took place in a seemingly never-ending present tense. He was now asking the killer question to establish where their relationship was heading.

Their relationship had resembled that of two seven year olds who meet on a beach on holiday and are inseparable for three weeks. They play together and live in a fantasy world of sand castle building, paddling in the sea and getting up to endless mischief. There is no script, no plans, no questions, just fun and beautiful present tense nonsense. The nonsense ends when the parents have to go home, taking their respective kids with them amid much wailing, screaming and kicking of little feet. Neither Nat nor Maria had parents to take them to their respective homes, so one of them had to decide to become one and Nat knew that he was fated to suddenly be the no-nonsense father who knew when their kids had just had too much of a good thing.

At least she gave him an honest answer to his question:

'Are you really Kosta's sister?'

'No, Nat. You know I'm not.' His next question was obvious.

'So, who are you then?'

She must have been prepared for this and she launched into a detailed description of her life so far. It was an intriguing and exciting tale of civil war, displacement, good luck and bad luck, moving between parts of former Yugoslavia and landing on a Greek Island where Kosta's family, committed members of Amnesty International, offered her a safe place to hide. Somewhere in the middle of this bewitching tale of gypsy-like living and surviving by the skin of her teeth was a period of stability during which Maria got herself a first-class education. She omitted to explain how this was financed, just as she skilfully managed to avoid any details of the role of men throughout her proclamation. Nat thought it might be in his own best interests not to know.

Maria had Albanian citizenship, which wasn't going to get her very far in Europe. Nat had one more question, which would have gone like this: "Maria, are you here now because you love me or because I might be able to help you?" Nat feared the answer before he had asked the question, so he decided not to ask it. He realised that Maria was reading his mind and she looked away as if she was telling him that the game was up. So he asked her to leave. He had had his three weeks of care-free bliss and he was about to look the ultimate spoilsport called reality right between the eyes and start chewing on a grisly, tasteless chunk of it.

'I think you will find a good woman one day, Nat, because you are a good man. If you were ten years younger, I would be digging my heels in now. Is that what you say in English? But I will go now.'

She gathered up her belongings in a very large overnight bag and headed for the door. It had taken him more than forty years to be able to make a decision like this: saying goodbye to an utterly desirable woman to prevent further pain. It reminded him once again of the boring fact that the head made better decisions than the penis. He had made a breakthrough and it was an important one, although the beauty and intensity of Maria was going to make him seriously question the sagacity of his decision for a long time to come. Her "ten years younger" quip had cut him to the quick, but it was another vital reminder of reality.

She left the house without closing the door. Nat's eyes stayed on her during the three and a half minutes it took Maria to reach the brow of the hill. The mystifying mixture of sensuous power and elegance as she glided along the stony path was torturing him, as it sank in that he would never again share intimacy with a woman of such ripe perfection and goddess-like beauty. Every thirty seconds a voice in his head screamed at him to go and get her. Three minutes were now up; if she had turned round and waved, he would have been out of the door like a rat out of a sewer, as in some cringe-worthy Hollywood love story. She didn't turn round. She didn't wave. The rat remained in the sewer. He closed the door.

4

He wanted to leave Greece in the knowledge that he had conquered at least some of his worst demons: he still had a long way to go, but there was cause for optimism. Too often in the past he had based important decisions on the principle that he would rather regret having done something, than *not* having done something. It was a principle which happily embraced risk, something which had always excited him and made life vibrant, producing exciting highs. However, if the risk-taking wasn't accompanied by good fortune, you could be left high and dry, something he had experienced too frequently for his own liking. He was, as Maria disappeared over the hill, high and dry again, but this time the short nature of this particular intermezzo would, he hoped, keep the resulting pain manageable.

Nat found it interesting *and* puzzling that both Maria and Kosta had described him as being good. What did this mean? Was it a typical Greek turn of phrase or a genuine sentiment? He wanted to believe that they meant well. Looking back, it was clear that Kosta's offer of help in the form of the Albanian cleaning lady and then his "sister" were his well-meant attempts to solve Nat's problem of loneliness. Presumably, a Greek man believed that a man living alone in his early fifties was a problem. If Maria was also a good woman, Nat may have just committed a terrible blunder.

He still had to see Kosta one last time before he left the island, to hand in keys, pay outstanding bills and book the house for the following September. He had decided to say nothing about the turbo-charged relationship with Maria and he was hoping Kosta had made the same decision. Thankfully, he had, and they settled up, exchanged the usual pleasantries and pretended nothing had happened.

'One for the road, Nat?' said Kosta as he made for the drinks cabinet.

'Thanks, Kosta, but I'm having a break from the booze.' Nat exchanged a longer-than-usual look with Kosta, who looked momentarily uncomfortable. For a second, Nat was anxious that he was going to mention Maria. He didn't, the moment passed and they shook hands and embraced.

'Thanks for everything, Kosta. See you in September.' And he meant it, just as Kosta had meant it with his "Albanian" solution. Their peculiar friendship was still intact and both of them now knew a lot more about each other's intentions and direction of travel.

Nat also meant what he said about the booze; he was going to be in Liverpool for two months and he planned to be dry for the whole of the first one. Hitting the bottle would not help him forget Maria, but rather push him into a self-made hell.

Nat's good work in Greece in establishing a healthy and sensible lifestyle had come to an abrupt end when Maria over-turned everything; the only exercise he had been getting was through excessive sexual exertion. "Shagged out" was the only banal expression which sprang to mind when describing the present state of his body; his state of mind could be blandly, but accurately, summarized by the quaint old phrase "mixed up". He had blown it, lost the plot, been a fool, but just staved off complete disaster. Deep down, he had always believed he was a fool, so it came as no real surprise. The fact, however, that he was now an *old* fool troubled him more.

He hoped to be able to turn things around in Liverpool, the place he had turned his back on all those years ago. The large family of cousins, aunties and uncles were either dead, missing, or missing presumed dead and he had no idea where any of his old friends from school or university were. He presumed that many of them had also fled Liverpool, just like him.

One auntie remained, Samantha, his dad's brother's widow and he was going to be living in her spare room for the next couple of months, until the summer equinox. He would have a bed, a table, a chair and a view out onto the street. He would pay her for the pleasure and expected no food and drink except cups of tea around the clock.

In the terraced house she had had lived in since before the war, she had two rooms downstairs with a TV in each - the perfect solution when they ran out of conversation, which Nat feared might happen well before the summer equinox. His aunt was a lovely woman, kind and gentle, but with the awful tendency of talking non-stop. She asked questions but rarely waited for the answers. As a conversation partner, you were superfluous; you were simply there to subject yourself to non-stop questioning and long, wearying stories of banality and tedium. But with a TV room and bedroom at his disposal, there was the permanent chance of intermittent escape; he cursed himself for thinking that way.

He was less sure how he was going to cope with the fact that his uncle was no longer around. Ebullient, carefree, daft Bob had an innate ability to stay awake forever, remain cheerful and always drink until last orders or the last bottle in the house was empty; he was like Keith Richards without the rock 'n' roll, but with the same eternal and unquenchable thirst for fun. Nat always found Bob's lust for life infectious and uplifting and he couldn't imagine the house without him.

Sam was teetotal, a fact his uncle stubbornly refused to accept during their fifty-year marriage and endless turbulence was the result, especially when Bob went on his regular benders in his younger years. The Maria story would have captivated him; Nat had not the slightest intention of sharing a word of it with Sam.

He got into the taxi for the airport, full of the best intentions but the same doubts. He was disappointed, to use football jargon, to have thrown away a two-goal lead through bad marking and a soft penalty and then concede a ridiculous own goal in stoppage time. In a moment of football Nirvana, a thirty-five-yard rocket into the top corner of the net made it three-all as Maria left the building. Nat and his imaginary team lived to fight another day. At least the next match was at home.

Branigan's boys and girls

Teenage smut, a battered city shouting at him to get out, and a beautiful ignorance of the world all form a deliciously shaky foundation for further exploits. What can possibly go wrong for young Nat?

Unlike his wife, John Branigan had no problems with Saturdays, the busiest day of the week. Hitting the sales target by the six o'clock closing time in his Ranelagh Street branch of Jackson the Tailors in Liverpool was one of the few real pleasures left to him. His wife, June, was finding the double burden of a full-time job running the shop and the menopause a bit more of a challenge and John took the brunt of most of the outbursts she wasn't always able to suppress during the long working day as she struggled to deal with irritating customers and male staff who were either infantile, macho or plain boring.

John dearly wanted June to give up work, but they would sorely miss her income. They still had one daughter living with them, twenty-four years old, flitting from one bloke to the next, showing little interest in steady jobs or steady boyfriends; she enjoyed life a little too much for their taste. They had managed to get the elder daughter off the premises – she had married an ambitious fellow a few years older than her who was the manager of the furniture department in Owen Owens, a well-known Liverpool store just round the corner. The Branigan's were now impatiently waiting for their first grandchild but realised that their eldest daughter also appreciated the bene-fits of two incomes: she was doing well as the manager of a car-hire firm on the edge of town. If Linda, the younger daugh-ter, could find herself a suitable partner and fly the nest, the Branigan's could save money, sell up and move into a smaller house, perhaps a cosy bungalow. With their tidy nest egg, June could afford to have her well-deserved break from working life. That was the vague plan, but John feared it was going to remain vague for quite some time.

Just before ten o'clock, a young man was ushered into John's minute office in the corner of the shop.

'Mr Coupland sent me,' said the young man. John discerned a slight stammer but liked the look of him.

'Oh yes, Jack Coupland,' said John. Nat knew him only as

Uncle John but presumed they were talking about the same person. Mr B (his unofficial title in the shop) gave him the shortest of inductions:

'Ten till five every Saturday. £2.48 paid in cash when you leave. You'll be working downstairs in the made-to-measure department. Mr Wilkinson will look after you. You'll have to get yourself a suit, Nat; we'll fix you up with a tie for today. Roger, can you fix this young man up with a tie?'

Roger was the assistant manager and he shook Nat's hand, and reappeared a few seconds later with an unpleasant-looking brown tie. Nat was then introduced to Bill Wilkinson who showed much patience in explaining the basics of made-to-measure tailoring and how to address customers and deal with their questions.

'Please call me Bill' he said, but added: 'But call me Mr Wilkinson when customers are around.'

As Saturdays passed Nat got to know the other members of staff, each one giving their views on how to do things in the shop and Nat stuttered himself up to something resembling competence. By the beginning of December, he was wearing his first suit, a brown two-piece made to measure garment for £14.99 (after his 25% part-time staff discount). His mum paid for it as an early Christmas present provided he stuck at the job for a couple of years ('You can't let Uncle John down,' she convincingly argued). He was shaping up, mixing and inter-acting with people outside of his customary circle of school friends, teachers and family and it was toughening him up, raising his confidence weekly.

The conversations with the other fellows were a revelation for Nat. Full-timer Pete from Birkenhead related his sexual exploits in detail while also expressing a fair amount of shame as a lapsed Catholic. 'You see, Nat,' said Pete, pointing at the central area just below his belt, 'the pope thinks you should only be using this for creating children.' Nat appreciated this graphic and down-to-earth way of explaining Catholic teachings on sexual morality but wondered why Pete had so blatantly ignored such doctrines himself. He thought it wise not to push the point when Pete was in full flow.

Jed, another Saturday part-timer, two years younger than Pete and one year older than Nat, hated Jonnies as much as Pete and just didn't bother with them at all. 'I just take a chance,' he admitted. He talked less than Pete and was curious to know what Nat was up to. Nat was amused when Jed asked him, 'Have you been up, up and away with your girlfriend yet?' Nat had never heard that expression before and never heard it again; it had an almost poetic ring to it. He bluffed an ambiguous answer and tried to change the subject.

But the subject never seemed to go away in that shop. Even the oldest member of staff, already pushing seventy and who only came in during the pressure periods of the menswear year, couldn't resist explaining the annual run on suits in the early months of the years as a result of "too much shagging at Christmas parties" where intoxicated women were letting themselves go with equally intoxicated and sloppy boyfriends. The wedding suits were being hastily ordered for the rushed Spring weddings, he explained. He added that September and October were also busy months after young folk, plastered on cheap foreign booze in the sun, were sowing their wild oats with the usual consequences. The fluctuation in menswear sales figures neatly explained by the sexual shenanigans of young Scousers: who needs economists, sociologists and fashion experts?

The other members of staff were all interesting in their own different ways. Bill Wilkinson, the man assigned to taking Nat under his wing, was retraining to become a history teacher after spending years in the rag trade. Self-assured, patient, calm and subtly witty, his quaint Lancashire accent had a soothing effect on Nat. He could answer any question a customer had. Cec Hale was the eloquent middle-aged Scouser who had a more cut and thrust approach to dealing with customers.

'What colour suit are you looking for, sir?'

'I don't know.'

'Ah well, that makes two of us,' was his usual follow-up comment. Nat was also impressed by Cec's stupendous general knowledge, his wide variety of vocabulary and smooth tongue. 'Educated by self-learning and life rather than school and university,' Nat concluded. He wondered whether a university would ever get him to that level of eloquence.

Nat's contact with Mr B was infrequent and fleeting. Round about one o'clock he would slip a pound note into Nat's hand, always uttering the same words. 'Get us a couple of meat and potato pies, will you, Nat?' The only place for pies was a family business in Hanover Street which Mr B had been patronising for the past twenty-seven years; the first time Nat went for the pies he slipped up badly, buying them at the nearby Sayers branch instead. He didn't make the same mistake twice.

Nat was surprised once by an unexpected question in a rare moment of intimacy with Mr B.

'Got yourself a girl, have you, Nat?'

'Yeah.'

'What's her name?'

'Linda.'

'Same name as my daughter.' Mr B walked away without any further comment; Nat guessed that Mr B had something on his mind, but couldn't imagine what it might be. It was the longest conversation Nat had ever had with him and it was the most puzzling one.

A few weeks later, when Nat was working in the shop during the school holidays, he met one of John Branigan's daughters, the Linda one. She was the female version of her father, attractive and bright, with long dark hair. Tantalisingly, she was almost the dark-haired version of his own Linda, which momentarily destabilized him. He was just about to take the stairs up to the off-the-peg department to prevent further distress in his own mixed emotions department, when Mr B said,

'Nat, this is my daughter Linda.' Nat was unsure of Mr B's motivation for telling him something he already knew and he was, as was so often the case, tongue-tied. He could hardly say: 'Hello, I have heard so much about you' (A lie). Or: 'You remind me of my girlfriend, but you have dark hair, whereas my Linda has blonde hair.' (The awkward truth) or: 'I can see where you get your looks from.' (The highly inappropriate truth which would not make him very popular with Mrs B). He weakly said, 'Hello,' without a handshake and all three people realised that twenty seconds of their lives had been wasted and it had all been Nat's fault. Linda smiled awkwardly and no further words were exchanged.

Nat had come a long way since he started working at Jackson the Tailors, but he clearly still had a long way to go. Why couldn't he just pass the time of day with Linda Branigan and relax? It wasn't possible because he was still a nervous, spotty seventeen-year-old who was still in the painful process of shaking off, rather unsuccessfully, the last shackles of debilitating puberty. So why shouldn't he find it difficult to talk to an attractive woman six years older than him? And she was, after all, the boss's daughter. He wondered again what Mr B was up to; the idea that he was trying to get Nat off with his own daughter was too ridiculous for words.

Before he could ponder further he was brought back to earth by Pete's dulcet Birkenhead tones behind him, 'Luvverly melons, eh?' Nat realised immediately that he was referring to the breasts belonging to the afore-mentioned Linda Branigan, the manager's younger daughter. Nat nodded his agreement and the conversation quickly dived into the usual Scouse cesspool.

The relief and sharp upward movement of his spirits at five o'clock on Saturdays marked the beginning of the weekend proper. He turned left out of the shop, walking past the ancient barrow woman sitting next to her huge stand of fruit and veg. She was a frightening sight: virtually toothless, a white scarf wrapped round a small weasel-like face, with bulbous eyes and almost always a dribble of saliva rolling out of one side of her mouth. Her massive frame was thankfully hidden behind a thick overcoat as she screeched out the prices of various items in a cackling Scouse which put every passer-by on edge. She only smiled when punters gave her the money for their items. Nat never saw her standing up, never mind walking, and had comic-surreal visions of somebody heaving her up at the end of the day and somehow managing to roll her home.

As he made his way across the shopping streets towards the bus stops, he often wondered where people like that came from; she seemed like a remnant of the Victorian age of dire Dickensian poverty when Liverpool was teeming with barrow women like her, along with the many losers of Irish immigration or the Lancashire lumpenproletariat. She was a ghost from Liverpool's grim past and Nat had always felt infected by her. Couldn't he see his own mother battling to flee from the world these unedifying sights had not yet left?

The litter and dirt under his shoes, the harsh language of the people on the streets and the decrepit buildings his bus would pass as it struggled slowly eastwards through neglected suburbs always made him think and he always came to the same conclusion: something's wrong here. People in his hometown had only just begun to free themselves from the triple nightmare of Victorian squalor, thirties' poverty and the Blitz while getting ready to face the post-war death of the docks and the disappearance of huge tracts of production industry. Men and women used the tried and tested methods of escape: sex, booze and football. The unavoidable truth was that the masses knew they couldn't change anything, so they decided to have as much fun as possible trying to forget that inescapable but simple fact. Of the three escape hatches, Nat had the most experience with football but was hoping the other two would one day create a holy trinity to make life meaningful.

At that stage in his life, he didn't know what cares were - the pursuit of carnal and emotional pleasures were the only things on his agenda. And they could easily be achieved by the purchase of the next Pink Floyd album, a particularly sensual time with Linda or a late winner for Liverpool in an important home game. He didn't know he was born, which was probably just as well; illness, loss and anxiety were such vague concepts that they had little or no meaning to him. However, something nestled uncomfortably in his mind and occasionally caused him a trace of anxiety: he would one day have to leave the place he loved *and* hated.

His time in the world of John Branigan taught him two important things: learning to interact with fellow human beings will get you somewhere. Secondly, ending up working for Jackson the Tailors would mean a life sentence in a world that Nat was already unconsciously planning to leave. The actual shape of the world that he was heading for was still unknown to him but he was far from discouraged as he stepped off the number ten bus and wondered what was for tea.

5

Home. A place you can never go back to, as a famous German writer once said. Nat never fully understood the saying but started to get his head around it when family members started dropping like flies in the place he called his hometown. The Irish language has a word to describe a state of being when everybody you have grown up with is dead. The idea depressed him but he had to give credit to the Irish for having the morose ingenuity to describe a situation which creeps up on anybody lucky enough to live long enough to feel that way.

Maria. He had had a long and serious conversation with himself on his last evening in Greece at the end of which he swore he would not permit himself any further thoughts on the matter. His saving mantra was, as all good mantras are, short and pithy: *You did the right thing.* His first month in Liverpool would be free of the evils that had been a drag anchor for many years: booze, self-pity, late nights, a confused mind and general self-neglect. The Greek campaign had been turning things around nicely until Maria appeared, so with her excluded from memory, he would just pick up the pieces and restart from where he left off on the Friday afternoon they met. The extreme emotions exploding inside him during those last three weeks had invited back the confused state of mind, but he was hopeful of being able to restore reason relatively quickly. A month of Liverpool concrete reality on the wagon would cure him of three weeks of Greek fantasy. Everything else would look after itself. At least, that was the plan.

Liverpool. He knew what to expect: the Good, the Bad and the extremely Ugly, which would include a roller coaster ride sweeping him up to the giddy heights brought about by the beauty of surreal Scouse moments and rolling him back down to the miserable pits of grim Scouse reality. His past would be chasing him everywhere; he would curse his obsession with it and knew that he would be drawn to every corner of the town where he had spent carefree hours with friends and people he loved. To ensure maximum stability, he planned to lay low, take regular exercise in places where there were no pubs, write, watch telly, with or without Sam, and dig in.

'You're looking well!' shrieked Sam. Nat was never at ease with the formalities of greeting his eighty-two-year-old aunt and gave her an awkward hug; she had never been a touchy-feely sort of woman.

'Do sit down and tell all,' which meant, 'Sit down while I interrogate you.' Nat sat down and was duly interrogated during which his eyes kept drifting to a half-empty bottle of Scotch on the top of the fridge in the dingy hallway. He realised it was the bottle he had given Bob the last time he had seen him, just under two years ago. By not asking Sam to give him a shot, he felt he was letting Bob down. Under Bob's command, half a bottle of Scotch would be empty within an hour, by which time Nat would be striding down the main drag, with a twenty-pound note pushed into his palm, to seek the nearest off licence for fresh supplies of beer to wash the Scotch down with. Now he just sat and listened to Sam talking. And talking. If she had offered him a shot, he would have gladly broken his no-booze rule on the first day. Two hours later, tired and weary, he made the usual excuses and retreated to his box bedroom.

After the relative spaciousness of the Greek house, his sleeping quarters for the next two months resembled a cramped box. He peered out of the window down the narrow street and reminded himself that some people, in fact, most people, stayed in the same street all their lives and were happy with that. He just presumed that he was a nowhere man who had just lost his bearings and strayed once too often. As his eyes became ever heavier, he convinced himself that he could survive the view for two months.

The next day he flung himself into the grey Liverpool rain with an enthusiasm which startled even himself, and within seventy-two hours he had an initial plan up and running which was doable, sensible and a Liverpool version of his Greek routine, with less fresh food, a very different sea air and no booze. The open spaces, healthy-looking people and a dry climate were also gone and Nat reassembled his inner forces.

Setting up the food schedule was the first thing on his to-do list and he meticulously put together his dietary plan after checking what local supermarkets had on offer. His daily exercise would be a one-hour walk in the park at approximately five p.m., after which, every other day he would return home for his Marks and Spencer's ready-made meal which went into Sam's brand new, impressive-looking microwave. On alternate days he would frequent an excellent Thai food fusion joint which cooked everything from fresh. As they were closed on Mondays, the weekly eating cycle would begin with the microwave fare. Every second micro wave meal would be a vegetarian option, as would every second meal in the Thai place. He planned to treat Sam to a Sunday lunch every week somewhere in town.

As in Greece, this planned strait jacket of a routine was designed to keep him from losing his mind and the plot; it also prevented him from having to think very much, which always increased the danger of moroseness, and that fatal overdose of self-doubt, leading to self-loathing. If he could fill the remaining bits of the days with quality writing, it would all be worthwhile.

He knew that the first month would be make-or-break and he summoned every ounce of willpower, praying that he could pull it off. He navigated himself through the first few days with relative ease. He slept well, soon got used to the different diet, chatted amiably to Sam when the need arose and even enjoyed his daily walk in the park, interspersing his brisk stroll with bursts of jogging, pleased that he could get his out-of-shape middle-aged frame to that level of forwarding movement without too much pain and discomfort. Then back to writing.

The evening chats with Sam were usually one-way and therefore soporific: the perfect way of inducing necessary tiredness for bed. She would reminisce about a past unknown to Nat, a time of sweet innocence when she dated numerous men who courted her in a way no longer customary in the twenty-first century Western world. In her twenties she saved up for coach holidays, first in Britain and then later to Europe, always accompanied by a girlfriend or work colleagues. Words and expressions like "courting", "on the continent" and "coach holidays" were no longer used by Nat's generation but were still alive and kicking in Sam's time-warped lingo.

'So you were quite happy as a bachelor girl were you, Sam?' was a question he dropped into the conversation one evening. A bit cheeky perhaps, but he couldn't resist.

'I was actually, Nat.' Sam suddenly looked sad and he regretted the question. By the mid-sixties Sam had probably resigned herself to remaining alone and looking after her elderly divorced mother: her two elder brothers had married years before and left them alone. And then she met Bob, the widower; they married at the end of the Flower Power Era and she was suddenly looking after three people as Bob brought along his seven-year-old daughter, Leslie. Together they formed a nervy team, more like three individuals invariably on the brink of civil war. Against all the odds, she managed to keep the peace, skilfully juggling her triple role as understanding second wife, efficient step-mother and caring daughter.

'Bob liked the women, you know,' she continued. Nat nodded in agreement: her statement was tantamount to saying: 'The pope is Catholic' or 'Richard Burton liked the odd drink.'

'You know he had an affair, don't you?' Nat didn't like the direction the conversation was going. 'Did he?' was the feeble lie he offered. Nat knew all the details of the affair, as Bob had happily described them on a number of occasions. Nat could see pain in Sam's face and he desperately tried to think of a way of changing the subject, but before he was able to, Sam lightened up.

'He was a handsome man, though. Especially when he was younger.' Before Nat was able to make the obvious point that most of us were quite handsome before the ravages of time got their hands on us, Sam continued her homage.

'Oh yes, he had lovely dark hair. That's why I fell for him. And he was charming. He could charm the birds right out of the trees.' Sam loved clichéd sayings and her voice always rose to the occasion when she used them as if she was performing for her speech therapist, or in an amateur production of *South Pacific*, pronouncing every syllable with real delight. Nat was just relieved she was smiling again.

Nat said goodnight, dragged himself upstairs and shuffled into his box room. As he snuggled under the duvet, sadness slowly invaded him and as he stared out into the street. He started sobbing; nothing hysterical, but steady and rhythmic, deep and rich and potentially there for the long haul. He tried to remember when he had last cried and decided that it must have been while watching a Liverpool match on TV, probably with his dad, who was probably crying, too. They were the moments when they both pretended that they weren't breaking up and avoided eye contact and communication until they had pulled themselves together again.

As the baby-like sobbing subsided, his thoughts drifted downstairs towards that bottle of Scotch on top of the fridge. Thirteen steps and he could have it in his grasp. He calculated that he had been in bed about half an hour, just past midnight. With a bit of luck, Sam might have dozed off. He would only be caught red-handed if she was going at that particular moment to either the kitchen or the bathroom. In deference to the fact that Sam had presumably only ever seen one man naked in her whole life, he pulled on a pair of undies and tiptoed down, every inch the thief in the night. Furtively grasping the half-empty bottle, he gleefully ascended the stairs.

He was momentarily breathless as he plonked himself on the bed. *This is how alkies behave,* he thought. Before this disturbing thought took further hold, he found a paper beaker, eagerly filling half of it with the glistening brown liquid and, before he raised it to his dry lips, he braced himself for a good long think. Or maybe he would make a short silent speech. Or say a prayer. Or stare out of the window again. In fact, he did all those things, then rounded it all off by thinking about the last time Bob and he shared the same Scotch he was now about to slurp down. It had been downstairs, in the same room in which Sam was now slumbering. In the course of that evening, Bob raised his glass and, out of the blue, said, 'Here's to your dad!'

Nat quickly repainted the scene, raised his beaker, and, in one pulsating five-second burst, every moment he had ever spent with these two men rattled around his body and soul, much like the way your life is supposed to flash past you in your last mortal moment on earth. The difference was that he was very much still alive, invigorated even. Then his body momentarily shuddered and one second later the wardrobe in the room did the same. After such a long break from alcohol, the Scotch was making swift inroads into his body and mind. He knew one was enough. Beaker empty, he settled down for the night and he no longer felt pain or fear. Drifting off into sleep, he started dreaming of kicking a ball around with two men much older than him in a park a stone's throw away from where he now lay.

6

He had started drinking again after a twenty-four-day abstinence; he had been hoping to stay dry a full month, which
meant he had missed his target by a week. He realised now
that he would be spending more time in town, checking out all
his old watering holes. He was painfully aware of the potential
dangers of these sojourns but knew he had to do it: he hadn't
been in a Liverpool pub for almost a year and the bitter he
drank there and the atmosphere found there was something
unique and uplifting. But he would have to make moderation
his watchword concerning both alcohol consumption and
obsessing about the past: too much of both and his plans for
mental and physical stability would be severely endangered.

His daily schedule also needed revamping. When would
the drinking take place? Daytime drinking was decadent and
slowed him down for the rest of the day. On the other hand,
it was traditionally moderate and he would be compelled to
consume sensible amounts if he wanted to get any writing done
later in the day. His big fear was appearing like the proverbial
sad bastard, silently and self-consciously supping in the corners
of half-empty pubs.

On good weather days, of course, he could just walk. The
walking would keep him out of the pub and in shape. And
there was the river, which meant he could never get lost: he
would simply walk north and south on either peninsula, turn
back to the ferry terminal on either side and find his way home.
Nothing could be simpler and nothing could go wrong.

That evening, Nat was almost out of the front door, on his way to the Thai place for his evening nourishment, when he heard Sam's voice behind him.

'Nat, do you know what happened to that bottle of whisky? It was on the fridge.' He hadn't properly completed his clandestine operation from the previous evening by putting the bottle back in its original place and now he felt foolish.

'Oh, I had a nightcap and didn't want to disturb you,' was his nervy, but honest reply.

'Oh, that's fine,' she said. 'I thought that John might have got his hands on it. I can rest easy now.' John was the next-door neighbour whose behaviour took a downward spiral whenever he got Scotch down him. Sam and John's wife had spent most of their adult lives preventing John from getting his hands on any. Sam was grateful that she had spared Pat, John's wife, another whisky-charged meltdown.

Alcohol. The eternal friend and potential enemy. Having a drink together was the easiest thing in the world, socially acceptable and enjoyed virtually the whole world over; the longer in the tooth he had got, however, the warier he had become of alcohol's destructive potential. Keeping their blokes out of the alehouse had been a mammoth task for women in his home town since time immemorial. Sam had done her best coping with the fact that Bob liked a drink, but she had never even come close to persuading him to drink any less; this had been the sad fate of generations of Liverpool wives. Nat feared that his nocturnal tipple might have disappointed Sam, making her conclude, perhaps, that all men were boozers and that Nat was no different.

And what was wrong with being like Bob? That was nothing

to be ashamed of. But Nat knew the paucity of this statement: Sam had suffered a lot from the effects booze had had on their marriage. Nat had only been around for the laughs, the banter and Bob's endless generosity at the bar; whenever Bob became a pain in the arse as the liberal quantities of alcohol kicked in, Nat was able to say goodnight and escape. That, presumably, was when the fun began for Sam. Nat suppressed such thoughts and walked down the street, turning right, down into the main road towards his unique little Thai café, a culinary haven in an otherwise grim suburb.

After the abrupt end to his period of abstinence and the disturbing and largely self-righteous meanderings in his brain about Bob and alcohol, Nat had to decide whether to pop into the twenty-four-hour shop to grab a can or two of beer with which to wash down his Thai delicacies. He kept on the self-righteous path, decided to do without and crossed over at the pedestrian traffic lights by the church and made straight for the café after casting his customary reverential glance at the church where his parents had married and he had been baptised.

It was a warm late May evening and he observed two winos sitting on the grass outside the Salvation Army Hostel on the other side of the road. He assumed that they had been to the same shop Nat was planning to get his beer from. Three men with two different aims: one to acquire booze as a cultured accompaniment to tasty food, two with the more existential concern of making it through another night as a guest of the Salvation Army. Nat didn't know what conclusions he was supposed to draw from this. Nipping the creeping paralysis of over-analysis in the bud, he instead concentrated on gaining access to a free table in the cramped dining area of the Your Thai Café.

If his memory was still serving him well, this was his thirteenth visit to Your Thai since he arrived; this meant that he had tried everything on their modest menu. Everything tasted good and the seat he was usually able to grab, with his back to the window, enabled him to watch a young sleek Asian woman cooking everything in her tiny open-plan kitchen. The order was made and the woman proceeded to bang away in various pots and pans until her petite, pretty Scouse colleague brought over the delicious fare in a time ranging between seventeen and twenty-one minutes. During these waiting times, Nat was usually able to read between approximately seven and eleven pages of any book he currently had on the go.

He was usually out of the door within the hour. This slavish adherence to daily routine was starting to perturb Nat and he had started questioning whether he was not going too far; it was doable in Greece as he could find some relief from the rigidity of his daily plan by walking on the beach or just staring at the blue sea or sky. Here in Liverpool, he stared at dusty potholed streets or barbarous concrete. And people scraping a living on the wrong side of town. Or watching winos crawling around on the other side of the street.

He thanked the waitress, briefly enjoyed her smile, wanted to utter something flirtatious, but thought better of it and left. Rather than turning right, which would have taken him back to Sam's place, he turned left to complete a mission he had resolved to do since his dad's death. He knew what to expect in the pub he had decided to visit: grimness, grubbiness, hopelessness and the realisation that life in his part of town was only known to people who lived there. But he knew he had to go there. Only once. Only one pint. Only to be able to say he had been there to say hello and goodbye. And then write about it so he could put it to rest forever.

The pub in question was the one where his parents had had their lunchtime wedding reception approximately sixty years previously. The Derby Arms, a place he had only ever seen from the outside and had never felt inclined to enter; the pub had survived while many around it had long since closed. The outer appearance was crinkly, wrinkly and lacking in style or charm. The interior was a slight improvement, helped by a fair crowd of buzzing people who genuinely seemed happy to be there. Nat made his way to the bar.

'Pint of Tetley's, please.' The barman's efficiency, as he made the fetching of the pint glass and the filling thereof look like one fluid movement, led Nat to believe that he must be the manager. Or perhaps just good at his job. Either way, Nat was impressed, feeling less hostile by the minute towards a place he had been avoiding all his life. He parked himself next to two couples engaged in animated conversation. The women smiled at him, the men kept talking. Nat enjoyed a few slugs of Tetley's. It was going down nice and easy. He carefully took in his surroundings and saw a relaxed, chatty congregation, all impatient to get their message across about anything that happened to be on their minds.

There was only one thing on Nat's mind: to view the room where his mum and dad had appeared as man and wife all those years ago. His pint glass now half full, he rose carefully and made his way to the left-hand corner of the pub where a door was half open. He approached it, peered inside and saw a fairly spacious room, now used as storage space for anything not in constant use by the pub. A couple of ancient darts boards, a large, dusty table and about a dozen crates containing full and empty bottles. In one corner stood an abandoned pool table and a very battered-looking kiddies paddling pool contraption. Nat's eyes flickered to an out-of-use serving hatch which now seemed to have no further link to a kitchen. 'Yes, this is it,' he murmured to himself. This is the place. His parents probably hired the whole pub for their special lunchtime event and this room, free of the debris now dominating it, would have been where sandwiches and sausage rolls were served up. And presumably, somewhere, a wedding cake. A young married couple, family and friends on a cold, blue-skied March day, a stone's throw from the church.

It was an anti-climax, as he knew it would be, and his attempt to visualize that scene from 1953 was brusquely interrupted by a voice behind him.

'Can I help yer, mate?' For the second time in the space of two hours, Nat had been caught on the wrong foot by a voice from behind, Nat could only stammer at the man who had served him his pint moments before.

Nat decided that the manager would not be interested in the subject of his reminiscing in a bereft, unused storeroom and lied that he was looking for the toilets. Mr Efficiency pointed him in the right direction. After pretending to have used the toilets, Nat returned to his seat, glad that he had achieved what he had set out to achieve, although sadly aware that places without people are just places.

He had only found out by chance that the wedding lunch had taken place there. His dad rarely talked about the past and Nat's attempts to discern how life had been for his parents in the immediate post-war period and beyond were largely a hit-and-miss affair. If he had ever attempted to write his dad's biography, he would have had to make most of it up: he had precious little to work with. Whenever he asked about the past, his dad's answer would invariably be, 'Oh, I can't remember. It's a long time ago.'

His pint glass now three-quarters empty, he was contemplating the ten-minute walk home. The glass was approaching the mouth, everything pointed towards tasks for the day completed, mission accomplished. Nat had done what he had to do, a quiet, civilized pint had been imbued and the successful operation could be rounded off by a pleasant stroll home. He would reach Sam's place at a respectable hour, then day two off the wagon would have come and gone without major incident, and his plan for stability and moderation would be up and running. The final drop of Tetley's slid down his throat and the muscles in the lower part of his body strained to heave him into a standing position. At the very same moment, 8.10 p.m., the door of the Derby Arms opened and in stepped Eric Keeler, born on the same day and in the same town as Nat Wilson in April 1957. The Derby was one of Eric's local pubs.

Nat knew that the quiet night was about to become loud. He wouldn't be allowed to leave anytime soon; the last orders bell, in just under two hours' time, would be the earliest release date. Before Nat could offer any form of resistance, a frothy pint was coming his way, enthusiastically transported by Ekky (Nobody, with the exception of Eric's parents, had ever called him anything else). Nat and Ekky spent six years together at Primary School and in the intervening time, there were only brief encounters once in a blue moon for the briefest of superficial chats. Ekky knew Nat lived in Germany, Nat knew Ekky had never left the neighbourhood he grew up in. And that was it. The danger of a parallel worlds' conversation was a real one: two people talking to each other without really grasping what the other one was actually talking about. Nat told himself to relax, drink and listen. He would only talk if Ekky wanted him to.

In his prime, Ekky was one of the best-looking blokes Nat had ever seen; a Scouse version of Robert Redford, but with more personality and charm. Thick flaxen hair, moderately tall with a taut figure, fair skin and flashing, mischievous blue eyes. Even at primary school, Ekky looked good. A great footballer, wicked left foot, quick, brave, skilful. Everybody liked him, nobody had a bad word. He had bumped into Ekky on an irregular basis around Old Swan in the fifty years that followed their primary school days, and they had never failed to exchange at least the time of day and to reassure each other that they were doing OK. Having the same birthday was a quirk of fate, but added glue to their superficial sense of complicity. The two hours that now lay before them would determine whether their relationship ever had anything more than brief emotional banter and the random fact that they had shared an almost identical Liverpool background during the first decade of their lives.

Whenever he had bumped into Ekky during any of those aforementioned encounters, the latter invariably had a jaw-droppingly, beautiful woman by his side. It is also true to say that Nat's sightings of him had always been in pubs, and

Ekky had been, more often than not, well under the influence. As the years went on, there was still no shortage of women, but they were, like Ekky, no longer looking quite as pristine and desirable as they used to.

Nat looked long and hard at Ekky: it would be going too far to say that he had lost his looks, but too much booze, not enough sleep, plenty of both end-candle-burning and probably a bad diet had all taken their toll. Nat still loved Ekky's smile and he could understand why so many women had fallen under its spell down the years.

The first pint of Tetley's had gone down fast and the second almost gave Nat the courage to just come out with it and start their evening with the outrageous question, 'Ekky, how many women have you actually shagged?'

An approximate and indirect answer to Nat's question naturally emerged in the course of their conversation as the two men gave each other a brief résumé of their private history. Nat's brief childless story paled weakly compared to Ekky's two marriages, three live-together affairs and (presumably) numerous one night stands which, all together, produced three children (all girls). He also spoke of seven stepchildren, who were, strangely enough, all boys.

'So you're the King Lear of Old Swan,' said Nat. The look of non-comprehension on Ekky's face and the inevitable 'Waddya mean?' made Nat rue his attempt at being witty. He would skip the literary allusions from thereon but still attempted to explain this one to Ekky.

'Well, King Lear had three daughters, didn't he?' He also regretted the "didn't he?", presuming, wrongly, that Ekky was familiar with the main characters of one of Shakespeare's major tragedies. Nat felt like a prat and moved onto more promising, accessible terrain. Football was the obvious direction of travel.

'The Reds are doing well, aren't they?' Ekky took the bait, showed his in-depth knowledge and passion and rambled on at top speed, but with utmost precision, presenting a hilarious history of Liverpool FC's ups and downs. And his views on modern football matched Nat's to the letter: football was business, the bond between players and fans had virtually disappeared and the game had become just another form of entertainment like holidaying, going to restaurants and buying drugs.

Nat was interested to know how Ekky had made his living down the years but wasn't quite sure how to put the question without sounding nosy and hideously middle-class. He wanted the Shakespeare allusion to be the only awkward moment of the evening so he opted for, 'What sort of jobs have you been doing?' Ekky had done virtually anything that paid the bills and facilitated access to fun and games, his sole problem had been reconciling his net income with his gross habits. He had been all over the country and much of North Western Europe, specialising in lucrative, dead-end jobs. His longest term of permanency had been running a second-hand furniture shop just down the road. It had been going quite well until the Inland Revenue started to ask questions he couldn't answer. His eyes lit up as he continued the conversation.

'I sold your dad a table a few years ago. He was made up with it! Has he still got it? How is he by the way?'

'No longer with us, I'm afraid, Ekk.' The brightness drained out of Ekky's face and he offered his condolences.

'My folks have both checked out, too,' he said. Nat went to the bar and got the next round.

'So you've been making a living in Germany?' asked Ekky, as they started their next pints.

'Yeah, mostly in the education sector.'

Ekky's smile returned.

'I always knew you'd do well.' Ekky didn't add, "unlike me," but Nat sensed that this was what he was trying to say. Nat waited for some more questions about his career, but was relieved when none came. Ekky's next question forced him into a brief description of social life in Germany which Nat had offered on numerous occasions to curious Scousers down the years.

'What's the nightlife like over there?' Nat had developed a standard answer containing two dodgy facts which satisfied most people.

'Well, the booze is cheap and the pubs stay open all day and night.' Nat embellished it this time with the ludicrous comparison, 'It's a bit like Amsterdam, but bigger.'

Nat was relieved to see that Ekky wasn't imbibing as ferociously as he thought he might be; their tongues, however, were starting to loosen. A long-legged girl in her mid-twenties floated over to him and pecked Ekky on the cheek. A few whispers were exchanged. She smiled at Nat, shook his hand and drifted away again.

'My youngest' said Ekky with justifiable pride. 'Got a great job at the airport. I'd be lost without Ava. Mind you, all my girls have been good to me. Especially when I had my health issues last year.' Nat probed no further and this time it was Ekky's turn to go to the bar.

Ekky returned with a double Scotch chaser. This time he raised his glass and said, 'Here's to your dad.' Nat had to gulp this down in one as the nasty bit of Deja vu momentarily decentred him. Ekky seemed impressed by Nat's efficient sinking of the double and followed suit. With ten minutes to last orders, Nat was still hoping to understand the life of his primary school friend.

The two men looked at each other and smiled. Perhaps the beauty of their brief time together had been in what they hadn't said, the thoughts they had kept to themselves. And what did alcohol-fuelled conversations about the meaning of life achieve anyway? They were both still alive, exactly the same age and reaching the final chapters; were either of them really interested in each other's earlier chapters? Come to that, was anybody interested? It was just a relaxing bevvy together.

Nat spotted Ekky's sumptuous daughter re-emerging and heading their way at which point he got up to get what he hoped would be the final round.

'Let me get you a drink, Ava. Same again for you, Ekk?' Ekky nodded. Ava followed Nat, saying, 'Let me give you a hand.'

Nat was glad of the help and lurched awkwardly towards the bar, almost falling. Ava held him for a moment; he steadied himself and told himself to get a grip. Her thick Scouse accent didn't contribute to her overall beauty yet the twang reassured. Yes, he was home.

'I've met yer dad. Luvverly man. He talked a lot about you.'

A Bombay Sapphire gin cocktail for Eva, a pint and a large Scotch for her dad and a single for Nat. They made it back to Ekky. The bell rang for last orders.

'Do you remember me mum, Ekk?'

'Yes, I do.' Nat beamed. 'Here's to her,' he whispered to himself. It was time to go. Nat hugged Ekky and placed the most delicate of gentle kisses on Ava's left cheek. She had her dad's smile.

'Be careful, it's cold out there,' was Ekky's parting shot. As Nat walked out onto the pavement, it struck him that it wasn't cold but he still got Ekky's message. There were still some intersections on their individual Liverpool roadways.

It was eleven o'clock. Sam might be getting worried and Nat picked up the pace. Of one thing he was sure: he had been in the Derby Arms for the first and last time in his life. He had swept up some remnants from his past and was doubtful whether they would help him with the present or future; instead, he was simply thankful that he was walking in a straight line again and that he would soon be sitting in Bob's chair in a room he knew well.

He had reached the other side of the road safely. It was the main east-west artery and a number of long side streets cut off at ninety degree angles to his left. Despite the late hour and his jittery need to get back to Sam's place before it got too late, Nat suddenly stopped and peered up the first street: Aviemore Road. The Catholic School and church of his dear mum, bearing the name St Cuthbert's. It stood where it had always stood, at the other end of the street, looking as imperious and cold as ever. A place his mother hated as a child, with its relentless brainwashing and fearmongering and cruelty but also a place she returned to many years later, in spirit at least, as she sat in her wheelchair, waiting for death, the local Catholic priest offering her the body of Christ as often as she wanted before she checked out for ever.

Nat felt uncomfortably enshrouded in the darkness of religion which still offered comfort before the final whistle; but he was also taken with half a century of Liverpool lives when people in this neighbourhood courageously battled poverty, sexual guilt, German bombs and ignorance. He had escaped; Ekky was still shooting in the dark on the same stomping ground, kicking the sexual guilt part of the DNA into touch, grateful for every pint and pound of delicious womanly flesh that had come his way down the years and now heading towards his own final whistle with women, ex-women, wives and ex-wives and daughters of his own. Nat didn't know whether to envy him or count himself lucky to have escaped it all.

The next street came into view as the coolness of the midnight hour created momentary clarity, steadying his mind and balance. Barrymore Road. Nothing here apart from the usual nondescript terraced houses and a barking dog. Chudleigh Road next, offered the same picture, this time without the barking dog. His befuddled mind had, however, spotted something and he stopped in his tracks, realising that he had walked past three roads with the initials A, B and C, in the correct alphabetical order. If his memory served him well, the next street was called Dunmore Road. It was. He tried to excavate the name of the next street from his childhood memory. He couldn't, but twenty paces onwards revealed the quirky truth: the street sign Endsleigh Road was now in full view. And Sam's road was called Frogmore Road. The first six letters of the alphabet. Why? This would be his first question for Sam back at the house; she would surely know the answer.

Nat was returning at an unusually late hour by his standards. Standing outside the front door, he saw the curtain twitch before he had even managed to extricate the key from his pocket. He was relieved that Sam was still awake: he had worried about frightening her out of one of her late-night armchair snoozes.

'Nat, you're late!' she screeched through the front room wall. He wasn't sure if this was a reproach or a conversation starter. He strode into the room as confidently as he could and hoped Sam wouldn't notice the effects of his session with Ekky. He was going to ask Sam about the street name story, but quickly decided that he first owed her an explanation for his lateness.

'Oh, I bumped into an old schoolmate of mine. We had a lot to talk about.' Nat knew Sam's conversation style and braced himself for interrogation on the subject of Ekky.

This time it was different. Sam seemed tired, lethargic and disinterested. Nat was allowed to elaborate on his evening, and even the vaguely scandalous nature of Ekky's lifestyle moved her little. Pangs of guilt were troubling Nat's boozed mind as he realized that he had selfishly overlooked Sam's need to be listened to since he set up base camp there over a month ago. She was grieving. As she opened up, Nat began to understand that the source of her grieving was not simply the passing of Bob, but also the passing of her life.

'Why don't you finish that whisky, Nat?' she said. Nat wasn't sure if it was a good idea, but he sensed that Bob was egging him on. Nat helped himself and dropped into the armchair and Sam kept on talking.

'I'm glad you're finishing that whisky. I didn't want to throw it down the sink. And Pam would have played hell with me if John had got his hands on it.' She smiled and seemed momentarily contented, but continued on a more melancholic path.

'I do wish Bob hadn't drunk so much. He just never knew when to stop.' Nat gave nodded half-hearted agreement as he slurped the Scotch, wondering whether *he* knew when to stop. Sam's next comment reassured him that he did.

'I've never seen *you* drunk, Nat. And your dad was a moderate drinker, wasn't he?' Nat agreed again, but didn't like the smugness welling up inside him and half-heartedly defended Bob.

'Bob had a lot of good points though,' was the best he could think of. Sam didn't take up the invitation to list any of these points and an awkward silence ensued. Then she continued.

'Perhaps I was too soft. But when you love somebody, you forgive, don't you?' As the generous portion of Scotch he had poured himself was preventing Nat from making any noteworthy contribution to the conversation, he grunted his customary agreement and hoped that she might start talking about something else. She didn't. There followed ten minutes of Sam relating a long list of all the mistakes she had made in her fifty-year marriage to Bob. Nat finished the Scotch.

Sam's main argument was that she had been weak. But she didn't claim that she could have been anything else. Even Nat, in his current state of advanced drunkenness, could see that Sam just wanted to be listened to. Sam always wanted to be listened to, but this time she was talking about something genuinely important: her failure to change the man she had married.

Nat had a decision to make: should he add his tuppence worth to the proceedings while he was still just about able? He decided against any intervention and started planning the thirteen steps up the stairs to his box room. She had gone quiet but was softly weeping; he had never seen his aunt cry before. He stared at her, helpless.

'Night, Nat,' was all she could muster.

'Night, Sam,' he echoed. Both of them pretended that she wasn't crying. He trudged up the stairs, relieved that the listening was over for the day. If he got up at a reasonable hour tomorrow, he would be able to avoid any further input from Sam for the rest of the day. He would only need to placate her one last time before bedtime when her inevitable "Did you have a nice day?" would oblige him to select and relate some of the happenings which might interest her. He was now too tired to think; he had had one too many and was close to collapsing. Getting his clothes off took an inordinate amount of time, especially his socks. It was a bit like a cat chasing its tail. The cat was the last thought of the day. It melted into the deep sleep which quickly enveloped him.

7

If Nat had learned to appreciate anything during his self-imposed, go-it-alone residencies in Greece and Liverpool, it was the power of early morning sober reflections, which were far more useful than the confused intensity of alcohol-fuelled philosophising late at night, either alone or with anybody drunk enough to philosophise with you. This half-truth dawned on him again as his eyes creaked open and he started to piece together the remnants of the previous evening. He tried to gather his thoughts but his valiant efforts were debilitated by a steady throbbing of his head and the disturbing movements of a mangled stomach.

He feebly tried to gather himself by peering down the street, which was glistening after a nocturnal downpour. The sound of the next-door neighbour's door opening and slamming shut in the space of approximately four seconds interrupted his incoherent thoughts. Sam's neighbour, John, was shuffling down the street at speed: a man with a mission. Nat remembered Bob's mocking tone when he used to tell him about John getting up 'at the crack of dawn' every day to get his newspaper. Nat blurrily looked at his mobile to check Bob's definition of 'the crack of dawn'. It was 6.25. The rising sun was indeed announcing the dawn and it struggled to make its presence felt over the western skies down by the Mersey but it just succeeded in momentarily bathing John's right side with an impressive beam. At that very moment, John turned a sharp right into Prescot Road and headed due East, where the nearest newsagent awaited him, approximately two hundred metres away.

John had moved into number 14 Frogmore Road a couple of years before Sam married Bob and was, after Sam, the street's oldest resident, along with his wife, Pam. Most people used the expression "rough diamond" when describing John: short and solid, a foghorn voice layered with the broadest of Scouse accents, the oddest sense of humour, a mound of mischief and, in his younger days, a phenomenal drinker. As pubs closed in the neighbourhood at the turn of the century and his health became less robust, sense and reason prevailed and he cut down accordingly. His one remaining weakness was the odd tipple of Scotch, which could transform him into a surreal but harmless madman once the tipple began to resemble a flow. Bob and John's Christmas Day whisky marathons had invariably ended in anarchic chaos down the years and had been unilaterally banned by Pam and Sam in the latter years of Bob's life.

Nat's early morning thoughts lazily stayed with John and he wondered how a man of his ilk structured his life. If he was racing down the road with such intensity at half past six in the morning, he clearly had some sort of agenda and Nat started sketching out a possible day in the life of John Ashton, based on what he still knew of everyday life in Liverpool life.

Quite why Nat was spending these early morning moments guessing how the daily life of a retired working class Scouser panned out was unclear. The pain of his hangover might have had something to do with it; pondering on how John gave his life meaning and structure had a soothing, almost therapeutic effect. It was also a pleasant reminder of his fundamental thesis that from routine a good life could spring, a life with the danger of unpleasant surprises largely removed. Nat was on the verge of awarding John's life plan an unremarkable seven out of ten, being critical only of its apparent lack of culture, when he remembered that John was a creator of culture. He sang.

God, yes! Could he sing? Watching him behind the mic in a pub, covering anything from Bing Crosby to Joe Cocker, was a sight to behold; a natural talent with real soul. Nat could never forget his rendering of "I Left My Heart in San Francisco" in a pub across the road many years ago. John belted out the final line and the crescendo of audience noise and emotion took Nat's breath away. John's fame had reached as far as Llandudno, on the coast of North Wales, where he and his wife spent many a summer weekend and where he regularly took the mic in the local pubs near their B&B. Nat mused that if the Welsh let you sing in their pub, and then ask you to come back and do it again and again, you must be pretty good.

Nat concluded his thoughts on John at the precise moment the latter returned with his newspaper. This time he needed a little longer to deal with the door: he heard an F-word as John's key did not find the keyhole immediately. The door slammed and silence followed. Nat lay back on his pillow and felt a faint improvement in his head pain, allowing him to upgrade the quality of thought and devote it more to the philosophical.

He started theorizing. John's singing was the passion that raised him above the mundane and this talent gave him pride and a sense of self-worth. He had a gift that few possessed: he could take people, in this case, a live audience, to another dimension. The power of John's song transported them to a world they might not understand but which they instinctively knew to be better than their place on Earth, temporarily releasing them from the routine and ordinary, the unpleasant and frightening. It was, however, only a brief respite from their daily grinds and worries and John, the singer, the artist, also had to re-enter the world of crack-of-dawn walks to the newsagent every morning.

And it was a truth that John presumably accepted: expressing himself artistically twice a month in an appreciative, rocking Welsh pub was all well and good, but he must always be aware that the real world would still be waiting for him when the applause subsided and the evening's performance was over. Keeping on a high long after their audience had gone home was probably something which John, wisely, never tried to do.

Nat was convinced that John would never have wanted a different life, no matter what glory and fame his singing career might have sporadically brought his way. Transcending his life as a plasterer and Pam's husband might have been possible, but never desirable; a rousing round of applause in a pub and a few free pints was enough. His lack of ambition had led to a contented, stable life.

In the same way, Ekky would probably never have wanted to leave the confines of Old Swan. Sex, drugs and rock and roll and enough money to finance all three was enough for him. Putting it crudely, buckling down to getting on any sort of career ladder was far less important than getting his leg over. Perhaps the closest either John or Ekky got to the truth was in sublime moments of vocal perfection for John, or sexual nirvana for Ekky. And when those moments were over they got back to the main task at hand: surviving.

They lived their lives, made the best of things, and didn't analyse or share their thoughts on politics, culture or climate change with anybody; they were too busy getting on with their lives. They were the *Somewhere* men who knew were they came from and where they belonged; they weren't even particularly worried about where they were going as long as they were getting their portion of bread and circuses, that ultimate appeaser favoured by the ancient Roman rulers.

So that made Nat the *Nowhere* man who had seen a bit of the world and had benefitted from the variety contained therein. Nomadic strains had got into his system. Friendships and relationships had lasted as long as he lived in any one town or region. Any roots he had were to be found in this part of Liverpool where he was now resting his broken head. But those roots were looking ever more tenuous and becoming ever more scarce. He respected and admired John and Ekky, the two men who were currently starting their day next door and a few streets away and wondered whether he envied them. He wasn't sure.

He lay his head back on the generous pillow, closed his eyes and enjoyed the early morning breeze wafting through the old-fashioned sash window. His hangover was easing with every tick of the clock. In the silence he was praying: thanks for the day, and for the rain stopping and the insights he had gently excavated from the previous evening's imbroglio with the help of the morning and its revelatory inspirations.

West-east, east-west

Nat refines the smut, revels in West German bourgeois hospitality, embraces the prosperity of the economic miracle and gets a free history and geography lesson. And all with a guilty, friendly smile on his face. He's coming along.

A balmy day in early summer. A busy couple on a long, spacious terrace were bringing all manner of interesting food and drink to their special guest. They were moving swiftly and with a purpose; well organised, as if they had done this sort of thing before.

'Anything I can do to help?' he yelled into their state-of-the-art kitchen, hoping they would turn down his half-hearted offer. Fortunately, they did, and he was able to concentrate on watching Gudrun's shapely form darting back and forth, smiling sweetly every time she passed him. They had recently got onto first name terms and she had just introduced him to her husband. 'You must come round for lunch sometime. My husband is dying to meet you,' she said after one of his classes. He wasn't keen on the husband idea, but could hardly say no. So he was sitting there, reconciling himself to the fact that the lanky, distinguished, gruesome-looking chap present had been fortunate enough to land a considerably younger, attractive woman.

Fuelled by his disappointment, and displaying gross unfairness, Nat immediately deemed the man unworthy of Gudrun; they were like the German version of Esmeralda and Quasimodo, except the husband was taller and didn't have a hump. And Nat had already discovered that the man's diction was far better than Quasimodo's and he possessed the ability to string together coherent sentences in an educated, entertaining and pleasing manner. This all belied an otherwise unpleasing demeanour. If anybody were to give you a photo of him, you would hand it back with the words, 'Ugly bastard, isn't he?' He also had a name that Nat didn't like: Rüdiger. Rüdiger by name, Rüdiger by nature, he thought, ungainly and lacking in grace. He rushed to consider theories about why he'd attracted Gudrun: his intelligence might have conquered her intellectual erogenous zones; she might prefer older men; he might have money. It certainly wasn't his looks.

Nat was rambling to himself again and needed to get back to being an appreciative guest. The food was ready.

There were endless tasty delights to choose from, ranging from salads, a staggering selection of bread, homemade soup and delicate, delicious finger food. Their flat was spacious, filled with all the trappings a double-earning couple with no kids could afford towards the end of the twentieth century in a Germany anxious to show off how well it was doing. They had functional but modern furniture and trendy modern art on the walls. Understated elegance and well-educated taste held sway. Beyond the balcony were dozens of similar houses backed off by neat gardens, well-clipped bushes and tall trees; their neighbours would all be enjoying a similar lifestyle. Leafy German suburbia never looked better.

Nat felt relaxed, serene and grateful, yet also guilty, as he thought of a very different life back home, hundreds of miles west of the place he was now sitting. There, they were probably about to tuck into beans on toast, with a poky, concrete yard as a backdrop. Here, Nat was revelling in the tangible fruits of post-war West German diligence and prosperity.

Rüdiger seemed to have something to say about any given topic and one of his favourite rhetorical tricks became clear within moments of his first monologue: repetition. Goebbels knew it worked and Rüdiger had made the technique his own in a big way. The first message he was determined to relay to young Nat was the importance of being lucky in life; without it, Rüdiger argued, you were pissing in the wind. Although he repeated his main message endlessly, he used different words and expressions every time, gesticulating like a court jester and employing a variety of facial expressions, exaggerated intonation, manic laughter and giggly grunts to great effect. Goebbels would have been proud of Rüdiger's dogged determination to deliver one simple message in as many convincing ways as possible until the listener relented and believed he was hearing the truth.

Nat did not feel that his German was yet good enough to offer any seriously coherent opposition to Rüdiger's bludgeoning style. And, anyway, who could possibly disagree with the notion that luck played a major role in the success we make of life? What was there to argue about? It was stating the bleeding obvious to the power of ten. Nat was also drinking Rüdiger's beer and eating his food on his immaculate terrace, hardly the time for instigating conflict with the man who was making it possible. There would be other times for locking horns; this was assuming, of course, that their friendship was going to last any time beyond this late Saturday afternoon in June.

Gudrun hinted that Rüdiger was talking too much. She had faded into the background as Rüdiger presented his thesis on the role of luck in people's lives. Nat attempted to engage her in conversation about her job - she was a teacher of German and art. He heard precise, concise insights into life in a German Secondary School. She knew her craft and sounded like a woman who had found her vocation and knew what to do with it. Nat was relieved she was back in the conversation.

Rüdiger realised that he had been hogging proceedings and thrust Gudrun back into the limelight, duly praising his wife's commitment to her job. He looked at her as a parent would a gifted child who had just pulled off a difficult Chopin piano piece. Not surprisingly, Gudrun didn't quite know what to say and a brief flurry of embarrassment ruffled her; she produced her customary coy smile. Then Rüdiger intervened.

'Nat, you wouldn't believe how many hours Gudrun spends preparing her lessons. She must be the best prepared teacher in Bad Oeynhausen!' Gudrun wasn't enjoying this but Rüdiger didn't understand why. Nat's rudimentary grasp on relationships told him that this was a mismatch, a marital accident waiting to happen.

'Would you like another drink, Nat?' was her way out. She fetched fresh drinks.

As the afternoon pleasantly progressed into early evening, Nat saw more icebergs on the Rüdiger-Gudrun Titanic horizon: Rüdiger was a drinker; a chain smoker; an oddball who didn't fit into society. Gudrun was none of those things, which added further fuel to his fears that their marriage would not last the distance.

Rüdiger worked in a bank; it was not his chosen profession. He'd always wanted to be an artist and he proceeded to explain what had gone wrong.

'It was what my father wanted, you see, Nat. He managed a bank a few miles from here and he wanted the same sort of thing for me. My brother studied pharmacy and became a pharmacist, so he insisted that I study economics and business studies with an eye to me becoming a banker, too.'

It was easy to see where Rüdiger's line of protest was going and it had a distinct ring of cliché about it: the creative child being held back by the sensible parent. If Rüdiger had been allowed to study art and become an artist, he would have lived a fulfilled life, driven by artistic passion rather than the need for financial stability and comfortable prosperity. Nat couldn't resist raising an obvious objection at this point.

'But you haven't done so badly, have you, Rüdiger?' he ventured, backing his observation with a cheeky glance at the salubrious surroundings and eye-catching wife. Nat had severe doubts about whether Gudrun would have been so taken by the starving artist version of her present husband.

'Do you see me complaining, Nat?' he said. Nat laughed, sensibly omitting to point out that yes, he had been complaining. It was the first time that he had noted the tendency of some Germans to suffer from a certain "having your cake and eating it" syndrome. Nat guessed that Rüdiger wanted to lead the carefree life of a paint-smothered artist rubbing shoulders with like-minded brethren and sharing bodily fluids with spaced-out female members of this bohemian community while enjoying the comforts of serious post-war prosperity. He felt it best not to take his line of argument any further; he was a guest in Rüdiger's home, and enjoying himself. Instead, they kept on talking and drinking. Rüdiger didn't take offence easily - he was growing on Nat.

Rüdiger asked him which part of England he came from and Nat tried to be clever, saying, 'Oh, it's a place about five hundred miles west of here.' Not to be outdone, Rüdiger said, 'And I come from a place about five hundred miles east of here.' The two statements had something wondrous about them and they both laughed. The guessing game started on where these places might be and Rüdiger won, naming Liverpool in double quick time. Nat took considerably longer naming Rüdiger's place of birth; in fact, he couldn't. His knowledge of East German geography beyond Berlin was, at that time, scanty. Frankfurt an der Oder was the best he could come up with. Wrong.

Rüdiger's place of birth was no longer in Germany, but in the Soviet Union. That sounded very east and definitely more than five hundred miles away. It wasn't. He was right in observing that Königsberg (now known as Kaliningrad) was, as the crow flies, almost exactly five hundred miles east of where they were now sitting - 820 kilometres, to be precise - and Liverpool (still known as Liverpool) almost exactly five hundred miles to the west (808 kilometres).

Two souls had travelled five hundred miles in opposite directions at crucial moments in their lives to be united on a sun-drenched terrace; this was a coincidence worth writing home about and it instantly roused Nat's imagination. Their paths spread from one end of Europe to the other: Nat had escaped Margaret Thatcher, and Rüdiger the Soviets, whose Red Army was about to take their first major German town, his hometown, in the most easterly part of the soon-to-be defunct Third Reich. His mother had pretended to be a nurse and talked herself onto an already overcrowded hospital train heading west, clutching her two sons, Rüdiger and Hendrik. It was January 1945, the war had returned home and Germany was sliding towards zero hour and the two young brothers to a new home in the west.

From where Nat was sitting, all he could see were two civilized people who had never known bombs, a hungry belly or the real misery of war. Nobody made any effort to fill the silence that resulted from their momentary mental excursion through space and time. Crickets were starting to chirp in the fading light. Gudrun looked on edge, her smile more fragile than ever; Rüdiger emitted an ambiguous grunt and Nat took his mind for a stroll across a thousand miles and thirty-five years of post-war European history. By his standards, Rüdiger was remaining silent for a disturbing length of time. Gudrun broke the spell.

'You must be feeling the pinch, Nat. Would you like us to drive you home?'

She had interrupted disturbing yet fascinating thoughts, but Nat accepted the offer.

'We must do this again sometime,' was his trite parting shot.

Rüdiger perked up, and with a customary snigger announced, 'We will, Nat, we will! ' They shared the look that only fellow refugees can share and followed Gudrun to the car outside. A quirky, beautiful relationship was creaking into existence and they would never mention war, or *the* war, again.

8

Nat would be leaving Liverpool in twenty-one days and he wondered what he had achieved since he had arrived. Had he wanted to achieve anything or was this just another chapter in the continuing story of structured drifting, made possible by a Lotto win and, during this phase, the tolerance of a lonely widowed aunt who seemed to appreciate his company when he found the time to listen to her?

In moments of listlessness and self-doubt, he had always put on the philosophical hat that enabled him to create something positive from what appeared to be nothing. He had grown closer to Sam than he had thought possible; she was a well-meaning and resilient soul who had endured much in her life without ever complaining. Nat was hearing her voice and understanding her for the first time.

She could be happy with little, reminding him of his dad who only ever wanted a good cup of strong tea, the back page of the Echo, a ciggie and the occasional pint and a live football match, even if this was only listening on the radio. Nat could probably learn from their ability to be happy with little and thought of the maxim that those who cannot be happy with little, can never be happy, full stop.

Their Sunday lunches in town were part of Nat's "less is more" education. Try as he may, Sam would never try anything new: same main, same dessert, same solitary drink. 'Oh, I couldn't, Nat, really!' she always said as he tried to nurture in her a new approach to cuisine. He gave up after the third

Sunday. Sam had what she always had: roast beef and Yorkshire pudding, followed by rhubarb crumble and custard and a cup of tea.

Nat was convinced that going out for a meal intimidated Sam and made her feel guilty. Nobody from her generation would go out for their tea every second evening as Nat did; nor would they have their Sunday roast out every week. In the eyes of his generation, of course, his weekly eating out arrangements would not be considered particularly decadent; perhaps just a little strange. Something you would do if you were a loser without a wife and kids or remaining relatives.

Well, he had a remaining relative and her name was Sam and they were getting on just fine. They accepted each other's opposing lifestyles and were filling a gap until he made his way to the airport on the twenty-second of June. The time for philosophizing for today was over and now it was time for him to redouble his efforts in devoting himself to another routine task which was supposed to take his mind off such thoughts and explain what had happened in his life: the book.

The book. His chance. To explain himself to the world. And to the generations to follow. It sounded like noble gestures, but the chances of the world and its generations wanting to read Nat's explanations were low. Very low. This troubled him little. If nothing else, the book kept him out of the pub and confronted him with the troubling yet amusing experience of working out what he had made of his life so far.

The book might even prove that he would not have done anything differently, even given the chance. Because he couldn't. His younger hands –like everybody's young hands – were tied by a lack of experience and an overabundance of lust and freedom. And the ability to be in the right place, at the right time, with the right woman was another party trick he had never quite mastered. That's where luck added its de-stabilising portion of absurdity, reminding you that the roulette wheel had the final say.

Nat was good at weaving entertaining structure into his book; he was less successful at putting meat onto the bones of the structure. If truth be known, he had not written much in Liverpool and he was sadly coming to the disturbing conclusion that the lack of booze was the problem. Although he had already rejected the dangerous idea of keeping up with those boozing literary giants, Joyce, Fitzgerald and Hemingway, he also knew that a few drinks always loosened his literary imagination.

He was going to follow the gut feeling idea that had appealed to him a few months ago: he would do proofreading and editing in a sober condition and seek creativeness and originality under the influence when he would write like a man possessed as the booze-inspired words would miraculously fill up the screen of his laptop. In other words, sober mornings for sober jobs and *moderately* boozy evenings to lift his book above the mediocre. He hoped this method would improve the quality of his work without pushing him into the dangerous waters of addiction. This also meant that he could spend more time with Sam, conveniently assuaging his nagging guilt that he had been selfish and neglectful.

Everything he had written since he landed in Greece nine months ago was from memory: floating moments hanging in the air which he injected either with a slick sharpness or an unclear haze. But they were often no more than shaky, cobwebbed memories. He fleshed out flimsy facts into fiction, decorated them with lies and half-truths and cooked them into some sort of tasty stew which he hoped would tickle the taste buds of any reader dipping their spoon in.

So far, however, he had only shot about seven thousand memory bullets, not a prodigious amount in the space of eight months, amounting to approximately one thousand a month, 250 a week, thirty-five a day. Couldn't he do better than that? Franz Kafka had to toil in an insurance company all day, battle ill health and an unsympathetic father and *he* churned out three novels and numerous short stories. Nat was a comfortable drifter who didn't need to work or care about anybody save himself and all he could manage was a miserly seven thousand words. Nothing much to be proud of there.

It was clear to him that anything too closely resembling an autobiography killed any idea of his book becoming a novel so he decided to dive into everything that was going on all around him. Instead of only cooking something up something from hazy, distant memories, he would stir-fry the fresh ingredients that he smelt every day. What was stopping him doing both, offering his readers a past and present picture show?

He had given himself a good talking to and the new remit fitted him like a glove. He was relieved that he could now tap into everything that came his way, enabling him to paint pictures on every page he turned, an endless supply of paint below his brush, just waiting to be dipped into. He started dipping immediately after his revelation and doubled his seven thousand-word total within a week, headed confidently towards twenty thousand. He was on a roll.

He noted that Sam was taking an increasing interest in his book, which was lifting her away from her usual reminiscing and maudlin ramblings. Her questions regarding the book were the sort he had expected, ranging from the easy ones like "What's it about?" or "Is it a love story?" to the more difficult ones like "Do you think I'd like it?" and "Is there a happy ending?" One particular question, "Do you think I would understand it?" saddened him because it made him feel as if he came from a different planet rather than the same town. Her question particularly rattled him because he was aiming for a universal audience: he wanted university professors, nuclear scientists, supermarket checkout assistants and security guards to get something from his book. Sam's reluctance to read a book which wasn't a story about people falling in love and living happily ever after dealt a serious blow to Nat's idea of winning over the supermarket fraternity.

'Why wouldn't you understand it?'

'Well, do you use fancy words?'

'Well, I use the words which best get my message across. But I don't use words you don't know, just words you don't hear very often. And I try and vary my words so it doesn't get boring.'

'Well, that sounds really interesting. I can't wait to read it. And what's it about again?'

'It's about a man who's trying to find out the best way to live his life.'

Sam now looked thoughtful and after a short moment asked: 'What about women? Has this man given up on women? I mean, he is looking for a woman. Is it a love story? Or has he given up?'

'Well, we never give up on women, do we?'

'I think that might be a very interesting read,' she said. 'When will it be finished? I can't wait to read it.'

Nat had found his first customer and decided to retire for the night while the going was good.

Soon he would be gone for another year. He felt a shiver but steadied himself with the knowledge that he had pulled things around. The book was going somewhere; Liverpool hadn't devoured him and knocked him off course with its customary invitation to wallow in the past; he'd thrown off Maria's scent and was ready for Germany again with its detached but familiar safety net. Then his first annual cycle would be done. And before he knew it, he would be staring at the back of a Greek taxi driver's head as he blurted out the usual question, 'Where you from?' Answering that one was a doddle; explaining where he was going would require a bit more work.

9

With twenty-four words of the book completed, Nat Wilson gave himself a week off before he left England. In the first half of the remaining days, he would edit, rehash and polish, but didn't envisage adding new words or action. Then he would go walking and see what happened; a non-committed observer, sniffing out the places of previous crimes, misdemeanours and wasted time.

On his first day of self-imposed idleness, Monday, he decided not to leave the house. The locals called it "Mad Monday", the day when people felt the need to extend the excesses of the weekend into the working week to squeeze out one last portion of joy. He couldn't face it and offered to help Sam with the weekly shopping and then carry the washing to the laundrette half a mile down the road in the afternoon, which left him so tired that he ended up having an early night. The second day was plagued by horrible backache, presumably caused by the lugging about he had done on the previous day. On the third day he felt unable to do anything, as if a colossal stone was chained around his ankle, preventing him from moving. Something had entered him, a silent but persistent voice telling him not to be a fool. Keep out of danger. Read a good book. Have an early night. Stay safe.

His plans to make Thursday the "breakout day" were thwarted by Sam asking him to stay at home as she was having her bi-annual visit from her brother and his wife, whose birth-day fell on that very day. Sam's comment, 'I've told them so much about you,' made him stay. They arrived at four. Sam later served up some Cornish pasties out of the oven, and by eight-thirty they were having a last cup of tea, before saying goodbye at nine-fifteen and heading back to the leafy suburbs of Cheshire.

Sandwiched in between that was painless conversation with thoroughly decent people who showed themselves to be both intelligent and compassionate. Roy, the brother, had been in the pharmaceutical industry all his life and Theresa had been headmistress of a local primary school. She expressed panicky concern that standards of parenting had dropped so rapidly during her years in teaching that she felt the country had a scary future ahead of it; she was glad she was able to get out when she did. Roy didn't mention his job once, possibly convinced that nobody would understand what he was talking about anyway.

The highlight of the evening came just before they left, when Roy made an announcement.

'We always used to bring Bob a bottle of pure malt, so we thought you might like to accept it on his behalf.'

On the spot, Nat forgave Roy for being a slightly boring chemist; he was touched and momentarily speechless.

They said their goodbyes and Nat felt guilty and sad - the bottle was supposed to be for Bob. He had had enough of drinking whisky alone.

Sam's unexpected praise eased his guilt as soon as her relatives were off the premises.

'I'm so glad you were here, Nat. I never know what to talk about with them.' He put the bottle on top of the fridge in the hallway and pledged not to touch it.

He watched News at Ten and went to bed, as sober as a

judge, and wondered whether he would ever make it into town again. The next day was Friday, dangerously close to the weekend, that time when Liverpool people stopped thinking about tomorrow. As he closed his eyes, he was thinking about tomorrow and steeled himself to venture into town the next day, carefully forage around and make it back in one piece. It felt like he was planning a reconnaissance in which only meticulous attention to detail would ensure survival. Or perhaps he was just getting old. Nat dragged his feet slowly through Friday, hoping Sam would give him something to do which would prevent him from getting onto the bus into town. She didn't. She watched her afternoon soap and nodded off. He didn't know whether this was customary; he had hardly ever been around in her afternoons to know much about her routine.

Guilt nibbled away at him again as he wondered what he had given her in the last couple of months. He had been writing, rethinking his past, procrastinating and trying to make sense of this square mile of Liverpool he had grown up in. During that time Sam had been doing all the things she had always done in her life and their paths had only crossed in quiet moments as the midnight hour approached when she talked about things she had never talked about before; Nat was unsure about whether he was supposed to offer an opinion or not. He usually didn't and half regretted now that he hadn't. Sam had been talking about her dead husband and a marriage that had lasted the course despite his uncle's reluctance to accept much responsibility for its success. She had opened up to Nat because there was nobody else left.

He was well aware of Bob's many foibles and failings, but he remained a family legend for Nat and Nat wanted, for better or worse, to keep it that way. Sam had had a chance to talk and presumably felt better for having done so. He reckoned that any other further interventions would have caused further pain. He could neither defend nor condemn Bob.

Sam was taking a long time waking up and he contemplated giving her a gentle nudge. Instead, he sat down, took off his shoes and drowsily waited. His eyes repeatedly closed and reopened and the gaps between light and dark became ever shorter until he himself dropped off and started dreaming.

Thwarted

Two generations intersect in a post office warehouse; for the first time in their lives, communication is stifled as uncle and nephew seek to make a living.

He was in a dusty, noisy late-Victorian warehouse, dragging Royal Mail bags across the floor before pitching them, with the help of a grossly overweight and cursing colleague with an appalling complexion, into the rear hold of a red mail van, now overflowing with similar bags. They gasped and the word 'Fuck' emerged from their dry gullets for the hundredth time that day. Their break was still ten minutes away: just time to fill another bag with parcels and bustle it onto the back of another van.

The thirty-man team had learned very quickly that overweight and underweight bags would be sent back by the overseer, so their job was made even more tedious by the need to weigh them first. And there was always a queue for the weighing machine. The overall tedium was fortunately reduced by the constant flow of inane, furious but ultimately hilarious comments about the overseer and their grim surroundings as the motley crew assembled around the much-coveted machine, hoping that their load was within the plus or minus weight range. After working there for a couple of days, many inmates regularly obtained a 100% success rate.

The overseer took the greatest pleasure observing unlucky packers repacking and never missed a facetious comment for the unlucky ones who had got it wrong. The urge to kill the overseer was strong amongst the men but as it was a temporary job for the three-week Christmas pressure period only, nobody had weakened; they were further pacified by the thought of their pay out on 23 December, their last day, when they could blow most of it in nearby city centre shops and pubs. The tea breaks every ninety minutes with their banter, banalities and obscenities were the other vital escape valve.

They spewed out new swear words and dragged themselves and their filled sacks once more to the weighing and loading area. A new van backed up, the driver's door swung open and a cheerful gent jumped out and, almost in a sprint, opened the rear doors.

'It's all yours, boys!' he beckoned, pulling out a packet of fags and stepping back to allow the rabble to fill the back of his van with their dusty sacks. He too had a gentle but fiendish look, not unlike that of the infernal overseer.

Their eyes met. 'Nat! What…' No more words were forthcoming from the driver's open mouth as his nephew struggled to get the final pre-tea break sack into the designated area. Any chance of further communication was thwarted as the overseer bellowed, 'Tea break! Back in fifteen minutes!'

Nat waved and Bob tried to say something. They never got

to speak; Nat went one direction to the area designated for tea urns and break time and two minutes later, Bob was driving off his van down Victoria Street, heading towards the Mersey Tunnel, hoping his nephew was going to get through the day in one piece.

Nat woke up.

'All right lad?' Nat opened his eyes, sat bolt upright in the armchair and there stood John Ashton, Sam's neighbour, right in front of him in the middle of the living room; Sam was hovering just behind him. Dream over, it was now time for a real tea break.

'We're going to have a cuppa. Would you like one?' she asked.

He wasn't sure how much of John he could take sober; he finished his tea in record time and said, 'I'm going to say good-bye to Liverpool.' He cringed at the over-the-top pathos of his announcement, but Sam seemed rather taken by it. 'Nat's a writer, John' she said, explaining Nat's dramatic language. John looked unimpressed, muttering a sarcastic, 'Is he now?'

Sam decided to see the writer to the door and wished him a nice evening. She hugged him. The hug was unexpected and he was unbalanced for a moment. He shuffled away at a brisk pace and didn't look back. The need for a drink was growing by the minute. He saw a bus pulling up at the bus stop at the bottom of the street and sprinted towards it like a man on the run. He jumped on. Sam was still at the doorway, saying goodbye to John. It was almost five-thirty. He trudged up the stairs to the top deck and bagged the front window seat. A little boy again, he drank in the familiar view of the A57, aka Prescot Road, pointing due west towards the centre of town and the river beyond. The heavy traffic emerging from the opposite direction was making slow progress as shoppers and workers headed home to their suburbs in the east; he felt strangely invincible and privileged.

The buildings flanking both sides of the road were rundown, some desolate with boarded-up windows. Others offered dubious pleasures: a spacious Wetherspoons, a drive-in McDonald's, a dozen or so betting shops and numerous dodgy take-away outlets. Only a couple of original pubs still existed on this main road through Kensington, boasting grand regal names such as "The Princess Alexandra" and "The Prince of Wales". The building coming into view immediately after them had always represented the sole moment of quality in hundreds of journeys Nat had made on that bus into town: Kensington Library. The combination of Victorian architectural elegance and the message in gold letters above the main entrance had always moved him: "Reading maketh a full man; conference a ready man and writing an exact man." The quote was by Francis Bacon, a seventeenth century writer of some repute. Yes, Kensington Library was always the only thing worth seeing on this stretch of the A57, and it was still trying to convince the local inhabitants that education was the answer.

He knew where his first port of call had to be: The Carnarvon Castle. An old people's pub, for people like him. No music, with considerate, gentle folk eager to strike up a conversation with you if you so wished and remain unobtrusive if you didn't. So if your soul was after solitude, you could slowly ease down your bitter as the pub soothed you down and took you in its imaginary arms and let you rest in its beer-perfumed breasts. He thought of all the people who had shared time with him in the Carnarvon. Most were dead and, he wondered, like a small child wonders, where they were and how they were doing. Whether they ever looked down on him, to use the naïve phrase that people always use when they claim that somebody was looking down on them. Those left behind tended to claim such things and feel better for saying them and Nat was no exception. He went to the bar and ordered.

He had to get something to eat; he would go primitive and get a portion of fish and chips with mushy peas in a plastic container, complete with plastic knife and fork. He was wilfully going to smother it with salt and vinegar and then abandon the plastic cutlery after consuming it. He would probably end up spilling half of it on the street. It didn't matter. There was a place selling such delicacies for less than a fiver just around the corner. *Fuck refined and healthy cuisine served in tasteful surroundings*, he thought.

He would cruise the town centre brandishing what much of the local wildlife brandished: fish and chips with plastic cutlery. That way, he might not stand out as the mixed-up kid who had started his life amongst them, escaped, muddled his way through a solid, decent education, read a few books, found gainful employment and met interesting people in a selection of towns along the way and ended up achieving the dubious privilege of being able to call himself classless whilst pretending to be part of a German middle class who had now taken him into their homes, taught him about the finer things in life and regarded him as one of *their* own. Despite these life-long self-doubts and accompanying confusion, he was, at least on this particular Friday evening, home, the place which had, together with his parents' gentle mentoring, given him everlasting values. Germany had finished off the job and he desperately wanted to believe that he had become a decent human being.

But this was not the time for soul-searching and self-analysis: getting a greasy lining on his stomach was the priority and only then would he be able to mingle with his fellow Scouse citizens in the fury of a Liverpool Friday night. He plonked his empty pint glass on the bar, prompting a 'Thanks, luv,' from the barmaid. He bade her goodnight even though it wasn't yet quite 7.10 p.m.

Standing in the fish bar, he remembered the Roger McGough poem, *Vinegar* about the bloke who *sometimes feels like a priest in a fish and chip queue quietly thinking as the vinegar runs through how nice it would be to buy supper for two.* Nat wasn't so sure whether it would be nice. But it wouldn't be bad either. He heard a voice in his head saying, 'You'll never finish that,' as the young man behind the counter handed him the overflowing mess steaming in its industrially produced container. He would give it a go. He manoeuvred his way past a couple of sharp-dressed men who were girding up their loins for the challenges of the night ahead.

They would have their plan in mind, he was sure of that. *His* plan extended no further than finishing the fish and chips and walking; having another drink; walking more; stopping once more for one more. By which time he would be thinking about getting back up the A57 in an easterly direction. The two gents he had just squeezed past would have a different plan: they would drink at least ten times more than Nat and – this was the vital difference – they would be trying to spend the latter part of their evening in the company of the opposite sex with whom they would exchange a flurry of words and gestures and, if their luck was in, considerably more when their night drew to its weary conclusion.

Nat had a minor exhaustion attack just thinking about the endless patience, energy and ingenuity they were going to need in their mission to make the night a success. The obstacles in their way as they combed the partying areas like minesweepers would be formidable and he felt not the slightest touch of envy or even desire to attempt the same.

He sat down on a bench and attempted to operate the plastic knife and fork, always fearful of one or both of them snapping at any given moment. He concentrated, chomped and, to his own surprise, enjoyed. It was the first thing he had eaten since his Spartan breakfast about eight hours before and he felt strength returning. His dad was right, he wasn't going to finish it all, and he scuttled towards a litter bin before a vicious gull nearby started its attack. He dumped the messy leftovers and the gull did the rest.

He started marching. Unlike the two warriors from the fish bar now entering the fray, he wasn't "going over the top", yet he was on the alert, as Friday night warriors always were. He was on a reconnaissance, prowling, ready to run, duck, twist and weave when danger signs flashed. There were ground rules to guarantee his safety: don't stare, make no comments on people's appearance or opinions, avoid over-crowded places, don't knock people's drinks over (and if you do, replace them immediately) and don't drink too much. These rules came naturally to Nat after forty years of Friday nights in his hometown.

He had plenty to be grateful for: clement weather, a few bob in his pocket, a couple of frothy pints behind him, an over-generous portion of fish and chips inside him and the freedom to do what he wanted with the Friday night that stretched out before him in that new party paradise called Liverpool. He felt, however, a deep sense of unease and sadness. The volume of the Liverpool surrounding him was increasing dangerously and the noise would only subside completely when the last stragglers somehow found their way home by any means of transport they could get their arses on. From now until dawn, very few people in this square mile of frenzied hedonism would be making much sense or giving a toss about anything other than the pursuit of the pleasures of the flesh. He understood their needs but did not understand his part in the liberating explosion of piled-up passion and lust that was building up all around him.

So, what the hell *was* he doing there? He could hardly claim he was going out for a quiet drink. The chances of being able to converse with anybody were remote. The music on offer in the general bedlam would drown out sensible communication. The only maxim here was "to be drunk is to be happy" and the drunker you got, the happier you would be. He was there as a philanthropist, doing vital field work so that the observations he made would make the books he would write later all the more authentic. He laughed at the nonsense he was creating in his head to legitimize his presence on this urban battlefield.

Anyway, there were still a couple of places where he could find some semblance of soothing civilization before heading for home. He would drop in and have one drink in both. First, he thought he would risk a half-hour walk through the world of pleasure domes and excesses. The main square beyond Bold Street and the numerous streets running off it revealed dozens of bars and clubs that hadn't existed when Nat was the same age as the people boisterously screaming and shouting all around him.

He kept walking and reached St Luke's church at the top of Bold Street. There was a distinct change of clientele at this end, as dishevelled figures asked him for money while other impoverished creatures staggered around in a different way to drunks usually do; more dangerous substances had been at play here, he thought. He veered left down Brownlow Hill, and the Adelphi Hotel came into view on his right; he crossed Lime Street and entered Ranelagh Street, the thoroughfare that saddened and annoyed Nat the most: hamburger bars in pink lights, the ubiquitous McDonald's and Burger Kings, a low quality plastic Italian chain restaurant, a laughably entitled Egyptian bar and pseudo-Irish bars which hadn't existed a decade ago, all of them bereft of any authentic charm. Jackson the Tailors was now a branch of a building society.

When Nat was a lad, there were four solid Victorian and Edwardian public houses on Ranelagh Street, all situated on the right-hand side of the road, running down from Lime Street: The Central, The Midland and round the corner in Cases Street, The Globe and Coopers. Real public houses, frequented by real people who knew how to behave. They still existed and were, thankfully, still frequented by people who appreciated a quiet pint in turn of the century, elegant surroundings.

He turned the first corner on the right and slid into The Globe. Not too full, not too noisy, not too young, and boasting an Edwardian century décor which hadn't changed much since Edward V11 ascended the throne. The fifties and sixties music was loud enough to hear and enjoy while still allowing conversation. He escorted his pint of Guinness and double chaser on the rocks up the slanting floor and into the narrow vestibule on the right, plonking himself gently onto the low stool squeezed against the wall.

Nat could hear every word of an intimate conversation underway next to him. The couple talking were probably in their late forties. They once had hopes at various stages in their lives of changing the world. Or at least their town. Now they didn't seem so sure: they talked of the breadline existence awaiting them when they retired. Cynicism and defeatism coated their every sentence as if they were competing with each other to win the title of "most miserable bugger in the world". The woman went to the toilet and her partner exchanged a glance with Nat and suddenly started talking.

'Only decent pub around here, isn't it?' was his opening gambit. After spending so many years in Germany, Nat wasn't used to being spoken to by strangers and struggled for an answer.

'Yeah, it's all madness now,' was the best he could do. His answer was peculiar but honest and he hoped his new friend was on the same wavelength. He was.

'Yes, it's all gone beyond the beyond. I don't know where these young people get the money from.'

The woman returned and the men's conversation was interrupted. Or perhaps it had ended. Before anybody was allowed to decide whether it had a future, Nat stood up and picked up his glass. He felt relieved, at least, that other people were in town that night who felt as estranged as he did. He bade them goodnight. They looked concerned. Just like him. They had good reason to be; they had presumably decided to stick it out in the former Second Port of the Empire for the rest of their lives.

Before deciding where his last drinking hole was to be, he was going to suck in the sight of a thousand women in Liverpool on a Friday night. Every form of womanhood would be flaunting itself; women with the faces of Greek Goddesses and the bodies of porn stars; or either; or neither; fat, morbidly obese, ugly, vile, slim, skinny, primitive, vaguely pretty, very pretty, young, old, middle-aged, single, and divorced. They were laughing, crying, dancing, singing, shouting, staggering, falling, running, slouching, sprawled on the pavement, squirming in each other's arms, in strangers' arms, all in groups of at least two and many more. They all had two things in common: they would be wearing as few clothes as possible and they all thought they were celebrities. They were dressed the same way in deepest winter or at the height of summer. They wanted to be seen and wanted. And the male half of Liverpool wanted to see and want.

Not all of them were from Liverpool, of course. Now that it was Party City number one in the North West, there were all sorts of accents and dialects crowding the Liverpool airwaves: Lancashire, Yorkshire, Dublin, Belfast, Birmingham and North Wales were just the start of the long list. They were celebrating hen parties, birthdays, anniversaries, divorces and the start and the end of new and old jobs in a blurred frenzy of boozed up loud and lusty excess. Everybody agreed it was great fun.

Everybody except Nat, whose mood was taking a steady nose dive with every step he took through the never-ending supply of screeching Friday night flesh. He shouldn't have had that double chaser in the Globe. He was running out of places which might offer the final last drink in relative solitude. He squeezed down Mathew Street, saw a slither of space in North John Street and turned right towards Victoria Street. Then he saw his salvation: a number ten bus. *Let's get out of here!* was his only thought as he picked up the pace and joined the short queue being swallowed up at the bus's front entry point. It was three minutes to ten.

The bus made its way up London Road and reached Edge Hill. A young man was using a fake posh voice as he was getting off, telling the bus driver that somebody was smoking cannabis in row five. 'That's the chap, driver, he is smoking cannabis, I tell you. The world is going to pot! Dear fellow, please call the police!' His outraged but controlled outburst was so ludicrous and unexpected that it prompted every passenger to question the man's mental state; but he had got them all sniggering and admiring his theatrical grasp and feel for Friday night. This was the comic drunk, getting a last laugh before he left their lives forever.

And, so, he stepped off the bus. Nat was watching the young man's look of deep disregard of anything happening in the world on the pavement outside as the bus pulled away; then he realised that the man had been talking about himself. He was the offender, but it was a comical farewell Friday night party piece which lightened up an otherwise dull bus journey.

Not to be outdone by this thirty-second burst of absurd theatre, somebody at the back of the bus began to sing; a deep, sonorous voice which was growing slowly in intensity and volume. Nobody was complaining. Nat could just make out the words: ... *where the evening shadows fall, there are people dreaming of the hills of Donegal.* Trust an Irishman to get in on the act, he thought. He knew the song but couldn't name it or the singer, but it was doing him the world of good.

Nat was almost at his journey's end. He didn't look around as he made his way to the door as he wanted to create his own image of the man singing and make up his own story about why he was giving us all a song. He caught the last snatch of a line as he passed the driver: '…to ease their lonely hearts.'

Nat stepped off the bus and was alone. He didn't have the slightest idea who or what was going to ease *his* lonely heart but he would see what he could do for Sam. He felt pleasantly intoxicated and glad he had escaped. He longed for Bob's armchair again and as he made his way up the street, he searched briefly for his key, feeling vaguely pleased with himself for getting home before dark. The creaking of the neighbours' door barely a yard to his right stopped him from putting the key into the lock of number sixteen. John's gruff tones were gruffer than usual.

'Yer better get down to de Royal, lad. Sam's been taken bad. We dunno what's goin' on.'

Nat hated himself for just feeling inconvenienced about having to get himself down dreary Prescot Road for the second time in the space of a few hours. The only feeling he should have felt was worry. "Sam's been taken bad" sounded bad.

'Will do, John,' he replied, putting the key back in his pocket and retracing his path down the street. He hailed a black Hackney cab and scrambled inside. 'The Royal, please.' The taxi pulled away. The cab driver's opening salvo mystified Nat.

'Well, at least you're getting down there before the pond life does.' What on earth was he talking about?

'Sorry?'

'Well, not everybody's pissed in town yet, so it'll still be quiet. After midnight it's like Omaha Beach. Mind you, it's nothing compared to Saturday night.'

Nat said nothing and puzzled about 'pond life' and 'Omaha Beach'. OK, Omaha beach was about massacre, blood and limbs hanging off, which presumably happened most Friday nights in the centre of Liverpool. But the meaning of 'Pond Life' was still escaping him. He plucked up the courage and requested clarification from the driver.

'What do you mean by Pond Life?'

'Oh, sorry mate. Well, I mean people whose brains are the size of tadpoles and all those little creepy crawly things that hang out in ponds.'

'Oh yeah, I've got you now' Nat stammered. Pond life. Liverpool life. Nat wished he was somewhere else.

They were at the Royal Liverpool Hospital in eleven minutes and Nat's stomach tightened as he approached the main entrance. Main reception. He was told that Sam was on the seventh floor.

When he got there he was told to take a seat, then a doctor appeared and asked Nat to follow him into a room where he gave him the news.

'I'm afraid your mum passed away about an hour ago. Massive complications after a stroke. She died peacefully.'

'She wasn't my mum, actually. She was my auntie.'

'Oh, I didn't realise.'

Sam was nobody's mum. Sam was gone. Nat was numbed and hoped he had done enough for her. He knew he hadn't but he knew he never could. It was his last aunt, the end of the family road and he knew what that meant. She would never get to read his book. He would never find out why the five streets leading to her street were in strict alphabetical order. He could never enjoy her perfect diction again.

'Do you want to see Samantha?' the doctor asked.

'No, thank you. I'll inform her stepdaughter tomorrow and she'll be in touch.'

'My condolences, Nat.'

'Thanks. You people do a great job.'

Out of the main entrance, he turned right and decided to walk home. Kensington, known as "Kenny" to the locals, would be the transit zone for the next half-hour or so. He threw one last glance behind him to take in the view of the Royal Liverpool Hospital. His dad, Uncle Bob and now Auntie Sam had all left the world in the building he was now moving away from at speed: he was desperate to leave it behind him. He was seeking a reasonable walking pace; if he didn't find it, he might lose the plot.

He gave a cursory glance at the house where five Liverpool lads made their first record, going under the curious name of "The Quarrymen". One of them lost his mother the day after that recording. His name was John Lennon, his mother's name was Julia. He kept up the pace. Once again Kensington library; he could just make out Bacon's golden words above the entrance. The boisterous Wetherspoon's just about to close. The drive-in MacDonald's was doing well. Across the next junction and on the right was the launderette where he had helped Sam drag the washing a few days before. Not far now. Past the Police Social and Sports Club where policemen played football every Saturday, sometimes watched by Bob from the bedroom window.

He had made it in less than half an hour and was covered by a thin, even glaze of sweat. He knocked on John's door and his wife, Pam, answered. She covered her whole face with her hands and sobbed when Nat gave her the news. No sign of John. Nat awkwardly changed porches and looked for his key once more.

He slumped into Bob's armchair: there was nothing left to say. The song from the bus haunted him again: '…they brought their songs and music to ease their lonely hearts'. He wanted the man on the bus to be with him now, singing just for him. Something pushed Nat out of the chair, down the short hallway and made him ring the neighbour's bell. This time John appeared, spluttering his condolences.

John had become an animal about to be ensnared by a hunter whose resolve and determination for the capture would not permit escape. Nat instinctively produced the Scousest of Scouse accents and threw the net over his bounty.

'A godda 'ave a bevvy wid yer, John! Dis 'as dun me 'ed in!' (Translation: 'I really must share an alcoholic beverage with you, John. This news has had a serious impact on my emotional and mental state').

'OK, lad, but only one!'

John trundled in and Nat carried the bottle of Malt into the living room and victory was within his grasp. He filled two tumblers with dangerous quantities; they raised their glasses and drank the first portions down like it was lemonade.

'Good stuff dat, lad!' Nat took this as a request for more. He filled the tumblers up again and they savoured every last drop. The two men sat in silence, staring at the walls.

'A nightcap, John?' It was a stupid question. They kept drinking and the bottle was soon half empty. Nat moved in for the kill.

'John, do you still do "I left my heart in San Francisco".
Would ye sing it fer me?'

''Aven't done it for ages, lad, but I'll 'ave a go.'

'Would you, John? For me and Bob? And for Sam, of course.
And me mum. And dad. And, well, for everybody.'

Considering the amount of malt he had knocked back in
the short time since Nat had opened the bottle, John's response
proved that he wasn't quite the clown the world thought he
might be.

'No lad, I'm singing dis just for you. Everyone else 'as
checked out, 'aven't de? De *you* know where de are, coz I don't.
Fill up me glass, will yer?' This time, the hunter was the hunted.
Nat did what he was told and John started singing.

The loveliness of Paris seems somehow sadly grey
The glory that was Rome is of another day
I've been terribly alone and forgotten in Manhattan
I'm going home to my city by the bay…

The shadows of self-doubt, the sadness of the day, the
despairing thoughts about his city and the final loss in the
family chain were eased out of Nat's soul as John lifted
the song into the heavens. Nat felt strength returning and
grasped that art, combined with passion and compassion,
were vital answers. The final line, 'Your golden sun will
shine for me', made the walls quiver and Nat was ready to
leave his city by the bay with renewed hope and the belief
that all would be well.

Nat pushed the bottle into John's hand as he left for the
front door.

'Thanks. Night, lad.'
'Night, John.'
'Night, everybody, everywhere.'

10

His hangover was vicious and merited. Nat dragged himself around the house in constant, searing pain. Endless mugs of tea and tap water. He found some paracetamol in a drawer in the kitchen and while he slurped two of them down he cursed himself for his overindulgence, just like he had done hundreds of times before. He decided to put the ironing back till later in the day. The clean washing was in two baskets in two neat piles in the front room; Nat remembered watching Sam meticulously separating the clothes when they had come back from the launderette a few days before.

He walked around the park and thanked God that the sun was shining. He discovered a greasy spoon café near the old abattoir and ordered the unhealthiest and biggest fry-up they had. The former abattoir was now a cold storage centre; the men working there were streaming in and out between shifts. They were full of jokes and nonsense, talking about football and rubbish in loud voices. He envied them and tried to imagine the homes they were going back to. Nat remembered his Berlin home with mixed feelings and a generous portion of debilitating doubt.

He had two phone calls to make: to Sam's stepdaughter and Sam's brother. He paid for the late breakfast and crossed the road to Frogmore Road. He found Sam's phone book and searched for the numbers. He was going to keep both calls as brief as possible. Both would begin with the words 'I'm sorry to say to tell you that…' They would continue with the briefest description of the circumstances of Sam's death, and end with the words, 'The key to the house is next door with John and Pam in number fourteen.' The first persons to arrive at the house could claim the key, the rest of Sam's possessions and responsibility for anything that remaining relatives needed to bear. He completed both phone calls in just over one and a half minutes; he felt like a bastard but he was at least a relieved bastard.

He brushed his teeth and sat down to write down anything that came into his head. This went on for hours. He drank tea and wrote. Four, five, six, seven hours. After the seventh hour, the sinking sun was still in the ascendency outside the house, and the few clouds on the horizon were changing colour from scarlet to purple against a surreal blue background. Dusk was closing in. With 5,056 words registered on his laptop, a record for one day's writing, he closed down for the day, booked a taxi for five o'clock, set his alarm for four, picked up the key and took it next door, explaining to John that somebody would be picking it up soon, but he didn't know exactly when. They wished each other all the best. He gently slid the un-ironed washing into his bursting case and went to bed. If his alarm clock did its job, he would make his 7.25 a.m. plane to Berlin-Schoenefeld with ease.

It was a perfect Sunday morning and the roads were deserted. They sliced south through the only leafy suburbs that Liverpool had to offer: green lights sped their passage. Silence all around, nobody in sight, no hangover and trees thick with green leaves nestling all around Calderstones Park. Thankfully, the taxi driver wasn't spoiling the soothing tranquillity; apart from the initial Liverpool taxi driver inquisitiveness about origin and destination, he had remained silent. He even made Nat smile (and proud) by claiming that he hadn't lost his Scouse accent.

Check-in and security over, Nat emerged into departures and hit a very different Sunday morning. People were consuming in industrial proportions: pints, shorts, cocktails, cheeseburgers, steaks, bacon butties and all those treats destined to ensure the travellers' lives were going to be that little bit shorter. The departure hall reminded Nat that modern life demanded one thing only: thou shalt consume. The volume of the music was starting to induce mild hallucinations and he believed he could see people dancing. Since when do you dance in an airport? Some of the travellers were clearly already off their heads and it wasn't yet six a.m. Friday night repeated on Sunday morning, this time within the confines of an airport departure hall.

Sam's death had been sandwiched between the routine madness of Liverpool behaving badly on Friday night and Sunday morning misbehaviour and Nat wanted to flee. But this time, there was neither a number ten bus on which to make a getaway nor a long straight Prescot Road to walk on; he would only be safe after take-off - and that was at least an hour away.

He looked up at an expansive screen above him and was able to steady himself by staring at a beautiful singer with long, black, thick hair; she was moving her perfectly-shaped and amply proportioned bottom inside a tight white silky trouser suit. She was naughty, turning around regularly during her dance routine to ensure that Nat could get a better view. He seemed to be the only person looking at the screen but he felt that it was his only chance of surviving surreal happenings inside a sealed building on a Sunday morning where outside, only half-an-hour before, nature had been gently stroking his soul at the start of a perfect midsummer day. From where he stood now, the only thing being stroked was the singer's bottom; well, in Nat's confused mind at least. No one seemed to care that Nat was behaving like an ogling old git.

Her performance over, Nat pulled himself back into reality and devoted himself to more mundane matters: he decided to buy a large bottle of mineral water, which would be free if you bought The Sunday Telegraph. He quickly overcame his aversion to the Telegraph, handed over his last pound coin and small change and found a comfortable seat as far away from the music as possible.

He knew in a flash what he was going to do in his first week back in Berlin: fast. Jesus did it; the Catholics tried doing it between Pancake Tuesday and Easter Sunday; the Muslims did it for a month during Ramadan and doctors actively encouraged it. A no-brainer, to use the irritating new jargon. The idea of doing without food and booze for five days, surrounding himself with silence, deep in meditation and seeking guidance from the Great Beyond seemed, at that moment in time, the only chance of rescuing anything worth rescuing from the remnants of the project he had started the previous September on his Greek island.

The flight to Berlin was on time. He disagreed with everything in the Sunday Telegraph. He thought of Sam and cursed himself for being in a pub when she was dying. He cursed Bob for being in the pub far too often. Nat was nursing a festering guilty conscience.

He quickly googled "fasting" before boarding and decided that the first statement he found was all he needed; he didn't care about its source and on what medical evidence it was founded:

"Fasting for a few days probably won't hurt most people who are healthy, provided they don't get dehydrated. But fasting for long periods of time is bad for you. Your body needs vitamins, minerals, and other nutrients from food to stay healthy."

Let the fasting begin: you can never have enough new starts.

The Hanover Ring or the blue orange

Nat's "it doesn't get any worse than this day". The "I am in the wrong film day". The "please can I die now day?" A football match in which the referee was bent, where the goalposts moved whenever you tried to put the ball in the net and at the end of the match your team is relegated to hell from which they will never return to play another competitive match. At the final whistle, Nat realised that questioning anything about the meaning of life and the peculiarities of people's brutal ways was futile and would only result in further pain. The Blue Orange Day that changed the nature of the game called life.

Nat had flown into the airport on a rescue mission which seemed as important as life and death itself and his stomach churned as he walked through the arrival doors, fists clenched. She wasn't there. Caught up in traffic no doubt, Friday at five was a terrible time. No point wandering off anywhere. Just wait.

He had spent three weeks replaying the past, bringing himself to the point of physical sickness, refusing to believe the contents of her letter. Naïvely, romantically, he believed he had the answer and he was here to take the wrapping off and start the future. He could hardly wait. There have been better backdrops for such monumental occasions than Hanover airport, he thought, but it would have to do. Yet dangerous portions of doubt were writhing in his unsettled gut. The vision he had was beautiful in its simplicity but liable to be no more than an excursion into make-believe if she decided not to buy a ticket to join him. But the love conquers all battle cry had gripped him obsessively in those gruesome three weeks during which he had not been able to reach her once on the phone. The pent-up frustration had turned him into a modern warrior, a sort of romantic missionary. It was as if his previous life had merely been an insignificant prelude to this, the real thing. He looked at his watch and paced impatiently up and down the arrivals area.

Airports. There are only ever three reasons for being there. You're picking somebody up, you're being picked up, or you're going somewhere yourself. Nobody in their right mind wants to be there any longer than it takes to do any of those three things and after twenty minutes Nat Wilson was sick of the place. He watched the tourists coming through the same doors he had come through on the short flight from Berlin-Tempelhof. Their suntanned, relaxed faces annoyed him as they were greeted with overdone hugs and kisses which only served to heighten his awkward, self-conspicuous loneliness. Probably only been to Majorca for a couple of weeks, he thought. He sneered at the cheap superficiality of it all and felt smugly superior. But the constant stream of people happy to see each other again was getting to him.

Half an hour gone and his jerky gaze was doing overtime. Still no sign of her. If someone was late, half an hour was the just about acceptable, so she'd be showing up any minute, he thought. Perspiration-producing moments, just before the moment of truth. A song came into his mind he and Jane had heard a lot recently. They mockingly delighted in the melodramatic words of the old blues singer who was waiting at the quayside for a ship to come in, hoping against hope that his girlfriend was on it. After waiting a whole night, he could make her out on the gangplank, coolly, slowly, tantalisingly coming ashore. The fact that Nat was rolling this image around his brain revealed to what extent he had slipped away from reality. No ship. No gangplank. No song. More to the point, no woman.

Nat was surviving on the shaky belief that the Hanover Ring was the only thing standing between him and happiness.

Forty-five minutes gone now, half-time in footballing terms. Football. She even liked football, understood the offside rule, and supported his team. Come to think of it, she liked most things he liked, something he had rarely experienced with other women. But Jane's emancipated façade had lulled Nat into a tragic sense of false security, otherwise known as taking a woman for granted. Nat wanted her to be here and now so that everything that should have been said in seven years could now be said. But she wasn't and until she was he was nothing more than a silent, desperate figure in arrivals clutching an overnight bag and a heart full of hope. His vision was not going to get past the planning stage if he remained alone in this anaemic arrival area much longer. He was becoming part of the place, being eaten away by debilitating doubts which were growing by the minute. He was slowly realising that the Hanover Ring wasn't the problem.

Another batch of tourists pushed their overburdened trolleys past him and the annoying ritual started all over again. Where the hell was she? *Surely she got my letter. She didn't tell me she wasn't coming, so she must be coming;* his comforting logic seemed unbeatable and he calmed down again.

The arrivals hall started to imprison him but he didn't dare leave its confines in case she arrived at that very moment. He quickly decided to slip into the gents and throw some water onto his face. He refused to look in the mirror and shuffled out again quickly. Another half hour passed.

Six-thirty and into injury time. This game was fast becoming a lost cause but he decided to play half an hour of extra time. He was painfully close to the grim realisation that the game had been postponed or had never even been kicked off. The extra half hour was nothing more than a quietly desperate attempt to get on terms with the reality that would be revealed to him at the final whistle. Seven o'clock. He gathered some change and found a public telephone. His shaky hand punched out the number and Marianne answered.

He asked if Jane was there. No, she wasn't. Any idea where she was? Gone away for the weekend. Where to? She didn't say. But she knew I was flying to Hanover? Oh yes, she got your letter. Thanks. He put the phone down and walked slowly away, nausea flowing rich and thick. Final whistle, mate.

Some people maintain that the whole of your life flashes past your eyes just before you die. In his case, the rest of his life flashed ahead of him. What he saw was chewing at the final portions of strength still at his disposal: a starving soldier gnawing on his shoe in the trenches. The next moments were going to be crucial and survival instincts took over.

He managed to leave the glaring lights of the airport and found himself on the dark pavement outside at the head of a row of waiting taxis. He put his hands in his pockets and sobbed for a few minutes. The seasoned taxi drivers didn't flinch.

The tearful release of tension steadied him. He forced himself to dig out a spy hole from the ugly mass of despair descending upon him and to think of his next step. Find the railway station and get on the next train back to Berlin? The last thing he wanted was a further four depressing hours on a train, another night alone after achieving nothing and knowing nothing more than he did before he had set out on this ridiculous journey. Anyway, he had a plane ticket for a flight back on Sunday night. He decided to stick around and find a bed for the night. He actually knew somebody in Hanover; had known him for years and had often crashed at his place. Back to the phone box, strengthened slightly by the thought that Peter might be able to feed some crumb of human compassion to a Friday which had started with an uplifting clarity about the meaning of life and was now threatening to push him into the abyss.

'Peter? Nat. I'm at the airport. Can I crash?'

'Yeah, sure. I'll be there in half an hour.'

He made his way back to the exit area and waited. Beneath the searing pain of rejection and the fact that his romantic notion of taking his loved one to blissful nirvana for the rest of their lives had been dashed, there lurked something sickening and premeditated about what had happened. She knew he was desperate to see her; she knew when he was arriving and how he would be standing there, waiting. Wherever she was between five and seven o'clock on that Friday evening she could, theoretically speaking at least, look at her watch and imagine every step of his painful awakening. It would take years for him to come to terms with this, but he would never understand it. It was like seeing a blue orange. And this surreal little monster orange was now blurring his vision, transporting him into a world where there were no rules anymore. As he staggered to the pick-up point his mind was panting at the thought of somebody he loved doing this to him and the words, "You are being treated like this because you are a bastard," were scraping at his conscience. They were to do so for a long time to come. The words "You're are being treated like this because Jane is a bastard," didn't yet exist in his mind, but were to play a significant role in his recovery later. A few years further on he concluded that the truth was somewhere in between these two assertions, heaving him into a long period of philosophical navel-gazing, resulting in a stronger but more cautious Nat.

Peter arrived and casually asked, with the hint of a grin, what the trouble was. They got into his car and headed into the town centre. Nat tried to relate the sequence of events which had led him to be standing at Hanover airport waiting for somebody to arrive who never had the slightest intention of ever arriving. Peter listened patiently and said nothing. Being a man of no little experience himself, he probably knew that the crumpled mess sitting on the passenger seat next to him wouldn't be listening anyway.

Peter was a friend of a friend rather than a friend, but Nat had known him for a dozen years or more. He remembered Peter having the one girlfriend for so long that people never mentioned his name without mentioning hers, too. Then suddenly it was all over and Peter had transferred all his efforts into his job, his drumming, his mates and pursuing women for frivolous pleasures of the non-committal but physical kind. He remembered Peter telling him on a recent visit that if any woman attempted to transport even one piece of clothing across his threshold, the relationship was terminated forthwith. The bachelor life, or so he claimed, suited him fine and served him well. The way Nat was feeling at that particular moment, he found it all very hard to believe. Peter was the sort of man Nat had seen flashing in front of him at the airport after his mission had ended in horrific failure. But if the bachelor life was to be a consequence of that failure, Nat had better start learning the rules fast.

They got to Peter's flat and he took a first faltering step towards getting accustomed to life after zero hour by asking Peter a fundamental question. 'How long does it take to get over a woman?' Peter opened the door of the fridge and took out a bottle. 'Some women you never get over,' he replied casually while he searched for a corkscrew in his chaotic kitchen.

It was definitely time for a drink.

11

His last memory on the plane was the sight of Liverpool Bay, bathed in sunlight, a rare sight, looking as blue as a bay can look in North Western Europe. The view was a fleeting one as, they crossed the Lancashire coast, heading east. His city by the bay was gone; he fought a brief pang of regret and fell in and out of sleep. He was awoken by the jolt of the landing in Berlin-Schoenefeld airport. He gathered his senses and braced himself for Berlin's gruffness, its over-the-top boulevards and scruffy side streets.

He was on a local train before he knew it, heading west. He always had to make a superhuman effort to suppress all the memories Berlin held for him. If he weakened, they would take over, debilitate him, render him useless and squeeze out of him any remaining strength. Berlin was a monster he had to fight every minute of every day and if he was not up to the fight, he better leave town on the next train out.

The fitful snatches of sleep on the plane had at least taken away the worst of his tiredness and provided him with just enough strength for the struggle. Forty-five minutes later, he was in the centre of Berlin, on the central eastern side of town, a taxi ride away from his twenty-storey block of flats in the Fischer-Insel area of the former capital of the German Democratic Republic. On the fifteenth floor, he left the lift and made his way to apartment number 15.007. He always laughed at the numbers 007.

A frugal living room awaited him, containing only a simple

armchair, a large, ugly, solid dining room table with two chairs and a small desk and a matching wooden chair looking out of the bay window with an impressive view of the nineteenth century buildings stretched out along the river Spree. He planned to work here on his book, a task made easy by a lack of distractions.

The adjoining room was another matter. Thick carpet, long sofa, extra-large TV screen, state-of-the-art stereo system and three walls of elegant bookshelves packed with books, most of which he had actually read. An armchair, equipped with a reading lamp, completed the opulent picture.

The long room containing the kitchen was another space to admire, displaying all the latest gadgets, most of them unused and in virginal, pristine condition. He had used a not inconsiderable proportion of his Lotto win to fit out these two rooms to impress. The remaining bedroom was back to basics: bed, wardrobe and bedside table. The bathroom also covered only minimum requirements.

Nat had fixed all this before his late summer move to Greece and observed everything now with a certain sense of street-wise satisfaction. He had bought the flat at a very reasonable price at a favourable time slot in post-war German property-buying history. The Berlin Wall had only been down a couple of years and few people were interested in touching a building built by Communists for Communists; the local authorities almost gave it to him as a present. It was a writer's retreat high above Berlin with views of the old rather than the new, because he knew that anything he wrote would be investigating the old.

The neighbours never bothered him. He was sure that a certain number would be ex-Party members, a few of them

Bohemian types, others suffering post-reunification blues, a condition brought on by being too old to be of use anymore to the New German free market economy. All in all, they kept themselves to themselves and were rarely seen or heard. There were deathly silences in the lift and the occupants of his floor seemed at ease with the natural capital city anonymity; Nat became used to it and accepted it as a fact of life. He had reached an age when the desire to meet new people had abated anyway.

He knew plenty of people in Berlin, of course. In a previous life, he had been a resident there for over ten years, at a time of his life when meeting people came naturally; a time when being alone was never an option. A female colleague, Marie, a few years older than him, Cockney roots and a slick line in giving no-nonsense advice which always made perfect sense, once said to him, when he was churning around in a particularly thick pot of emotional self-pitying pudding, 'You're in your late thirties, intelligent, single, fluent German speaker, you don't look like Quasimodo and you're living in one of the most exciting capital cities in Europe! Can't you think of a few interesting things to do?'

So Nat did "interesting things" and dived into the countless attractions Germany's new capital city had to offer. But new facts had emerged since Marie's pep talk all those years ago: he was older and things that were interesting then were less interesting now. He could dig up all sorts of people who would open their doors to him, be pleased to see him and offer a beer and maybe more. It was the "maybe more" bit that worried him. He had planned to stay undercover here in the next two months; if he was dragged into worlds he had left years ago, he may not re-emerge alive. Kosta was waiting in Greece and the second cycle was due to begin on the day that war began about sixty miles down the road in Poland. The temptation to become a real hermit in Berlin for two months was beginning to gain ascendency.

Discipline was the key: he lost it in Greece. He lost his aunt in Liverpool and if he wasn't careful he might well lose his mind in Berlin. He had a room with a view, a kitchen to cook in and a room to write his book in. This was a sort of home. There were no impediments to progress. He had savoured the excesses of Berlin life once upon a time; to be dragged under again during this late summer (and at his age) might result in embarrassing fiascos. He was free to make sensible decisions: Sartre's maxim that we are condemned to freedom meant he would have to give this freedom some meaning and structure.

It was one o'clock: he needed to breathe in the awful Berlin air, listen to the aggressive Berlin murmurings which would soon be engulfing him down on the street below and begin coping with a street culture liable to slap him in the face at any time.

He knew the route he was going to take, a path that would never drag him more than half-an-hour away from home. The beauty of living in a high rise is that it was difficult to lose sight of where you lived when you left the place you live; as long as you knew the block number you could never get lost provided you didn't drift too far away.

He started walking and he was soon gazing up at the magnificent Prussian eye catchers as he followed the curve of the Spree heading west. The Nicholai Church and Berlin Town Hall on the other side of the river and the TV Tower shooting up beyond that. Staying on the South bank, he was soon approaching Berlin Cathedral and resisted the temptation of taking a sharp left down Unter den Linden, which would have taken him past the Humboldt University and the square in front of its library where Nazis started burning books on May 9th, 1933, as a useful warm-up to burning people in the subsequent twelve years. Perhaps this Sunday was not the day for asking the usual eternal question of "why?".

Instead, he continued along the Spree and was impressed for the thousandth time by the museum island crowned by its ageless jewel, the Pergamon Museum. He was less than five minutes away from the spot in Berlin that he called his own: the Weidendamm Bridge. When he got there, he clasped the bridge's railing and the usual breathlessness took over. He stood there, transfixed, for about ten minutes, ogling Friedrichstrasse to his left, as it headed due south until it reached Checkpoint Charlie, formerly the end of the world for East-Berliners, now a normal junction on the former West Berlin border. A glance to the right and Friedrichstrasse snaked north past the Friedrichstadt Palace and on and on until it took you past the small cemetery where Brecht lay. In the pre-war days that stretch between bridge and cemetery was frequented by prostitutes, pimps and punters. By all accounts, business was still thriving, albeit on a smaller scale, well into the Fifties. The building of the Berlin Wall in 1961 heralded the end of such antics as East Berlin's border guards were taking more interest in any movements anywhere near their new construction.

Berlin Cathedral was now behind him. The three edifices straight ahead represented for him the heart of Berlin. On the left of the Spree, Friedrichstrasse railway station, the first step by local train inside the former capital of the German Democratic Republic; on the right the Berlin Ensemble, Brecht's theatre, built to bring the performing arts to the proletariat, determined to build a just and better future. Beyond that, normally just out of view, but somehow always present, the Reichstag, where the West used to start. And within the square half-mile from the spot where he now stood, a hundred pubs, bars, restaurants and cafes offered anything thirsty, hungry or entertainment-seeking punters could wish for.

Every time he stood on that bridge he mentally tried to scoop up a generous spoonful of Berlin's twentieth century history and culture and every time he succeeded because everything that was Berlin circulated all around him: sex, low and high culture, decadence, totalitarianism, the centre of power, overground and underground railways, the river, and gritty urban sharpness. He shivered, as he always shivered at this moment. He walked down the steps and made his way onto and along the narrow river bank, walked into a large bar and ordered a large beer.

The first German beer after months of abstinence was always a moment of inner celebration and quiet satisfaction: he was back in the land which still upheld the Purity Law of 1516 forbidding anything other than barley, hops, malt, yeast and water in the brewing of beer. He was reassured as the pure taste engulfed him.

The events of the last forty-eight hours, the early start, the culture shock, the thousand thoughts swirling around his brain and the oppressive weight of guilt after leaving Sam's few remaining relatives (three, to be precise) to deal with the bureaucratic haze of death in the family, all combined to paralyse, sadden and confuse him. He had done a runner, reneged on the responsibilities a nephew presumably had in these sorts of situations and had fled to the Fatherland on virtually the next flight out.

He attempted to piece together the reasons why he was in such a hurry to get out and the only one he could find was the short sentence that had been loudly pounding away in his head from the moment the doctor told him the news two nights before: 'That's the end.' The end of Liverpool. The last tie. From now on he would have to stay in a hotel whenever he visited; doing that in your own hometown was a sad thing to ponder. This simple sadness pained him, but he had to accept it.

It was approaching six o'clock, the sun had gone in, and it was getting cool. He consoled himself with the fact that he wasn't a tourist in Berlin and to prove it, he was going to take himself to a place just off Friedrichstrasse which served tasty homemade grub at reasonable prices to people who were normally not tourists. He was still doubtful whether this meant that Berlin was home, but at least he wouldn't be ripped off - people rarely got ripped off in their hometown. Afterwards, he could sleep in his own bed in a flat which belonged to him in a part of town he knew well and he could cook food of his own for the first time in eight months. He started to feel better.

He arrived at the eating place, a real Berlin tavern: a long bar on the left as you entered, all the bar stools occupied by men sharing nonsense with the two barmaids who knew their trade and how to deal with their boisterous male customers. There was a free table in the backroom and he wearily plonked himself at the thick wooden table, almost missing the comparatively delicate chair accompanying it. Tiredness was setting in and he was in need of something substantial inside him; the powerful purity of barley, hops, malt, yeast and water had started to weaken and destabilize him.

The barmaid arrived and he ordered his plate of heart attack food: fried meat, thick gravy and spuds. He felt that this culinary indulgence was justified as a last meltdown before his five-day fast, due to start in approximately twelve hours. No one would begrudge him one last blast before making abstemiousness his new religion for a few days. The beer arrived and he tried to make a decision on whether it was to be the last drink of the day. No. He would have a final tipple before retiring.

He had to force himself not to eat too quickly because the food was too good. Just too good. Too good. Delicious. Good wholesome fare. Strength seeped back and he now believed he could get himself over the weekend finishing line and look Berlin in the eye on his first day back. He now had two months to knock himself back into shape before the second Greek cycle.

The waitress appeared, asked how he had enjoyed his meal and gave him something approaching a warm smile, a rare occurrence in Berlin, a town renowned for producing people with the charm of an alligator, and tongues spiked with venom. He praised the food enthusiastically, which immediately put her back on the defensive: her Berlin sense of deep suspicion that anybody could wish to say something pleasant and positive and mean it gained the upper hand and she responded with the bland and deflating: 'If you say so.' *Yes, I say so*, he thought.

He thought better of engaging her in further banter and asked for the bill. He paid, without tipping, hoping she would read his mind, but knowing deep down that she wouldn't: Berlin women like that would be marching through the rest of their life with guns blazing, taking no prisoners and never feeling remorse about rubbing anybody and everybody up the wrong way. He would be a fool to imagine that a brief talk on human relations would change anything for this particular exhibit of Berlin sardonicism.

It was cool in the Berlin dusk and for the second time that day, he shivered. He considered going straight home, without the final tipple. It was approaching nine o'clock and he felt lethargic and unpleasantly bloated and the temptation to just go home and crash was making its presence felt. But he needed one more hour to process the three days just ended and the five about to begin. And, after all, he was barely ten minutes from home, an acceptable staggering distance.

The crowded streets in the centre of former East Berlin seemed to be full of non-Berliners, judging by the accents and languages swirling all around him. This area now offered entertainment a go-go with countless bars and eating places every few yards; before the wall came down, the same streets embodied dismal urban decline from the interwar years with crumbling buildings, pot holed streets and desolate, empty premises. Since 1989, twenty years later, every available square yard had been transformed into a space to satisfy the whims of any self-respecting twenty-first century consumerist, culture vulture.

Nat entered what could only be described as a long narrow room with a small and simple bar at the end. The chairs and tables on each side of this glorified corridor were old, didn't match and lacked any trace of elegance and style. Large, black and white professional-looking photographs hung from both walls, showing guests, past and present.

There were plenty of free tables and seats on this particular Sunday evening; he found a seat with his back to the bar, allowing a full view down the "corridor" to the door. That way he had better chances of survival in case an armed terrorist entered from the street. If they gained access via the window of the dilapidated toilets behind the bar, his chances would be correspondingly worse; it was a chance he was willing to take. He presumed over fatigue was creating these ridiculous thoughts.

He focussed on ordering a double Dimple with one ice from the waitress who took his order with a cheerful smile and returned almost immediately, placing the one-iced Dimple in front of him. He fancied a bit of meditation. He strained everything still available for straining and attempted to stop thinking of anything for one minute; this entailed closing his eyes, which he hoped would not disturb any of the guests lounging around the tables in front of him.

His one-minute journey was black and uneventful. He then filled the empty space with the only data he needed to process in the next twenty-four hours: the death of Sam, the impending five-day fast and the putting-in-place of some sort of structure for the next eight weeks in Berlin.

He felt bad about not feeling bad enough about leaving Sam's house just over a day after her death. He wouldn't be flying back to the funeral – he had overdosed on funerals in the past few years and no longer saw the point. He would think of Sam every day for the rest of his life and felt proud he had spent every day of the last weeks of her life with her. And he would remember the last hug before he raced for the bus; the only hug of hers which ever felt natural and right.

He was apprehensive about the five-day fast but would first seek advice at a local health food store before going ahead with something he had never done before. When the fast was over he could at least start cooking his own food in his own kitchen, something which would largely answer the question of how he was going to structure the Berlin campaign: make mealtimes the ceremonies around which the days could unfold.

That sounded worryingly fatalistic as if the only thing he had under his control were mealtimes. This meant that there were spaces in between which could be filled with dangerous undertakings. He recomposed himself when he factored in the hours he would spend writing, similar to the Liverpool writing rhythm. A couple of hours walking or cycling through the historical wonderland of Berlin, shopping, cooking, washing up and general housework would also help prevent his thoughts from turning to self-destructive pranks and dangerous larks.

After the third slug of Dimple, a new concept for assuring his mental and physical safety began to distil in his mind. The title of this promising idea was "safe houses", which broadly referred to places and homes where little or no harm would come to him. He defined harm as actions which would damage either his mental or physical health or derail him in his efforts to write his book. The colossal error would be to spend the next two months in Berlin half-heartedly reliving his hedonistic past, sleeping irregularly, drinking excessively and falling into a vat of pleasurable but self-destructive treacle which might be the final death knell to any plans he had to get through his raging mid-life crisis and toughen him up for the dreaded twilight years where potential fears turn into the dismal, debilitating facts of an old man's life.

He used to laugh at the whole idea of a mid-life crisis but was now sure of its existence. He once read somewhere that it lasted from the age of forty-five to sixty-five; in footballing terms, he was well into the second half after a scrappy first half that had been a stop-go, nervy affair with plenty of goalmouth action and a few gilt-edged chances which had all been wasted. The score was 0-0 and Nat didn't seem to have team mates for encouragement and support; he would be relying on his own instincts to make up some second second-half tactics. The 'safe houses' tactic seemed like a decision which would at least enable him to hold the 0-0 draw and take a point. At this stage, his ambitions extended no further than that.

He was about to sink the last drop of whisky when a young woman asked whether the seat opposite him was free. She took off her jacket and elegantly plonked herself down. Her face was make-up free, her complexion clear and enticingly pale, her hair not quite blonde and not quite red. Her breasts looked perfect. Encased in the customary prison called lust and desire, Nat tried not to stare and laughed to himself when he remembered the saying on a T-shirt worn by a fellow sufferer on a Greek beach many years before which read: "Can you please tell your boobs to stop staring at me?"

He gulped down the whisky, concentrated on not staring, and asked for the bill. Unfortunately, the waitress was taking her time. He unconvincingly feigned interest in the pictures on the wall, checked his wallet three or four times, gazed down the room again and turned round several times in the direction of the bar area. The waitress finally turned up with the bill and Nat paid then dragged himself upwards and onwards. To his surprise, his beguiling table partner said goodbye in a soft, gentle tone and with the faintest of smiles, either out of pity or perhaps relief that her time spent in the world of Nat's lustful glances was now ending. Or perhaps Nat's years of practice at watching without being watched had got him off the hook, or perhaps she was vaguely pleased by it. It would be politically incorrect to think she had been enjoying it, so he scrapped that idea immediately. Or perhaps she had got used to it and didn't give a barman's fart. At this stage of the day, he didn't either.

Whichever direction the wind was blowing the barman's fart, the disturbing fact was that Nat had started the day entranced by a woman's bottom in Liverpool John Lennon Airport and at the end of the same day, this time in a Berlin bar, his eyes had travelled no further than a few inches up another woman's body to another area much frequented by that wretched male gaze. And again he had been transfixed and depowered.

This was not a new thing: it had been happening to him and men for thousands of years and the vast majority had learnt to cope. Those who hadn't had become the slaves of their drives, leading to imprisonment, disastrous decisions and madness. Nat vowed to redouble his efforts to avoid such frightening fates. For some reason, he bade her farewell in English and she smiled again.

It was unpleasantly cool for midsummer and Nat picked up the pace, happy in the thought that he would be in the safest of all houses within ten minutes. If the definition of home was cooking your own food in your own kitchen and sleeping in your own bed, Fischer Insel 007 was it and would keep harm at bay for the next two months. It would soon be pitch black and he would be ascending to the fifteenth floor, clambering into bed and letting the night take care of everything else.

And so it came to pass: he ascended, entered, clambered and closed his eyes. He was finally free of nagging doubts, over-ambitious plans or self-recriminations. Like the summarizing paragraph of a well-constructed essay, he had a clear conclusion: Berlin was there for the taking, unless he himself decided to clutch defeat from the jaws of victory. Yet a final, familiar, nagging thought, which had accompanied him for over fifty years, briefly delayed the smooth transition from the waking hours to his first sleep back in Berlin for over a year: tomorrow is never what it is supposed to be.

Swingtown

A romantic disaster of colossal magnitude – even by Nat's standards - deserves an empty room with all his earthly possessions heaped in disunion in its centre. He didn't deserve it, but he'd certainly asked for it.

It was late. Midnight slowly creeping. Late winter. The decorator's table stood in the middle of an empty, gloomy room, on the ninth floor, in the middle of a housing estate, yet a stone's throw from East Berlin Zoo.

The three-bedroomed flat was empty save for a hastily-arranged pile of possessions in the largest room, forming a ragged circle around an out-of-date pull-out bed. This sofa had provided one night's uneasy sleep and was likely to play no further role in its occupant's life.

The only light was provided by a small lamp on the window sill and added to the ghostly atmosphere; two bottles of beer next to the lamp suggested a human being had decided to make the courageous attempt to inject a flicker of humanity into the formless, unfamiliar surroundings.

The occupant drank the beer from one of the bottles and circled the decorator's table. The steady, circling, hypnotic rhythm of his steps on an uncarpeted floor provided a solitary crumb of stability in a world of unreturned beer bottles and an unmade pull-out bed.

12

Nat awoke after a particularly disturbing dream, and got himself to the bathroom where he had his first shower back in the capital city. This was not Sam's simple but cosy bathroom, this was Berlin. Time to knuckle under, toughen up. Nat was girding up his loins for sarcasm, snappy comments, miserable faces. All those tedious things Berlin had thrown at him down the years.

The first step was to get down to the bakery-cum-kiosk just around the corner, devour a salami roll, slurp down some extra strong coffees and build up some sort of strength to prepare for the five days without solids which lay ahead of him. He was determined to carry through the fasting experiment despite the fear now slowly starting to envelop him. On the other side of the street was a beverage market from which Nat planned to wheel a crate of mineral water with the help of a trolley that the non-German gentleman who ran the store had gladly lent him in the past for similar purposes. Nat had never worked out what nationality the owners were but their easy-going attitude was always a welcome change to the snarling belligerence of other shops in the neighbourhood. A few metres further down the road was a health shop where he might be able to obtain advice on his fasting plans.

This was all pretty mundane stuff, but even artists needed to attend to the mundane sometimes. And if you didn't have your health, you had no art; in fact, you didn't have anything at all. Nat's attitude to his health in the past few months had been a hit-and-miss affair; the only consistent building block in his overall plan to stay reasonably healthy was to take regular exercise, which consisted of walking every day. He had regular drinking relapses and, once again, he still found it hard to imagine a day without a beer.

A doctor many years ago had once advised him to drink beer rather than anything else if the need for a drink came over him as it contained the least amount of alcohol; he also advised going for a brisk walk for half-an-hour a day. His one final important message was to lose weight. 'The fun starts, health-wise, at sixty and the less weight you're carrying by that age, the fewer problems you'll have,' he casually pronounced. He then proceeded to present a lengthy list of ailments, diseases and sicknesses, all sounding distinctly unpleasant, others life-threat-ening, all of them lining up to pounce on you, particularly if you were carrying more weight than you should in your later years. When Nat asked him how to lose weight, he replied: 'Eat less, drink less alcohol and do a daily half-hour walk.' No ambivalence with this physician. He was a good doctor, talking in plain, simple language that even the most disbelieving of patients could believe.

Having collected enough water to keep himself afloat during the fasting days, he dropped into the health shop. He approached a woman in the shop who looked like she might know what she was talking about. He briefly revealed his fast-ing plan to her and she gave him the usual look that Berliner's reserve for people they believe to have a screw loose. She had some questions.

'Any underlying health issues? Are you overweight?' (Her withering look suggested that she thought he might be). 'Have you spoken to your doctor about this? Have you done this sort of thing before?' Nat's spluttering, incoherent replies to all these very legitimate questions did not encourage her to carry on the conversation. Her innate sense of Berlin impatience was starting to froth and Nat felt she was about to dismiss him with a curt, 'Go away and think about it, sunbeam,' or the Berlin equivalent thereof.

She surprised him by handing him a slim brochure with tips on fasting and minimum calorie recipes with delights such as Water Slim Noodles and Pasta. A second brochure advertised special offers in the field of detoxicating supplements, including "Bootea" and a seven-day teatox Slimbione Thermos in Strawberry and Lime flavour. They all sounded disgusting.

'You see,' she added, with a first touch of human compassion, 'you have to take in some sort of minerals if you're doing this sort of thing.' Nat would have to have a re-think; he mumbled incoherent thanks and made towards the exit.

'You wouldn't want to overdo it now, would you?' she called after him. She smiled as if she cared. This was getting creepy; by Berlin standards, this woman was showing signs of humanity way beyond the normal call of Berlin duty. Nat wasn't ready for this sort of thing on his first day back in Berlin; rather just the opposite. He felt anxious about relaxing, lest the woman disappointed him the next time she saw him. But for the time being, he felt a pleasing warmth entering him and he wasn't complaining. He was encouraged. She also looked good. And during and after the smile, she looked considerably better than good.

Back at the flat, he opened the balcony door and stepped out, staring and pondering. He had hastily concocted this five-day fasting lark while he was in an exhausted, confused state at an overcrowded departure hall at Liverpool John Lennon Airport yesterday as he was entering a trance, brought on by the erotic perfection of a woman's silk-clad bottom. In the cool light of a Berlin Monday morning, he was only just starting to sober up and the chip implanted deep inside his brain called "Pull yourself together, you dickhead" was also finding its feet. He found his feet and began pacing up and down the living room.

After two minutes of gentle pounding across the floorboards, Nat had a revised plan of action up and running for the next five days. Breakfast would be tea without milk and sugar and a bowl of low-fat yoghurt; crispbread with low fat spread for lunch and a bowl of tinned soup for dinner; fruit and raw vegetables to kill the hunger pangs throughout the day and the crate of mineral water he had just dragged up to the fifteenth floor. And, of course, no booze of any kind. In other words, a fast for cowards, avoiding the intense pain of total renunciation. He darted out of the flat before he changed his mind again.

On the way to Aldi, something made him halt his hectic trajectory precisely outside the health food shop. He gazed at his new contact through the window, now sitting at the cash desk. He wondered whether she had a partner (it was an obsessive game of his). Did she marry her childhood sweetheart? Was she happy? A mother? A single mother? An independent-thinking, hard-core feminist? She had presence; she looked as if she could take care of herself. She wore clothes she looked comfortable in but which also made her desirable, with a minimal amount of makeup. And she had something many women didn't have: a hairstyle which perfectly suited her. It was brown, shoulder-length and enticingly thick, and a fringe that regularly slid across her forehead. It was always on the verge of impairing her vision, but she seemed to enjoy flicking it back with her left hand whenever it threatened to do so. Her skin was pale and clear. He hoped her eyes were brown.

He felt the need to go in, wasn't quite sure why, and was hoping to find a reason in the time it took to get to the entrance. He knew that the more he thought about his decision, and the unconscious motives behind it, the more awkward everything would be. He entered and calmed his nerves by telling himself that he simply wanted to thank her again for her help. Hey presto, he had his reason for approaching her again. His nerves calmed and a skeleton plan for the next few seconds flashed in front of him.

He saw her explaining something to a little old lady at the checkout. *Good*, he thought, *her soft side will now be activated*. He feigned interest in a box of porridge which had just entered his line of vision on the shelf to his left and started reading all about its unique goodness and the wonderful things it would gift his body. He thought of using the porridge as a reason for approaching her. Did he need porridge to approach her? It depended on the reason for approaching her. The old lady had left, the shop was empty, she had spotted him and he had the next three seconds to decide whether it was porridge or proposition. Her smile encouraged him to sod the porridge and go for the proposition. He had reached the checkout, still holding the porridge, not underestimating the protection it still might be able to provide.

Her eyes were very definitely brown, the brownest he had seen in a long time, causing him to drop the porridge on the floor. He managed to get the box onto the counter.

'Do you want to buy this?' was her matter-of-fact question. If her soft side had been activated with the previous customer, something had subsequently deactivated it.

'Er, yes, please.' He was a stammering, puberty-infused teenager again and they were back into the dithering customer and clear-headed woman scenario. Out of the corner of his eye, he saw another customer entering. He didn't have much time to pull this thing around. It was time to start making sense.

'Thanks for your advice before. I really wasn't sure what I was doing.'

'No problem,' was her curt reply, displaying that old Berlin need to keep things brisk and non-committal. The porridge transaction was over and it was now up to him to turn porridge into something else. His next line could have been lifted from the definitive book of clichés but it was the best he could come up with considering the minimal amount of time at his disposal.

'I don't normally do this sort of thing, but I was wondering whether we could have a coffee together sometime.' She looked up at Nat with the faintest of smiles and made him wait for a long time before giving an answer. Her answer turned out to be a question.

'You're not from here, are you?'

'Well, not from Berlin, no.'

There was another excruciating pause.

'Do you know Café Kant on Kantstrasse?'

Before Nat could reply, she continued.

'I've got an hour or two to spare before my afternoon shift on Saturday. One o'clock?'

Nat, enthused, was monosyllabic in his reply and shuffled

off the premises. He hadn't had butterflies in his stomach since he first set eyes on Maria on the south-eastern side of Europe a number of months before and he floated towards Aldi to get his basic supplies for the week. Saturday would come soon enough.

The drastic reduction in food consumption over the next five days nudged Nat into a vacuum of minimalistic lightness which weakened him physically but sharpened him mentally. After the first two days of hungering for richer and more substantial amounts of food, his body started to adjust to the new regime. On the third day, he ventured out for a one-hour walk which turned into two and a half hours. He timed the walk to start exactly one hour after his last intake of food; this way he just had enough energy to reach Tiergarten in the West or the southern reaches of Prenzlauer Berg in the East. And then back to solitude and frugality, something he could cope with for five days.

Strolling in the neighbourhood of Prenzlauer Berg was a challenge in the form of a kiosk selling, arguably, Berlin's best "currywurst": *Konopke*. Curried sausage, an invention designed to deliciously kill any hunger; a double portion kept you going for the day. It would be sensible to avoid this part of Prenzlauer Berg altogether during his daily walk but something in him got a kick out of the masochistic ordeal of smelling and imagining.

He had hardly missed alcohol at all. He believed that one explanation was the food he was eating. Who would really enjoy a glass of wine with a portion of crisp bread? Or a cool tasty beer with a stick of celery? Or the same to wash down a tin of Aldi pea soup? He felt lighter without the booze and he could process thoughts more easily, with less chance of finding himself wallowing in an alcohol induced-pit of confusion. He slept better and was able to hit the one thousand-word mark fairly effortlessly whenever he sat down to write.

He listened to music in the old-fashioned way, which meant putting a CD into his machine, sitting down and listening to it from start to finish. Then he would put it back where he had found it. He possessed approximately one thousand CDs. He decided to rank them, artist-by-artist, starting with *Hunting High and Low* by A-Ha, an excellent Norwegian Combo who had some high-quality hits in the eighties. He would then work through the remaining 999 until he came to *Eliminator* by ZZ Top, that irrepressible trio from Texas, who all wore beards, apart from the drummer, who was, surprise, surprise, called Frank Beard.

A quick check on his pocket calculator revealed, however, that this was not going to be possible in the time remaining to him before moving back to Greece. He had an idea. He went to the "Z" section again and started counting his Frank Zappa CDs. He had twenty and he needed to purchase twenty-eight more to own the complete (official) works of the late, great man. Fifty-four CDs in sixty days would be doable. And probably highly therapeutic to boot. Feeling rather proud of this new building block in his search for the most suitable occupational therapy, he sat down to sort the complete collection chronologically. This took him an hour and he resolved to make a start the following day.

So, on Thursday evening, he sat down and listened to *Freak Out* (1966); it wasn't the first time he had heard it, but it hadn't grown on him. Diffuse, twee songs, little or no direction, but listenable and containing two-stand out tunes and an overblown final ten minutes, dominated by calamitous percussion. Not an album you could listen to sober, he thought and overall it represented a bit of a disappointment, especially after all the praise lavished upon it down the years. He noted two stars out of a possible five. With a few drinks down him, he might have given it three.

Undaunted, he turned to *Absolutely Free* (1967) and was much more taken: equally as freaky as its predecessor, but far better song quality. Five stars out of five. Two down, fifty-two to go. He was tempted to have a drink and move onto the next album; he had one bottle of beer in the fridge. He resisted and decided to have an early night. The couple humping away upstairs depressed and distracted him at the same time, so he changed tack, dragged himself back into the living room, put the headphones on and sank his teeth into *We're Only In it for the Money*, Zappa's piss-take on late sixties Hippy Culture from 1968. The album had a reasonable bunch of surprisingly catchy songs and vaguely funny lyrics. He gave it three stars out of five. Then back to bed and silence.

Listening to Frank Zappa and expecting to fall asleep immediately afterwards is a big call and Nat lay there wondering what he could do to drop off. Counting sheep always seemed to be a ridiculous idea, so he changed it to counting the former women in his life. As he pondered, he realised how easy it was easy to remember the exact shape and feel of all their bodies. He didn't even have to try particularly hard; he felt them next to him as he lay there. It took him a while to drop off.

He had no idea where the date with the health shop woman was going to take him, but he knew that he was just happy to spend time with people again before he became as weird as the

Zappa albums with which he was force-feeding himself. Who else could he spend time with? Keeping strictly as possible to his safe houses policy, he chose the safest house he could think of and decided to phone Bill, a Scottish friend from his early years in Berlin.

He hadn't seen Bill for a few years, although he had known him for many. Nat admired him for his honesty, discipline, common sense and desire for a drink. Bill's wife Karen, however, seemed to keep him on a fairly tight rein, a fact which Bill actually seemed to appreciate; he had, on more than one occasion, admitted that he didn't like himself when he had too much in him although Nat had never noticed anything particularly obnoxious about Bill when they had been drinking together. Bill now had two kids and his life was all the better for that. Alcohol was a civilized accompaniment to quality food and uplifting conversation; nothing more and nothing less. Bill had become a pillar of society, and this was good.

Nat dialled, Bill answered, and Nat felt a kind of boyish enthusiasm oozing out of Bill at the prospect of meeting up.

'You know my folks, don't you? Well, they're here at the moment. Come round for dinner next week, why don't you?' Nat felt that he would be safe, surrounded by a sound Scottish family, more than willing to bury the hatchet after hundreds of years of bloody conflict with their neighbours from south of the border and offer a warm, hearty welcome to Bill's Sassenach pal. And in the middle of it all, a no-nonsense German lassie from the Baltic sea coast who had cured her husband's occasional excesses. This was the embodiment of what Nat had termed a "safe house" and he felt a soothing glow inside him; a lost traveller gazing up at a house with smoke wafting out of its chimney, a huge fire flickering its warmth through the curtained windows. He could almost smell the Scotch broth. He was looking forward to the following Tuesday.

13

He had got to Friday and had achieved a pleasing degree of stability. He had lost a few pounds, kept demonic thoughts at bay, got back into the swing of Berlin again and felt vaguely at home. The people inhabiting Zappa's world regularly screwed up and his music reflected this fact, the primary message being that you can't take anything seriously.

Nat was feeling as happy as he had been feeling in a long time; Zappa's music was helping, in the therapeutic sense. And not a drop of alcohol had passed his lips in five days. He still wasn't sure whether he was looking forward to meeting the health shop woman. This wasn't a blind date in the Maria sense of the word back in Greece, not erotic sublimity dropping on him from the skies; rather a date with an interesting retail shop assistant. The prospect of anything else happening was uncertain. He briefly considered not showing, but that would mean never entering her shop again, forcing him to surreptitiously shuffle past her every time he passed that way. Mind you, if the date went badly, he would have to do that anyway. What did "go badly" mean anyway? He wasn't at all sure. *Fuck it, just do it*, was his concluding thought on the matter.

The Zappa therapy continued and would continue until he finished his stay in Berlin. The music today unsteadied him more than anything else; he shakily descended the fifteen floors, to make the half-hour trip across the centre of Berlin to Charlottenburg. At least he was sober. Very sober indeed. How did you prepare yourself for a meeting like this? What on earth were they going to talk about? What would she say? At this stage, he started to wonder whether a stiff drink might not be a bad idea. He spotted a kiosk across the road and he was a gnat's dick away from grabbing himself a miniature bottle of Schnapps to calm his nerves, but then remembered how far gone he had been on his last date and how that ended; he walked resolutely on and in twenty minutes he was ascending the steps of the underground. On reaching ground level, he was impressed, as always, by the grandeur of Kant Strasse, one of the mammoth avenues spread-eagling west from the Brandenburg Gate in the dead centre of the city.

Kant Strasse had changed little in all the years he had known Berlin; unlike their East Berlin equivalents, which had been transformed, sometimes beyond recognition, West Berlin suburbs had generally retained their sixties and seventies aura of grubby charm. He was fifteen minutes early; the place wasn't busy and he found a seat by the window with a clear view of the door. He ordered sparkling mineral water. When it arrived, he remembered that exactly a week before, he was ordering an English breakfast in the café opposite his auntie's street. That was Liverpool. That was death and it was lingering as he wondered what Sam would think of her nephew on a date like this. He thought she would find it romantic and decided she would put on her best amateur dramatics diction and say something crassly twee and antiquated like, 'Well, Nat, a faint heart never won a fair lady.'

Nat was momentarily overcome by a deep sense of sadness and loss when he thought of how she would smile as she gently, but dramatically, enunciated such lines. He would never again hear that voice and share the gentle joy she always felt when she was delivering to a selected audience. In the previous ten weeks before her death, that audience had been Nat.

The woman appeared and Nat hardly recognised her. This had less to do with the clothes she was wearing, but rather the fact that she was smiling. Really smiling. In the shop, her half-smile had almost been half-hearted, forced even.

'Been waiting long?'

'Just arrived.'

Nat stood up and rather formally offered a handshake. The first awkward moment as she didn't seem interested in such conventions; he nervously coughed and laughed as she dropped into the armchair opposite. Nat's thumb was in his bum and his brain was in neutral and only the most excruciating small talk seemed available to him as it painfully tried to squirm itself out of his mouth. He tried the antiseptic, 'Have you come far?' which produced: 'No, I live just round the corner.' What do you say next, he thought? 'That's good,' was his fascinating rejoinder. 'Nice place, isn't it?' was his next little conversational gem. He was getting dangerously close to the classic 'Come here often?' but was saved by the arrival of the waitress. Nat knew that he had to loosen up so he reverted to chivalrous, old-school ways.

'I'm treating you, so have what you want. It's very kind of you to join me in your free time.' This sounded like some sort of business deal; thankfully, she took it the right way and thanked him. They both ordered cappuccinos, which was a bit of an anti-climax after Nat's clumsy invitation to break the bank on her behalf. But he had the feeling that whatever he said at this meeting was going to sound awkward and mildly ludicrous.

She put him out of his misery and said something real, efficiently cutting through the bullshit.

'I knew you weren't a Berliner, or even a German when I saw you in the shop. Don't ask me why.' He didn't.

'You didn't even look like one of our normal customers; you know the bourgeois do-gooders and the ecological nutcases.' Nat was at least relieved that she hadn't placed him in the "nutcase" category. Yet.

'It's very rare,' she continued, 'for customers to talk to us at all. They all seem to know what they want before they get onto the premises. We barely get the time of day out of them. I was glad to be able to help last week; you seemed a bit out of it.' "Out of it" was putting it mildly, he thought, but he didn't feel this was quite the right moment to explain anything.

She took her first sip of cappuccino.

'I'm Martina, by the way.'

'Oh, I'm Nat. Nat Wilson. ' Her name suggested that she was probably around forty – "Martina" had been all the rage when he arrived in Germany but was dated now.

'Isn't Nat short for something? Isn't it a girl's name?' For the first time in their brief relationship, Nat knew something she didn't and he was happy to explain that it could be short for "Natalie", the girl's name, but that his name was short for "Nathan". She repeated it a couple of times and seemed to like it. Nat liked the sound of her voice and the smile that appeared as she said his name; it gently moved something in his mind and body. Mostly his body.

Martina was dead right about him being out of it the previous Monday, but he wasn't altogether sure that he was back "in" yet. She was the first person he had spoken to since then and that conversation had only consisted of confused ramblings about fasting and today's hurriedly planned rendezvous. He was out of practice communicating with the human race and it was showing. Martina was opening up and he decided to bide his time until it was his turn to say something worthwhile.

She had grown up in Potsdam and had moved to West Berlin after the reunification. She had looked after her auntie during the last stages of her multiple sclerosis journey to death and inherited her flat in Charlottenburg, together with a tidy sum of money. Martina's parents were expecting a cut of the cake and when Martina didn't oblige, they disowned her. Her only son had been studying in Hamburg for the past four years and she was supporting him generously. The father of her child had died in a car crash on the day before their seventh wedding anniversary. She enjoyed the part-time job in the health store and was planning to start travelling the world now that her son was getting to the end of his studies. She loved doing anything she wasn't able to do in her former life behind the Berlin Wall.

That was Martina's story and there was a lull in the proceedings as Nat processed the tragic simplicity of it all and the possibility of a happy ending. He realised it was his turn to talk although the urge to ask Martina a thousand questions lingered; but this was a date, he presumed, which meant that she would also want to know some basic facts about him. He decided that he needed a drink before he started his condensed life story.

'If I wasn't working today, I'd join you.' She smiled. Nat liked Martina, her smile, her soft voice, easy way, her thick hair, her playful vulnerability beneath the brashness of her mild Berlin twang. While Martina was talking, Nat had been observing her intensely. Yes, he could imagine. Yes, he was imagining. He needed a beer to imagine a bit more and he cursed his weakness, his inability to look at a woman and not imagine. Assuaging his guilt about the fact that he was drinking when she wasn't, he reminded himself that his last drink was six days ago. Martina didn't seem to object.

He reckoned that she had spoken for about five minutes in all, so he resolved to present his personal CV in half the time. He had done more things in life than she had, lived in more places and with considerably more madness thrown in, but he decided to keep things as comprehensible and presentable as possible. He remembered having his hair cut once and telling the German hairdresser about his nomadic lifestyle, causing her deep distress. He would never forget the grimaces in the mirror as she rejected the whole idea of not living your whole life in the town you were born. Well, Martina had made it to Charlottenburg from Potsdam and wasn't a hairdresser. There was hope.

Martina looked at him expectantly and he decided to tell her what he wanted to tell her rather than what she might want to hear. She would hear about a skeleton with selected pieces of meat on it that had contributed to him ending up where he was today. Born in Liverpool. Difficult place to find work. Parents and him did their best. Got a good education. Liked the idea of teaching. Got to Germany. Liked it. Lost mum. Lost wife. Didn't lose the plot. Kept going. Kept finding work. Re-found the plot, lost the plot and many other things. Kept going. Enjoyed the joy and floundered in the despair, but kept on his feet. Kept finding work. Lost dad. Won money. Had a long think and started an experiment. Was still thinking. He stopped and said, 'God, that beer tastes good.'

She listened carefully until the end of the oral stroll through his life and searched for a comment. It was now her turn to be on shaky ground; the first time in their short, stuttering relationship. Nat resisted the temptation of offering any facetious extras like, 'Will that do for today? Have I whetted your appetite for more? Do you want to say goodbye for ever now?' She just smiled, offering an uncommitted, 'Hmm.' His speech seemed to have been a conversation stopper.

Nat broke the silence with a mumbling apology, although he wasn't sure what he was apologizing about. In a situation like this you were, at some stage, required to say something about yourself, and whichever way you did it, it was going to sound stilted and clumsy. Still she said nothing, which prompted Nat to show concern.

'Are you all right?'

'Yes, but I was just thinking. Do you write books? What you just said sounds like a book to me.'

He realised that almost a year of thinking and writing had turned him into a being who now communicated in stories. He had lost the hang of talking to people; instead, he produced narratives and people were supposed to make of them what they wanted. But Nat was impressed by her instinctive grasp of what he was doing. He owned up to being a writer.

They still hadn't quite got over the awkward silence but Nat was encouraged by the fact that Martina seemed to be thinking, rather than switching off, but panicked slightly when she let out a long 'Well.' This was followed by the banal but important point that she would have to start thinking about making her way to work. The "well" was not ushering in a statement to the effect that men who try experiments at his age and start writing books are experiencing a particularly bad dose of mid-life crisis. Instead, the down-to-earth Berlin mind-set had kicked in and Martina confidently rounded off their hour together by saying something that encouraged him.

'I'd love to hear about your writing next time. That is, if you fancy a next time.' Nat fancied a next time and told her so, hoping she didn't notice how pleased he was about her wanting a next time. They exchanged mobile numbers.

She got up, thanked him for the cappuccino and placed a brief but tender kiss on his lips, which surprised him but made him feel good. She faintly blushed, but she even managed that with self-confidence, and then she floated out of Café Kant. Nat felt dizzy for a moment, steadying himself by sitting down. He liked and fancied Martina and tried to fathom what had happened during their brief encounter.

Nat was also relieved that she was from the East. He found their women self-confident without being arrogant, emancipated without the need to remind you of the fact at every available opportunity; more down-to-earth, less spoilt and less likely to use sex as a weapon. Nat was never quite sure what he actually meant by this, but it probably had something to do with East German women taking a more pragmatic view of the whole caper.

The hour enjoying her relaxed self-assurance, natural smile and way with words had pushed buttons which switched on positivity and had gently pulled him towards her. If Albanian Maria had been lust at first sight with an explosion of irrational madness thrown in, Martina's effect on Nat had been slow, steady and gradual. There was no taxi waiting outside Café Kant for them, only the underground to take Martina to her

afternoon shift at a health shop. No three weeks of unadulter-
ated decadence in a lonely Greek cottage on a hill. This was
Berlin, and Nat and Martina had jobs to do. Saturday was
almost half-over and the westerner would be sleeping in the
east and the easterner in the west.

His next stop was at the nearest big supermarket where
he would get his week's shopping. He couldn't wait to work
through all those old recipes waiting for him in a book he had
kept for thirty years. He had enough of them to keep him well
fed until he left Berlin. The therapeutic benefits of cooking and
regular eating times would also give his experiment its next
portion of structure.

Tonight he was looking forward to goulash and one glass of
red wine. The next Zappa album, however, *Just Another Band
from L.A* (1972) didn't complement or match up to the culinary delight; he was angry that a sloppy set of live songs with
inane, unfunny ramblings from the band was detracting from
an otherwise great day. After the second glass of wine, he stared
at Martina's number, saved in his display. And he wondered
whether he should ring her. No, he shouldn't. An early night
would do him the world of good, the Zappa album getting a
desultory one star.

14

It was Sunday, and up at dawn after a perfect night's sleep, Nat started writing again. He had had a week's break from the only thing, apart from music, which maintained his sanity and he was feeling calmer with every word he wrote. In the last ten days, there had been too much of everything, with no day resembling another. He now knew how a boxer felt, ducking and weaving and dying for the bell. The bell in his case was going to bed, the only time he was able to lock himself into a module which kept everything else out. The alcohol-free days were improving the quality of his sleep and also seemed to be keeping bad dreams away.

He had only dreamt of Sam and Liverpool once, on his first day back in Berlin. It was the sort of guilt-producing dream he had been dreading in which Sam was asking why he was going out and leaving her alone. He stood in her doorway producing one reason after another, all of them lacking the slightest sliver of conviction. Guilt gnawed away at him as he saw Sam slowly disintegrating; he then bolted for the bus and his feet effortlessly lifted him to within inches of the cheery bus driver whose face he knew so well. Bob said, 'I'm knocking off at eight, d'you fancy a pint in town?'

Tonight's dinner was to be chicken lasagne. A new recipe, a new challenge, another way of taking his mind off things. As the chicken lasagne project looked like a two-hour affair, he was confident of being able to multifunction through cooking and listening to the next batch of Zappa albums. *WakaJawaka* and *The Grand Wazoo*, two stonking jazz-dominated monsters, both from 1972. As he removed the lasagne from the oven, he gave both albums four stars. The food wasn't bad for a first-time recipe but it was too creamy, too rich and most important of all, too much for one person.

The dishes lay in the sink, and he knew he had to attack them straight away or they would be there to haunt him first thing the next morning. He moved as best he could to the rhythm of Zappa's music, and that, together with the disgusting lyrics, reduced the pain of the gentle tragedy of a man cooking an elaborate meal just for himself, washing and drying alone and sadly contemplating what the hell he was going to do with the final hours of Sunday.

It had just turned five. The three hours between now and eight on a Sunday had always crawled all over Nat for as long as he could remember, injecting him with a subtle dose of melancholic poison which spread through his mind, causing a feeling of vulnerability and fear. Thankfully, it wasn't winter; this always increased the pain of the poison. Berlin was always an unforgiving place in winter, being considerably colder than the western cities of Germany and dominated by either old or new concrete. In the Berlin Wall days, East Berlin became particularly dangerous as most street lamps were switched off to save energy. It was either another Zappa album or face outdoor Berlin. Looking out of the balcony window, he noted that it was cloudy but pleasantly bright.

He walked faster than usual, tried not to plan his route and turned into streets he didn't know. After half an hour, he found himself in Kreuzberg and wandered among hipsters, student types and the sort of ecological flotsam and jetsam that Martina had been complaining about the previous day. Some such people were sitting on the benches outside the numerous bars that were scattered across much of Kreuzberg. The late summer mildness and the sight of people enjoying it had already convinced him that he just had to settle down for a large beer at the next suitable watering hole that came into view.

The lasagne had brought on a mad thirst and he had to do something about it. He sat down on a bench outside a bar called "Rick's American Café", and waited. He decided to test the waitress with an old favourite which sometimes produced positive vibes and sometimes not. A positive vibe would lovingly and gently ease him into the home straight and his customary Sunday evening blues would be all but beat. A negative reaction would add extra burdens. He fancied the risk; the waitress had spotted him.

She arrived and smiled, indicating that she was ready to take his order.

'I have a problem' he said.

'What's that?' she replied, her smile quickly evaporating.

'Thirst' he said. This was a vital moment; her reaction depended on a number of factors. Had she had a good day so far? Did she have a sense of humour? Had she heard this opening gambit before? Did she just think Nat was trying to be a facetious smarty-pants?

'We specialise in solving those sort of problems,' was her more than satisfactory reply and Nat returned to normal waitress-guest dialogue, with the equally reassuring feeling that he was going to survive Sunday without too much distress.

'In that case, I'll have a Pils for adults.' The confusing

174

addition of "for adults" visibly irritated her and warned him of the limits of her tolerance of Smart-Alec guests.

'By "for adults", do you mean half a litre?' she snorted, Berlin impatience starting to get the better of her.

'I suppose I do,' he admitted. He had now adopted a naughty boy look. She smiled again and moved on to the next table. The couple there expressed their wishes using the conventional jargon and the waitress seemed relieved that she was able to get back to doing her job efficiently, without the need to conduct mini-interviews to get to the bottom of what guests wanted.

When she reappeared with the beer, she pleasantly surprised him.

'Your problem solver has arrived,' she said. This time, he was caught on the wrong foot, and let out a non-committal 'Oh!' The nonsense had been worthwhile; she had joined in the silly game and he felt better. She seemed to have enjoyed the banter after all and the transaction proved that people were supposed to interact, regardless of the superficial nature of the interactions. The risk had been worth it and the Pils tasted all the better for having spoken to another human being on subjects beyond the necessary.

Back at base, he blitzed through five albums, all of them crackers: *Apostrophe* (1974), Jack Bruce guesting on one track with a superb crackly bass solo; *Roxy & Elsewhere,* a rambling double live album from the same year, a veritable masterpiece from the following year, *One Size Fits All,* and then another live album, the riotous *Bongo Fury,* with Zappa's old school friend, Dan Van Vliet, aka Captain Beefheart, on vocals. And just before midnight, he squeezed in one final five-star masterpiece, *Zoot Allures*. He retired to bed; Zappa had, almost singlehandedly and at the death, elevated the day out of the three and into the four-star category.

Individual arrangements

When doing good things got you nowhere, why not do bad things to fill up the time before you got around to trying good things again? Like casual sex. As long as nobody else came to any harm. And as far as Nat knew, nobody else was coming to any harm. Lust, however, casual sex's motor, could sometimes do just that.

Friday evening at five was the usual time. She would arrive with a bottle of rosé wine. He would greet her nervously and go in search of the corkscrew. She elegantly slipped off her coat, flicked back her long blonde hair and settled down on her side of the sofa. He always let her sit on his left. That way it was easier to overlook her failing looks as the lamp behind her made the best of her moderate attractiveness. Her gaunt expression and thin face were a long way from his ideal picture of womanhood and he wouldn't have looked twice at her skinny figure on the street. Her saving grace was her long blonde hair which reached down almost as far as her delicate but well-rounded behind; that compelling roundness which started it all off a few months previously as she bent over to take a closer look at Peter's hopelessly out of date record collection.

So, Friday had come around again, the corks had been pulled, glasses filled and he let her talk. He sat back and nodded and chuckled in the right places. He took big gulps and re-filled the glasses whenever they threatened to empty. After half an hour he began to relax, by ten to six he was looking for the corkscrew again. The critical phase was deliciously ushered in as the alcohol took its decisive grip and he slowly sank into a floating world where Nadja wasn't so bad looking after all. She went off to the kitchen's open window for her pre-coital cigarette and he loosened his clothes in preparation for the forthcoming exchange of bodily fluids.

She came back and started to remove his clothes. For some reason, she never failed to remark on the colour of his underpants. The accompanying smile always rankled but never put him off the task in hand. He assumed it was just a filler.

They usually started the main course on the sofa and finished off in the bedroom. Although her thinness sometimes bothered him, her natural greed and lithe flexibility always made the event an enjoyable one, despite the lack of real meaning or feeling.

She was married and he was between girlfriends, so commitment was strangled at birth with both parties squeezing an extra portion of seedy pleasure from these sobering facts. She occasionally talked about the death of her marriage. He avoided the subject of women altogether. Otherwise, it was two thinking people filling empty spaces with a few whimsical thoughts. They had sex, he reached for his underpants and she for her cigarette.

The post-coital lying together was always the trickiest part of the evening for him. He couldn't quite manage a token cuddle or caress and shot off to the bathroom as soon as was diplomatically possible. He returned, underpants donned and slouched on the bed for a few minutes. Their silence was the door to thoughts they were trying to avoid. She would then disappear for her second cigarette of the evening and he would join her in the kitchen. He felt more at ease there and was generally able to rest his hands on her shoulders with something vaguely approaching tenderness. Now it was his cue. 'Where are we going to dinner tonight, then?'

They dressed quickly, left the apartment block and went to the usual place.

By ten he was seeing her onto the bus. A few steps later he was in the lift.

Two sets of problems for two people had been solved for another week. He opened the kitchen window to kill the last niggling remains of her cigarettes and took a beer out of the fridge. He lay back on the sofa. He was always pleased to get back in time for the football highlights on TV. Fridays just wouldn't be the same without it, he thought.

15

Pankow, in the north-western corner of East Berlin, had never been embroiled in the gentrification process that had transformed most of the central districts of the former East German capital. It had refused to become trendy although its housing stock had been improved beyond recognition. But there was little night life to speak of, no funky bars frequented by funky hipsters, students, would-be artists and computer whizz-kids.

Nat's "safe house" was inhabited by Bill Campbell and his East German wife, Karen. Bill was a teacher and Karen a librarian, one of the lucky Easterners to become a civil servant in post-wall Berlin. Their two kids were now out of the house studying sensible subjects in Leipzig and Hannover. All the ingredients for a solid bourgeois household, an image Bill seemed to revel in a little too often for Nat's liking. Bill was always trying to get on and he was determined his kids should try and do the same. His elder brother was a high-flyer in the Diplomatic Corps, which had caused an unpleasant outbreak of sibling rivalry.

His parents had both reached the top of their profession to become head teachers back in Scotland, a position Bill was never going to reach in the German system; Bill was condemned, in *his* mind, to being categorised as an underachiever. Nat saw his role in their friendship as the joker who cajoled Bill to relax and take it easy and be happy with what he had. Nat had the impression that Bill was often on the verge of saying to him, 'Shut up. You don't understand, you're not from my class.' Inversely, Nat often felt like saying the same to Bill. Their friendship and the many things that bonded them meant that they would never utter such words.

Bill introduced Nat to his parents.

'I'm doing an intensive German course in Berlin,' his mother enthused. 'The last time I did German, Macmillan was prime minister, but the basics are still there. Somewhere.' His dad was a less effusive type; not unfriendly, but naturally displaying a distant steadfastness and wisdom, before he even uttered a word, reminding Nat that he was dealing with a retired Scottish headmaster.

The variety of topics they got stuck into at the dinner table was varied and impressive and the analytical depth they got to in record time admirable. Nat was able to hold his own on German post-war politics, but when the elder Campbells started to hold forth on Anglo-Scottish relations down the years, the influence of early Scottish settlers on North American literature and society and the manifold reasons why the Scots didn't want to achieve independence from the Union, Nat was lost in the slipstream. He almost felt like he was back at university and should actually be taking notes for the forthcoming Campbell follow-up seminar.

The seminar did indeed take place over dessert when Bill started questioning some of his parents' theses, causing a heated debate which almost prevented Nat from enjoying Karen's delicious rhubarb crumble. Nat seemed to be the only one taken by it and made an extra effort to lavish her with the praise she thoroughly deserved while the rest of the Campbells were now locked in mortal combat on a new point of contention: the future of the Labour party north of the border. Did these people ever stop re-examining, analysing and going into ever greater detail on every conceivable topic under the sun?

Nat thought back to tea-time in Liverpool, which was as different to the Campbell's' rigorous debating society as could be. The only thing that Nat and his folks got stuck into around their cramped kitchen table was the food served up by his mother. This was eaten in silence, the only sound being the jingling of the knives and forks. Back home, talking during meal times was actually deemed to be bad manners and communication was restricted to his mother's interest in whether they were enjoying what they were eating. Nat and his dad were always keen to be as generous as possible with their verdicts and Nat's reaction to Karen's crumble might well have been a flash from the past which was suddenly reviving Nat's old habit of praising the cook.

The Campbell kerfuffle petered out and the gathering made itself comfortable on the cosy couch in the corner of the room. Prompted by Bill's mother, Nat gave a shortened version of his life and career so far. At the end of it, she fell silent, for the first time that evening. This must have meant something, but Nat wasn't quite sure what. An atmosphere of unease was creeping in and Bill's parents both declined Karen's offer of coffee as they 'fancied an early night'. Karen thought she would do the same, if Bill agreed to devote himself to the washing-up. Bill nodded, looking relieved.

Left alone with Nat, Bill made a beeline for the drinks cabinet and brandished a bottle of Johnny Walker Black Label. Nat was mildly shocked by Bill's urgent need to get a 'wee dram' down him barely three minutes after the weary ones had said their goodnights; Nat insisted on some ice cubes, in case Bill had a thirst on him and was planning to go for a full tide. He just hoped that the thought of his having to do the washing up *and* getting up early the next morning might just prevent him from doing anything silly with an almost full bottle of whisky in his hand.

Glasses clinked, first gulps negotiated, and Bill started talking. It was a different Bill; not the self-confident, done-well-for-himself husband, father and son of the dinner table but a slightly weary-looking, troubled, middle-aged ditherer.

'Sorry about my mum,' he mumbled. 'She has a problem with people who see life differently to her. And when she realises such people aren't going to come round to her way of thinking, she pretends they don't exist. This is what happens when you've been running a tough school with an iron rod for forty years. It helped her survive and she hasn't yet realised that she doesn't need to do it anymore. Dad's almost as bad.'

'Hence the early night?'

'Hence the early night. Anyway, Nat, you seemed to have started a whole new life for yourself. Are you still playing the field?'

This was an old-fashioned expression and Nat didn't understand why a relatively young man like Bill didn't revert to the multitude of options modern media and young people offered.

'Did I ever play the field?'

'Well, you did have your moments, Nat,' said Bill, still sounding vague and slippery.

'Well, I put most of my effort into writing these days. This three-year project should do the trick. And then I'll see.'

'Do you really think you can keep up this-life-in three countries plan for three years? I mean, where are you going to stay in

Liverpool next year now that your auntie's gone?' countered Bill.

'I might just relocate to North Wales for the duration. My tenants are thinking of moving out at the beginning of next year. They're having a second child and need something bigger.'

Bill went into mocking mode, producing a sneering smile.

'Oh, so you have tenants, do you?'

'Yes, Bill. I have tenants. What am I supposed to call them? I've got to pay the mortgage somehow, you know. It's called the free market. I'm sure you've heard of it.'

Bill was silent, poured out and gulped down another large Scotch and looked deadly serious again; he obviously had something on his mind.

'Well, whatever you do with your life, Nat, don't let your dick rule your head, that's all I can say. I'm not one for giving advice but something happened since I last saw you that almost finished me off. I had two short, sex-only affairs with two different women in the space of a year and I haven't quite yet recovered. You're the only person I've told.'

This was a lot of news to take in. But Bill wasn't finished yet.

'Lust, you see, Nat, is a wicked thing.'

Had Bill gone religious?

'I could have lost everything if Karen had found out. And I have got to give ye something afore ye go.'

When Bill lapsed into the Scottish vernacular, it was a sure sign that he was starting to wobble, either caused by drink or emotion. In this case, it was probably both. Nat was anxious to know what was in the brown envelope that Bill had just carefully retrieved from an obscure section of his massive bookcase. Nat poured himself a second shot, without ice, to brace himself for its contents.

'These are fairly disgusting pictures of the two women,' he whispered. Nat swiftly transferred them to his shirt pocket lest any of the Campbells unexpectedly appeared through the living room door after sniffing the whisky down the corridor. Nat wasn't sure whether he wanted to see these photos. What was he supposed to do with them?

'I've never been able to throw photos away,' Bill said. 'It's an obsession of mine; I can never part with them. But obviously I've got to get them out of here somehow. Throw them away if you want. Just don't tell me if you do.'

Nat tried to understand but wasn't having much success. The only logic he could discern was the necessity to get the foul evidence off the premises.

'So all I'm saying, wee Nat, is that you shouldn't let this happen to you. Don't let lust get the upper hand.'

The patronising "wee Nat" annoyed him; he blamed the drink again. And the new double role he had been assigned as confidant and one-man church congregation learning about the perils resulting from the pleasures of the flesh from "Father Bill" was also wearying. Years ago, Bill had explained all the reasons for him being a dyed-in-the-wool atheist; now he seemed to be shivering in his boots at the idea that he had reneged on his matrimonial vows. He might be severely punished by a God he didn't actually believe in. Did he expect Nat to transform into a priest himself and forgive him his sins in this unlikely confession box in downtown Pankow while they gulped down generous doses of Scotch? It was a ridiculous scenario. He decided to give this failed atheist a shot of dirty pragmatic thinking.

'Look, Bill, this can happen to any man, you know. Your

middle-aged flings are over now, your balls are empty, and I take it these women are out of your system and off your trail. I also presume that you've got neither of them up the duff and that Karen knows nothing. And I am going to take these photos and blackmail you with them next Monday. That should get me a new cottage in Wales.'

'The second word is "off", Wilson, and the first one you know already,' said Bill. But at least he was smiling. For the first time that evening, the fucker was smiling a real smile.

It wasn't yet eleven o'clock and Nat was heading out of the door. They were both pleasantly on the inebriated side and Nat was genuinely pleased that Bill seemed to have experienced some sort of cathartic release during the generous nightcaps. He looked relaxed as he waved down from the balcony, even though he still had to tackle a sink full of dirty dishes and manoeuvre himself beside Karen into bed whilst ensuring that she didn't get the waft of Black Label of which she so strongly disapproved. He would be up the next day at six to get to the local secondary school where, according to Bill, the children seemed to be getting stupider and more disinterested by the year.

He tried not to think too much about Bill's predicament and focussed on getting the right underground connections home; if in luck, he could be there in twenty minutes. He wanted to fit in an intensive listening to *Zappa in New York*, a double live album released in 1978, and be in bed by something resembling a respectable time.

"Zappa offers an excellent look back at twelve years of musical creation in this live album, with excellent performances and, despite the unnecessary, unfunny gibberish between songs, it deserves a four-star rating." Nat wrote these words about *Zappa in New York* after his first mug of tea on the morning after he visited Bill and they gave him an idea for a book. A book on the recorded music of Frank Zappa; a short, witty, concise evaluation of his work which would prevent people from wasting their hard-earned cash on some of Zappa's more impenetrable and irreverent material. Yes, he would rank the fifty-four albums, describe them, and fit everything into 120 pages. Then get it out at an affordable price. "Zappa For False Beginners" might be a catchy title. He could easily write it alongside the novel he was currently working on, thus providing light relief from the more strenuous toil of producing "literature".

Thinking about Zappa also helped to take his mind off the evening at Bill's place. An evening that seemed to illustrate the middle classes at their worst, featuring meaningful conversation and the chance to cleverly display their knowledge and persuasive arguments and where the good food and wine were merely a sideshow to help maintain the eternal pretence that everything was perfect. The final half-hour of intense confession by Bill was at least authentic, entertaining even. Nat regretted being so soft on Bill by suggesting that these sorts of things happened in the best of families; he should have added that the holier-than-thou middle classes were particularly good at this type of hypocrisy.

Then he remembered the photos Bill had entrusted him with. He decided on the spot that he should open them, stone-cold sober, strengthened by Zappa's madness and the strong mug of tea he was just finishing. Bill had simply called them "disgusting pictures", which sounded promising. Nat's only fear was that Bill might feature somewhere in them, removing any retention value for Nat. He opened the envelope.

Nat was neither disgusted nor particularly shocked. Thankfully, there was no sign of Bill's private parts, not a sweaty male body part anywhere; instead, just two women undressed, in a sombre light, their poses titillating rather than pornographic. They showed off their firm bodies, attractive, smiling faces half-covered by hands and pillows. One blonde, one brunette; Nat scrutinised the brunette's photos more closely, clearly understanding Bill's weakness after she got her kit off. In classic terms, the blonde had a fitter body, but Nat kept returning to the more opulent form of the other. The blonde had got the lion's share of the fifteen photos, the brunette only featuring in six.

He didn't like the inordinate time he was spending with these photos and he wondered once again what it was all about. He remembered Bill's rationale that he couldn't throw the photos away. Nat had the same problem. Photos of ex-girlfriends were particularly bittersweet and Nat had kept them all. Hanging onto your past with the help of photos was no big mystery. Nothing sinister. Just a bit masochistic, or in Bill's case, masochistic and seedy. Perhaps seedy was too strong a word, but they weren't photographs taken in bright sunlight next to beautiful trees of two sweet lovers cuddling. They were photographs of women taken in darkened rooms just after or before dirty sex with a married man.

He put the photos next to the breadbin; he wanted to talk to Bill again about this. He was genuinely interested to know how it all came about, who the women were and whether Bill was really over them. Nat didn't believe he was; his ramblings seemed to indicate that he was trying a bit too hard to convince himself of the fact and the almost religious, self-flagellation course he currently found himself on suggested a man in turmoil.

This exposure to tasteful soft-porn made Nat decide to bring forward his call to Martina. He had no qualms about the link between naked female flesh and Martina. If an unhappily married man from a classic middle-class unit could get away with that, a failed bachelor, rid of the chains of wedlock, should be allowed another go at that wicked game called lust. He entered her number.

Martina knew a "cute little Italian place", very reasonably priced, near Bijouplatz. Should she reserve a table? Friday was always very busy. Seven o'clock? Nat wasn't protesting. And he knew that he wouldn't be protesting about any other suggestions he now firmly believed Martina might be making after the espresso and complimentary Grappa had been swigged back.

In the meantime, there was Zappa work to be done. He had listened to and ranked the first twenty-three albums; there were twenty-three to go. The album title of the next one was *Sleep Dirt*.

The underground was busy for a Saturday morning; there was no chance of a seat, and Nat squeezed down the middle of the train, making for the doors where there appeared to be some welcome space. He found himself standing directly opposite a face he knew well. The woman smiled and looked surprised.

'Hello, Nat. Haven't seen you for a while!' The smiling face belonged to Angela, an old colleague from his pioneering days in Berlin. Always upbeat, always laughing, time spent with her was always easy. She had a husky voice, pleasing to the ear, as King Lear said, *an excellent thing in woman*. She gave him a coy look as she added, 'I didn't know you lived round here.' He didn't. Nat smiled, Angela smiled and she knew what naughty Nat had been up to. The conversation and chance meeting ended at Alexanderplatz with the usual, 'We must meet up some time'. Nat changed trains. He spent the final short leg of his journey home suppressing a dirty grin, which irritated everybody in his immediate grumpy vicinity.

The childlike glee which dominated his return from Martina's place in Charlottenburg started to ebb in the course of the morning as the new reality eased in; the days would be different now and Nat didn't know whether to laugh or cry. His relationship with Martina had been consummated after their third meeting and Nat had only positive things to say about every minute he had spent with her so far. A relationship had been set in motion and he felt relaxed about everything.

Nat had been economical with the truth by not mentioning to Martina that in six weeks' time he would be heading back to Greece. He probably hadn't mentioned it because it wasn't set in stone. He was sandwiched between the garden of memories called Liverpool in his rear mirror and the isolation of Grecian island life ahead of him. And now things had changed in the present tense, as things always tend to.

He had pulled off a pretty impressive restart in Berlin: he had made steady progress on the book, had Zappa madness to save him from his own madness and there was the spin-off of having a new book project in the pipeline. He felt fairly invincible in his fully-equipped, comfortable flat. And now he was up and running with a woman. Bill's advice had been to reduce the "experiment" to two years; another voice in his head was at that very moment screeching at him to call it a day now, after just less than a year.

The other voice would be angry if he dropped everything now, settle into some sort of relationship, drift into a cosy routine and eventually shack up with a woman he had asked out in a health store in a moment of confusion, loneliness and fatigue. After banishing both voices from his thoughts for a few minutes, he tried to remember what the master plan had been a couple of years ago after his tidy Lotto win. "Have three years off and get away from it all". It was a banal, vague battle cry which was just dying to have some meat put on it by inexorable fate. He had already had the double whammy of losing a mysterious dream woman and his last remaining aunt; he was now on the verge of losing his freedom. So what?

Nat had seen the three-year project as an attempt to exercise solitary philosophical reflection during which he would try to make sense of everything that had happened in his life so far. He had suppressed the sober fact that events, twists of fate and the actions and presence of other people would inevitably get in the way in those three years; the snag was that Nat was happy to have people getting in the way. He could happily do without the negative twists of fate and events, but doing without people would be intolerable. Doing without women in the romantic sense would have been feasible for three years, but now that Martina had entered his life, with all those timeless qualities that sensuous, mother-of-earth women possess, he knew he had been de-railed.

The idea of going it alone in life seemed to possess anybody who has been disappointed by people and relationships and

Nat admitted to himself that he had unconsciously fallen into that category, although he had never properly bought into the idea in its entirety. Time had taught him that balance was everything, and not having somebody to love was the worst example of imbalance that he knew. He simply did not know whether he would be on that flight for Greece on the third of September.

The prospect of having sex twice in the space of twenty-four hours with somebody special to him was getting to him. It was foolhardy and ludicrous for a man of his advanced age with his dodgy past to be over-confident, but he suddenly found himself heading for the heart of Saturday night with renewed lightness of heart.

16

The weeks took care of themselves: life was balanced, easy. He was fighting to keep the mental and emotional chemicals which infiltrate anybody in love under control; if he didn't, any sense of autonomy and reason would be lost. That much he knew. In Liverpool, he hadn't allowed himself to think about Maria for too long. It worked, and within a couple of weeks, she was more or less out of his system. In Berlin, he was going to adopt the same system to make it work for a woman he *didn't* want out of his system.

Living in two different apartments facilitated this plan; in Greece, Maria was there 24/7 for the best part of a month and Nat was in emotional chains for the duration. In Berlin, he could increase and reduce the emotional volume with relative ease. He despised these reflections: emotional autonomy and volume, systems and facilitating plans sounded like the dry terminology of psychiatry rather than the inspired musings of a man in love.

In Berlin reflecting, thinking and even philosophizing were still part of his everyday life but it never became obsessive or debilitating. He learnt something tangible and useful from Martina: her stories told how human beings survive crises with dirty pragmatism, a cool head and the constant belief that things could always be worse. Her motto seemed to be: "Use the difficulty". A life of the usual deprivations in the GDR, losing her husband, bringing up a child singlehandedly, getting used to a new Germany, the strain of looking after a dying relative and finally, the acrimonious break with her parents. Martina didn't endlessly philosophize, stew in the unpleasant juice created by nasty twists of fate; instead, she reacted to events positively, used the difficulty to make decisions. And moved on. It was admirable, made sense and weakened Nat's resolve to resist feeling more attached to her.

Their first few meetings covered her own personal building sites and it was clear that she was constantly moving on. Martina was here and now and Nat was here and then, but already he was beginning to see the benefits of her "now" take on life. Martina didn't ask too many questions about his past and Nat realised that she had already learnt the lesson that dragging out wretched things from the past and mulling over them until they made you sick and tired was draining and self-defeating. And also plain boring.

Nat believed that his book was paying enough attention to his past anyway, so he didn't feel the need to awkwardly air his own wayward, error-strewn past in conversation. His past was driving the semi-autobiographical content of the narrative, personal therapy without the expensive fees of not-to-be-trusted shrinks. He let it all spill out onto the pages and he felt better for it. What potential readers did with it, made of it, or learnt from it, was entirely their business.

Right from the first meeting, however, Martina had expressed an interest in reading his work and her interest persisted. He had put her off by saying that she might have problems understanding his style; she countered that she had had contact with English-speaking people and that she often read books in English. Nat realised that he was going to have to hand over at least part of his manuscript sooner rather than later. He just hoped that it wouldn't interrupt the hitherto smooth flow of their relationship by provoking a stream of awkward questions. There may even be linguistic questions, plunging him back into the role of teacher again, not something he was anxious to revive and relive.

Martina's take on her past in the German Democratic Republic resembled that of most East Germans of her age and went something like this: "We had very little in material terms but we helped each other and made the best of things. The system was rotten, but what were we supposed to do? Not everything was bad: everybody had a job, nobody was homeless. We didn't know until after The Wall how active the Stasi had been and how many people were working for them. We were incredulous and elated when The Wall came down and nobody wants the old system back." This was the general verdict of the ninety per cent. There were still approximately ten percent who saw the collapse of their system as a temporary aberration and the most calamitous event of their lives; socialism would re-emerge with 100% certainty sometime in the future to clinch the ultimate and final victory. Socialism was, after all, all about believing, not thinking.

If Martina had been in the "ten-percent" group, Nat would have made his escape after their first date in Café Kant. There was a religious fervour about such people, with whom no reasonable discussion about contemporary German history was possible. Nat had had a couple of relationships of varying kinds with East German women of this ilk down the years in Berlin and they were all destined to failure after the first exchange of opinions on the subject. The vast majority of East Germans believed that things were generally much better, while the bitter ten percent sulked in the corner, refusing to join in the post-wall party, preferring to wait for the Second Coming of Socialism.

Berlin was the only place that linked him to the Web. Emails were few and far between since he disappeared off to Greece almost a year ago and he only checked his inbox weekly on his out-of-date computer. His mobile was the simplest he could find and sending text messages was his only link to anything which might be described as technology. His Friday glance at the dozen or so he had received that week threw up two worth reading, the sad one he had been expecting and a bizarre one which took time to make any sense of at all.

The terse statement attached to the first one read: "A celebration of the life of Samantha Wilson. Anfield Crematorium, 20th August, 2012. 10.30 a.m." Sam's stepdaughter had obviously found his email address somewhere. There was no other message attached but he took it as an invitation. He would send flowers. He slumped down and said a little prayer, which took the form of a brief conversation with Sam.

The other mail of relevance required more concentration. The content was strangely gripping and comical, the English employed idiosyncratic, misspelt and lacking even the pretence of punctuation. Everything was all over the place and he had to read it twice before his memory finally nailed who it was from. It was from Ian, a native of Leeds, whom he had met two years previously in Berlin when the latter was still just about mobile despite the creeping ravages of Multiple Sclerosis. He was the friend of a friend and had been riotously funny, raucous, and rebellious company for two weeks despite his dreadful disability.

Nat read the mail for the third time and concluded that this particular Yorkshireman wouldn't be dead until they had hammered the final nail into his coffin. The MS had obviously been progressing nicely in the two years since they had last seen each other. Ian had managed to get the following powerful gibberish to Nat.

hi natty how you doing pal well it is all happening for me I got my self a woman in the U.S.A we have been talking on the net for some time and on 1 august I fly out therefor 5 weeks for once in my life im taking Ods approach to life the the bank has plenty of money. Darling Karen is an M.S re like me and has a good job as a call center manager earns $635 a week after tax so I wont starve.

we intend to go on holiday together well she is in charge of were maybe Kentucky or Vermont. But it could be nashvill to see another ms er called connie who was a nurse prison guard ex trucker that sings country

but realy this has all just happened up to a few weeks agoe life was abit flat and now at my ripe old age having had sex like I never imagined albeit on the pc I am may be looking at a dual nationality

when I said I couldent get agreen card she said who cares I earn enough for us both and I said I wont get residency she said ther is one way sweetness but we will have to let my divorce settle so isort of said woooo there gali don't know the words to the star spangled banner

it's a plot im sure connie sent me a mail and said that if Karen likes you as much as in real life she wont let me go home. well old buddy it looks like THE FIRST BATALLION OF THE O'DWYER HORSE AND CART COMMANDOES WILL

HAVE TOLAUNCH A QUICK SNATCH OPERATION to recover what is left of me . ah well funny old world tuss ian

It was a confusing explosion of words and emotions from a man refusing to take terminal decline lying down; Nat was moved that Ian wanted to share his confused joy with him. Thinking of the effort required to get his disfigured fingers even as far as the PC keyboard with the meagre help of increasingly weakened legs made Nat sit down and pray for the second time in the space of ten minutes and it was a direct message to Ian, which he thought Ian would believe in.

Nat wrote: *Go fer it, yer randy bugger! Go out with a bang!* Nat hated his own pun, but knew that Ian would find it funny. He could almost hear him laughing.

Nat's days were full of creative purpose, while the hours listening to Zappa and the walks with no particular place to go were a necessary and enjoyable waste of time. The writing cleared his head and the walking beat lethargy. He always remained within a five-kilometre stretch of Berlin west and east of the former border, but always tried to produce a pleasing sweat by keeping a brisk pace. One beer would do somewhere to catch his breath and work out his thoughts and the most efficient way of getting back home was invariably public transport.

This was Berlin in late summer and there was no finer place for an urbanite to stretch his legs and retrace the steps of hundreds of thousands of people who had done good, bad and everything in between in the almost eight hundred years of this beautiful *and* ugly metropolis. The late summer sunshine covered up a multitude of Berlin's warts, but its wide, inspiring boulevards, intriguing, narrow side streets and bars on endless corners in sunshine kept a hopeless romantic like Nat walking and dreaming.

Berlin in winter, however, was the ice-cold efficient assassin, the bastard that killed at birth any traces of good mood or positivity. Colder and icier than anywhere else in Germany and virtually on the Polish border, concrete, screeching trams, tons of dog shit and endless building excavations dominated everybody's vision; the foul temper of anybody you wanted anything from completed the hellish picture of a place you didn't want to be in. He had survived one such Berlin winter when he barely clung onto life itself as his broken heart spread constant pain to anything belonging to the wrecked and weakened ex-member of the human race called Nat Wilson. The Berlin prison he found himself incarcerated in offered not a crumb of solace and the trauma of that winter still made him shiver and was the main argument for getting out of the place before the last summer month changed into September. He had five weeks to make up his mind.

He had fallen into a comfortable pattern of seeing Martina two or three times a week. As she was working every day, and her shop was nearby, she tended to stay overnight at his place. He would cook a meal and then they would talk. Nat hated himself for doing it, but he was filling many gaps in her grasp on history; the East German education system was no worse than the West German one, as Martina had noticed when her son was moving through the school system in West Berlin, but she also admitted that subjects such as history were presented in such a biased and selective way in the GDR that you ended up knowing little of any value.

From this ignorance sprang many intriguing questions about Britain which Nat loved trying to answer.

'Why do you still have a monarchy?'; 'Why don't you have identity cards?'; 'What's the point of the House of Lords';? 'Why doesn't Britain like Europe?' They were the sort of questions he longed to get from his former university students but never did; this was his chance to shine and he grasped it with both hands.

One morning, after Martina had left for work, he was horrified to see Bill's envelope still resting next to the bread bin. He didn't fancy having to explain that compact collection of soft porn to Martina. He prayed she hadn't seen it and looked inside. He put them in a safer place; he was going to have one last look sometime and then bin them before Martina's next visit.

Later that same day, he directed his daily walk to an area where he had met a true artist many years before. He had noticed down the years that the dozen or so artist ateliers situated below a number of renovated railway arches in the Tiergarten district still seemed to be going strong and he was gripped by the need to find out whether this particular character was still flogging his puzzling works to unsuspecting bourgeois punters. Nat had classed him as a true artist as he really did seem to devote all his life to creating paintings, none of which seemed to make any sense to Nat or his dad (who happened to be visiting at the time). The artist's ability to keep a young man (Nat) and an old man (Nat's dad) riveted to canvas was remarkable, especially as neither of them could make head nor tail of what they were staring at.

As Nat moved from one gallery to another, he desperately tried to remember the artist's name, just in case he was still there. They had exchanged correspondence ferociously for about a year after their first meeting, so he must have seen his name almost every month during that time; but try as he might, the man's name remained out of reach. He reached gallery number nine and there he was, sitting there, talking to a woman, a damned attractive one at that: long flowing hair tumbling over a loose summer dress. Somebody had forgotten to tell her that the era of free festivals was over and that Woodstock was never going to happen again. She seemed unconcerned; the artist had clearly not lost his knack of taking people prisoner and making them feel good about it.

As the artist looked up, it seemed to take him an age to place Nat but by the time he was within a yard of him, the word 'Nat!' echoed round the arches, probably frightening the lives out of genteel folk browsing in the neighbouring caves. He had certainly remembered Nat's name, but Nat was still none the wiser about his. A perfectly executed bear hug got the beautiful hippy girl giggling and Nat gasping for breath. The artist shrieked the German equivalent of 'Fuck me sideways!' two or three times and then they stood rigid, staring at each other. He looked as youthful and pretty as ever, although he was carrying more weight.

The woman stood up elegantly, saying: 'Same time next week, Holger?' Holger. Of course, Holger! She had inadvertently got Nat out of an embarrassing jam and before Nat could protest at her leaving, she had manoeuvred herself past antique furniture and memorabilia and glided out of view, hardly giving the intruder a passing glance. Nat had at least got the timing right: they both looked relaxed in a post-coital sort of way.

They talked. Holger filled two flimsy beakers with Scotch.

And they talked. Holger had been doing the same thing for the last ten years since their last meeting, the only difference was that he now had a small apartment round the corner. When they had met for the first time, he was living in something resembling a cubicle at the back of the gallery. There was still a bed there, presumably employed these days for purely daytime activities with female visitors.

'Did that woman ever come back to you, by the way?' was Holger's out-of-the-blue question.

'No, but *you* said she would,' was Nat's churlish reply.

'No, I said she would if you were on the same wavelength.'

'We were on the same wavelength.'

'Well, obviously you weren't.'

Nat was tempted to refer Holger to a taxidermist, but decided to put the topic to bed straight away: they were talking about events which no longer had any relevance. But still Nat felt rattled.

'I'd best be going,' Nat muttered. Holger bade him to bear with him for a moment. He shuffled off into his back room and Nat heard much cursing as Holger violently opened and slammed shut drawers. He reappeared, fiendishly grinning. He shoved half a dozen dog-eared pages into Nat's hand.

'You should remember these gems. You gave me them as a present way back when. Doubtless you wrote them under the influence, but they have a certain novelty value.'

Nat didn't know what on earth Holger was talking about. He put the pages in his mini-rucksack and decided to meet them head-on when he was alone, just as he had with Bill's photographic keepsakes. He had dug up two old friends and they had both shoved mysterious things into his hands for safe-keeping. Was it some sort of plot? A practical joke? Or just bad luck? Ian's anarchistic e-mail had already unsteadied him with its bizarre description of bizarre news; and now Holger was adding to the surrealistic pantomime.

The meeting had taken a peculiar final turn, a displeasing twist, brought on by unhappy memories and the two generous portions of Scotch Holger had served him. He would walk home, by which time he would be sober and be able to get on top of things again. He had invited Holger round for some food some time and promised to call but he somehow couldn't quite imagine Holger sitting down at a table enjoying good food, sipping fine wine and making polite conversation. Nat couldn't imagine Holger being anywhere other than here, underneath these Berlin railway arches, selling art, seducing customers and women and cheerfully fornicating. The bear hug goodbye was not quite as bearish as the first one of the day and Nat sped off, a slightly troubled soul.

Almost exactly one hour later he was home, almost sober, with a pleasant layer of sweat on him. He had a quick shower and started reading what Holger had given him. They were poems. Nat's own poems from a decade ago. Holger had got one thing right: they had seen the light of day with the help of liberal portions of the hard stuff, and he had given them to Holger as a gift to try and express the turmoil he was sloshing around in at the time. He suddenly remembered that he had been inspired by Holger to try his hand at poetry; if Holger could paint and express himself, he thought, why couldn't Nat write poems and achieve the same?

He slowly read the first one and couldn't believe the depth of intensity he had been able to get onto paper. Did he really write this over-the-top shit? It was entitled: "Jane or 2565 days". Dreadful title, but the contents weren't quite as dreadful, he thought.

And when they were over,
Loved to death by both of us
With stroking and French kisses
Heated bodies and words
Which we nailed to some stars somewhere
You looked around
And felt cold and desolate

Something was missing
That other half
That doubled ME
That unshaved something
And you damned your freedom
That little fearful freedom

It was morning with those pointed finger sunbeams
Which unexpectedly caught your face in the window
Pushing you straight into loneliness
Straight into uncertain future
And you picked up your pen to be alone

Condemned to be alone
Call me again
And we'll search for our words
Which we nailed to some stars somewhere

He hardly remembered writing this piece of work masquerading as a poem, although the awful title rang a bell and its sentiments provoked a melancholy shiver. The poem momentarily pushed him back into the freezing cave of despair, in that grimmest of Berlin winters. He resisted reaching for the strong drinks cabinet. Then he suddenly remembered the thick winter coat that his dad had bought him in the big department store on snowy Alexanderplatz. The coat that saved him. And there he was, praying again, for the third time that day.

Scully's client

In the history of the world, thick winter coats have often been in short supply, but there are always enough human beings around to make sure that they get onto the backs of the people who need them. One such human being lived in Liverpool and doing what came naturally to him eased the pain of an old Scouse gent. Just another day in the life.

Graham's decision to become a social worker was not a conscious one, but neither was it ever seriously in doubt: his desire to help people had been with him for as long as he could remember and was a natural, dominant element of his being. He wasn't clever enough to be a doctor, had toyed with the idea of becoming a teacher, which in certain parts of Liverpool is the same as being a social worker. He could never understand why other people didn't feel the way he felt about the injustices all around them; why they didn't care, why they didn't share his pain, why they weren't driven by the same need to relieve that pain. Sometimes he thought that his wife was the only other human being who understood him. Sue, who was also a social worker and understood him. She looked after kids from problem homes, or no homes at all.

There was no shortage of takers for the sort of compassion the Scullys had been supplying in abundance during their thirty-year tenure at Liverpool's Social Services Department. Demand had steadily risen during that time yet they could remember every case, every breakthrough and failure, and every client, as they were now requested to call them. Their patience, perseverance and optimism were endless, their devotion to improving the world unshakable.

It was late Friday afternoon, the prelude to Graham's favourite time of the week. The time when he and his wife cooked a meal together, a relaxing ritual they fell into and nurtured after the kids had finally got themselves off the premises. He was in charge of the main, Sue flexed her culinary muscles on a fancy starter; she amazed Graham by managing to conjure up something novel every week. Even if it wasn't entirely new, it was invariably a subtle variation on all the other starters she had created down the years. He stuck to a rock-steady two dozen list of winning favourites. He didn't go for experiments in the kitchen.

He had one more piece of work to attend to before Sue got in from work when they would start fussing in the kitchen; he picked up his slim briefcase, and after a brief forage, yanked out a three-page report on a client and plonked it on the coffee table. He poured himself a pre-dinner drink (always a Peroni, having become pleasantly addicted to it on their last two holidays in Italy) and started reading. The sober reading matter was an assessment of the needs of an eighty-seven-year-old man, living alone, who, on the initial recommendation of Graham, was to be offered a care plan. Graham had been visiting Mr Wilson for several months now, getting to know him and assessing how best to help him. The consultant now stepping in was a certain Dr Clive Adams, an Old Age Psychiatrist. He would back or reject Graham's recommendation and, if he was in favour, the latter would devise a programme best suited to the client's needs. Graham knew Adams personally and was fairly confident that he would see things as he did.

Graham had grown to like Mr Wilson: he saw him as one of those old-school, decent Scousers who had never lost their charm, innocence, self-effacing honesty and respect for other people. Mr Wilson's priceless gift was being happy with very little. Graham's own dad had been of the same ilk before he had succumbed to cancer about thirty years ago and Graham's talks with Mr Wilson closely resembled the countless talks he had had with Scully Senior. Graham understood his clients because he was from their world, albeit one generation removed (one of his favourite sayings was, 'I'll be old myself one day'). Most of them just wanted to talk and what they said was never boring. He never forgot what that generation had been through: the thirties, the war, fifties' austerity, outside toilets, no bathroom, hard work for low pay, Thatcher. The constant struggle to keep body and soul together, with little chance for much else. Mr Wilson had been a widower as long as Graham's mum had been a widow. Mr Wilson rarely mentioned his wife. Discomfort, receding physical and mental powers, were the only things on his mind now.

Unless it was absolutely necessary, Graham consistently rejected the social work ethos of always maintaining a profes-sional distance. His own feelings were the eternal and ultimate motivator and enabled him to survive in the job; no other approach would work for him. He cried when those he had cared for eventually died, but then he moved on; there were always new clients to help and he had to be ready for their challenges. Combining a professional attitude *and* being compassionate in the job was his special trick.

He took a sip of Peroni and started reading the report on Mr Wilson.

Reason for assessment: Seen by GP at home – poor mobility and arthritic pain. Also visited by Community Matron. Mr Wilson complained of poor memory. He lives alone. OKD 3, heart failure, IHD, hypertension and OA. Patient has catheter for BPH.

History of Presenting Problem: Mr Wilson was charming. He told me 'I'm just about managing. I've got this breathing problem that varies. Even my memory is going. I've got arthritis in the legs, shoulders and the pain in my arms is terrible. I've had a blood problem in the past.'

With regard to his memory, Mr Wilson told me, 'Yeah, it's hopeless. It used to be perfect. I lose track of conversations and it's a bit embarrassing.'

Mr Wilson told me that a girl called Sylvia who lives down the street used to do his shopping, but has now stopped and he doesn't know why. He then said, 'There's one other girl who does a bit of shopping for me.' But Mr Wilson could not tell me her name and I was left not sure that she exists.

Mr Wilson continued, 'My son is a teacher in Germany. He comes over Christmas and summer and phones me every night.

He stocked up my fridge when he was home over Christmas.'

Activities of Daily Living Skills: Mr Wilson told me that he eats pies and sausage rolls. He said he buys them from Asda and that is as far as he can walk. If he goes to Old Swan, he has to get a taxi. Mr Wilson admitted to over-cooking food but told me he had never caused a fire. He said, 'It's a bit awkward getting washed and changed, particularly in the shower. In the summer, I fell outside when I stood up from a chair. I'm gasping for breath at the top of the stairs.'

Current Medication and Compliance: Ferrous Sulphate, Bisoprolol, Omeprazole, Aspirin, Furosemide, Ramipril and inhaler. Tablets were stored in a rather haphazard fashion, which caused me to have concerns about his compliance.

Personal history: Born and raised in Liverpool. Wife died about thirty years ago. Couple had one son, Nat, who works as a teacher in Germany. Mr Wilson worked till he was seventy-two. He was a milkman for twenty years and later was a security guard, working mostly in the Port of Liverpool. Mr Wilson told me that he has never been a heavy drinker and has not drunk any alcohol in the last twelve months. He smokes about seven cigarettes a day.

Mental state examination:
The house was cold apart from the living room where the gas fire was on. The stairs were steep. There were two bannisters. I found a halogen heater in the bathroom. Mr Wilson told me he has to use an extension lead from his bedroom. There was

a shower in the bathroom and a bath board. The living room was rather cluttered and the wallpaper was nicotine stained. The kitchen was also rather cluttered and the front of the cooker was splashed with fat. The fridge was well stocked, but one of the bottles of milk was out of date. Mr Wilson was unshaven. His fingers were nicotine stained. He was very pleasant, cooperative and euthymic. Mr Wilson was grateful for my visit. His mood was normal and there were no psychotic symptoms.

Cognitive examination:

Knew the current day month and year, but thought it was Autumn although we were halfway through January. Impaired attention, calculation and recall. Scored 22/30 on MMSE.

Diagnosis/Formulation/Summary/Initial plan of care:

Mild dementia, probably mixed Alzheimer's and vascular. ICD-10 FOO.1. Pbr Cluster 19.

Statement of care

1. I would be grateful if you would arrange for Mr Wilson's medication in future to be dispensed in blister packs.

2. I will arrange for a therapeutic trial of Donepezil.

3. I will ask Linda Murphy, CHMT Co-ordinator to arrange for a CMHN to make contact with Mr Wilson's son.

4. I will ask Besa Selik, OT to carry out a home assessment including his function in the kitchen and bathroom and how he manages the stairs.

5. Mr Wilson made it clear that he would not be interested in a move to sheltered accommodation.

6. I will via this letter ask Social Services to arrange for a social worker to visit with a view to arranging a care package. I think Mr Wilson will require at least two visits per day for medication prompts, meal preparation and help with personal care and I will also ask social worker to arrange a shopper and help Mr Wilson to organise a private cleaner.

7. I will review as and when necessary.

Risk:
Inadequate social support. Poor diet and mobility, and risks of falls. Inadequate heating and halogen heater in bathroom.

Risk Management Plan:
OT home assessment and care package.

Graham found Adam's report fairly accurate and it boded well for a short-term, modest improvement in the quality of Mr Wilson's life. Notwithstanding the usual NHS and medical jargon and abbreviations, it went considerably further on the human level than most. This was the effect Mr Wilson had on people and even a hardened, slightly stand-off professional like Harvey had started to sound like a real human being. Graham hoped to have Mr Wilson around for a while longer. He was hoping to meet his son one day; Mr Wilson talked about him a lot.

He slid the report back into his case, placed it in its usual place and took his unfinished Peroni to the kitchen. With the kitchen to himself, he started thinking about the hour of cooking ahead of him while unloading the necessities from the fridge and pantry.

He didn't worry about Mr Wilson, felt no pangs of guilt about him making beans on toast while he was trying fancy cooking with his wife in a fancy part of Liverpool. Mr Wilson didn't do fancy, he did beans on toast and he had regularly told Graham that he was quite happy with his 'tin-pot life,' as he called it. It was Friday night, he would be having a good chat on the phone with his son (and perhaps with his twin brother down the road) on the eternal question of Liverpool FC. A ciggie before the live match on the telly, a good strong cup of tea at half time. At eleven o'clock he would summon up his last strength and heave himself steadily up the twelve steep steps to his bedroom. It was the nightly challenge he dreaded, but with which he defended the right to live on his own, independently, without anybody telling him what to do. Safely in his bed, his head down, he wouldn't think and he wouldn't worry about a thing.

The only thing Graham worried about was losing Sue, who would be fifty-five this year, the same age as Mr Wilson's wife when he lost her. He heard the key in the door, it opened, Sue walked in and Graham shuddered. Without saying a word, he was in front of her before she had time to get her coat off. His embrace was slightly longer than usual, his desire for closeness surprising both of them.

'All right, love?' she asked.

'Yes, I'm all right, love.'

17

He had been neglecting Zappa and so devoted himself to some of his more difficult albums. Four hours of complex Zappa had made him hungry for a simple meal and he opted for something more German than the Germans themselves: a "Strammer Max", a difficult concept to translate into English (it sort of meant a "Pissed Max"). He assumed it got its name from the idea that the only culinary creation an intoxicated German man could rustle up after a session of heavy drinking would be this: two slices of buttered bread with a couple of portions of boiled ham slung on top with two fried eggs to top it all. It was the sort of fare his dad would appreciate and he realised he was eating in the style favoured by him: hunched shoulders, concentrating on the contents of the plate. A cave-man with a knife and fork.

Nat occasionally talked to himself, spreading unnerving seeds of doubt in his mind about his own sanity. An extra worry was that he sounded just like his dad during such conversations: the light Scouse embellishments, the sing-song whine, the repeating of age-old truisms and deep sighs. His deceased dad was there when he watched football on TV: they cursed dodgy offside decisions and misplaced passes. This all added melancholy to the fear that once you had been living on your own for a certain length of time, you felt yourself starting to lose the need to give a fuck. Martina might help stop the rot, if that's what it was.

For some unknown reason, this got him thinking about an

LSD experience of an Irish friend who had died recently; he had only had one trip on this particular substance and he never took it again. After hearing his story, Nat understood why. Under the influence, Eamon was dead and was following his loved ones around down on earth, desperately trying to prevent them from committing sins; the torture of the trip was that however hard he tried, pleading and screaming, they couldn't hear a word. When he had first heard the story, Nat made some flippant comment about it being a 'typical Catholic LSD story', focussing on the Catholic obsession with sin and guilt. Nat was never tempted for half a millisecond to find out what his "Scouse-and-Vaguely-Anglican" background would throw up for him on *his* LSD excursion.

Nat was still curious to know whether anybody was trying to tell *him* something from the beyond; if they had, he hadn't noticed. His dad's voice within his own voice was perhaps the closest he was going to get to anything ethereal.

His eyes rested once again on the envelope containing the photos. Getting his priorities right, he first got a beer out of the fridge with his left hand, elegantly freed up the cold beer with his right hand, aided by his trusty Polish bottle opener, and made an equally elegant box stop at the adjacent bread bin. He re-assembled himself in his armchair to have one last look at Bill's amateur photography. It was time for the pictures to go.

Bill certainly knew his way around a camera, he had to give him that. The photos of the blonde, for example, were taken in such a way that nobody would ever be able to identify her unless they had intimate knowledge of her body. She was tastefully presented in a light which delightfully showed her impressive, petite, neatly sorted form; but you were left to deliciously speculate about the beauty of her face, which was tantalisingly half-hidden. The same trick was used to conceal the identity of the more opulent brunette appearing in the other photos. But this time it didn't work because Nat was already familiar with the naked body in the picture; he had been exploring it with a considerable amount of enthusiasm for the previous five weeks or so. It was Martina's.

Nat started shivering. Then he laughed hysterically. He stared into space, stood up, paced around the room and sat down again. There he sat for ten long minutes, stuffing the meat of this very mad, bad news through the mincing machine now grinding furiously in his overheated brain. The shivering was over, now it was time for the sweating session. He got up again, lurched towards the balcony, desperate for fresh air, and stared across the centre of a town which now seemed to be showing him its ugliest face again after being a relatively good boy for the last month or so.

He had to digest some harsh facts and then decide what to do next. He would have to go through every conceivable scenario and think through every possible decision until he found the least awful one and then take it. Even at this early stage, he knew that the number of choices at his disposal was limited.

So, what were the facts? Martina had been one of Bill's bits on the side. For how long? Did this question matter? Somehow, yes. When was she the bit on the side? Did *this* information matter? Nat thought yes. Was she his first bit on the side? Or was she the blonde's successor? The mere fact that Nat was asking these questions meant that he thought they were important. But he also knew that the only way of finding the answers was to ask Bill and/or Martina. Did he fancy that?

He'd rather eat his own balls than do such a thing. The potential for creating self-torment on an industrial scale was great. The list of questions Nat could ask was endless and he knew that asking for answers from the elicit lovers might destroy his relationship with Martina.

He could just call Martina, tell her the news that he was going to Greece and that he would understand if she thought a long-distance relationship like that didn't have a future. And hope that she agreed with him. As he had to tell her about Greece in the next few weeks anyway, this might be a solution; however, if she decided that she wanted to fall in with his plans, he would have to find another way of ending the relationship. Like telling her the real reason, i.e. her relationship with his old mate, Bill. Which brought him back to the dismal prospect of at least one of them knowing what he now knew. Or he could just disappear on 3rd September and never get in touch again.

The digestion of two possible courses of action at his disposal now complete, he finished his beer, fetched another bottle and started grappling with the next slab of ten-minute thinking. He now had two viable possibilities, which one was he going to use? The idea of him springing the 'I'm off to Greece at the end of the month idea, so goodbye forever' might create a discussion which could create the unfavourable scenario of his revealing what he knew. The second one was cowardly and outright bad behaviour. In any case, both variants presumed that he wanted to finish the relationship. He was now deep into the process of finding out what he wanted. His overtaxed brain was working overtime.

Normally, Nat had been able to kill off any torturous thoughts of present lovers' previous lovers by not thinking about such matters, which was normally doable by applying the due amount of discipline. But there was little trace of normality about this case: his present lover's previous lover, who just so happened to be his mate Bill, had given him alluring photos he had taken of Nat's present lover naked, presumably sometime before or after the sexual acts which had been committed within a seedy extra-marital relationship based on Bill's pure lust. No, these were not "normal circumstances". This was the crux of the matter.

Before entering the final straight in the race to make a decision before bedtime, he decided to change his liquid refreshment. To prevent unpleasant excesses, Nat never kept short, strong stuff on the premises of his Berlin apartment; but Bill, of all people, had slipped a miniature malt in his pocket as he left his Pankow abode all those weeks ago, presumably as a thank you for lending a sympathetic ear regarding Bill's hanky-panky.

He emptied half of the malt into a glass and vowed to make the necessary decisions there and then, despite, by now, being well under the influence. And he would not change his mind the next morning after sleeping on it. He was thus about to break two principles he had rigorously stuck to in recent years and which had, generally speaking, kept him in good stead: don't mix booze and life-changing decisions and always sleep on things before making those decisions.

There were other possible courses of action: suppress the memory of what he had seen and carry on. Or he could tell Bill how pissed off he was and threaten to spill the beans, perhaps – and it really was a big perhaps – providing himself with some degree of momentary, vindictive, uneasy satisfaction. Even as he was considering such childish meanness, he knew it could never really be part of his overall plan. This was the drink thinking.

So, suppression it was to be: his decision was to let things roll and pretend that nothing had happened. He had never seen any photos; he knew nothing of Martina's romantic past and wasn't interested in finding out anything more about it. He would complete everything in Berlin that he had wanted to complete as a writer, social romantic and sad bastard survivor and take it from there. He would ignore the photographic evidence of a seedy relationship, which now threatened to ruin a potentially perfectly good relationship. He had found this out through a freakish coincidence and he now had clarity at least: he would be returning to Greece in three weeks' time. With or without Martina.

Balzac was right, happiness has its roots in ignorance and Greece would be the place to nurture and wrap himself in that liberating, soothing ignorance. It was the one last bullet in his gun, the last card up his sleeve, the two fingers to fate.

He took himself off to bed and slept surprisingly well.

Messengers
Nat had almost forgotten one message from beyond and he had Yoko Ono to thank for it. And being at the right place and time.

Liverpool was gathering for live music at the Pier Head. The stage was set and the weather clement; a gentle, westerly breeze was rolling off the Mersey and the sun was peeking sporadically through high-scattered clouds. Fifty years before, sometime during the early days of 1940, a young married couple once again displayed their joyful lust for each other during one of the husband's intermittent visits from yet another lengthy escapade with the Merchant Navy. The man's wife, Julia, gave birth to their only child, a boy, on 9th October that year at the Liverpool Maternity Hospital, barely a mile from the place where today's guest of honour, Yoko Ono, was now standing. John Lennon would have turned fifty this year and there was no shortage of popular artists wanting, at worst, to murder his songs or, at best, give them an "interesting" new spin. Whatever the case, they all meant well.

Due east, three miles inland, he was watching on TV and wondered why he wasn't there; he couldn't remember any build-up in the media, knew nothing about ticket arrangements. Anyway, it was live, all-day TV coverage; why not be a lazy bastard for a change and watch it in the comfort of your own trusty armchair? He watched the crowds hanging around for something to happen. The whole event had all the makings of an amateurish attempt to cash in on Lennon's fame, despite the organisers' assertions that all the proceeds were going to an organisation working for world peace (what else?).

The TV camera bobbled nervously amongst the masses, before shakily landing on a startled Yoko, who, unprepared for this unexpected chance to make a statement to the expectant viewing public, looked straight into the camera, gave a huge grin and excitedly spurted out her feelings from the bottom of her heart with the breathless:

'Isn't this greeeaat?'

Nat was thrust back into his armchair and felt a bolt travelling up his spine, causing him to momentarily lose any sense of time and place. He looked at Yoko and knew that it was his mum speaking to him. Her Liverpool twang. Her natural enthusiasm. And Yoko's smile, tolerating no opposition to the joyous nature of the moment. For a split second, Yoko had sparked a reunion and Nat was spread-eagled across the couch as he realised that messengers were operating across space and time and he was on their wavelength. You only had to be at the right place at the right time to get tuned in. Being at home in front of the TV was, in this case, the right place to be.

He watched the rest of the show in a state of wild bewilderment but gained only moderate pleasure from any of the acts performing. Al Green's "All You Need Is Love" was a highlight, and "Power to the People" was delivered with full Lennonesque anger by Dave Stewart from The Eurythmics. Lou Reed performing "Jealous Guy" was deadpan and surreal, Ray Charles' powerful vocal on "Let it Be" was impressive, but oddly inappropriate, considering it wasn't even a Lennon song. But things went downhill after that. Kylie Minogue's disco version of "Help" was painful and Nat desperately asked John for forgiveness via his new between-the-worlds mediator, Yoko.

And the question of all questions was: Where the fuck were Messrs McCartney, Harrison and Starr? Presumably, they had better things to do than get down to the Pier Head and reunite with their Scouse roots. Their presence would have made a forgettable event less forgettable, maybe even unforgettable. One of the few people to look back with fond memories was Nat Wilson who had a soft spot for everybody's least favourite Beatle wife since that day.

Over the customary nightcap, another man born in the same hospital as John Lennon, albeit thirteen years earlier, cautiously looked at his son and muttered: 'Good show, wasn't it?' His son came alive and spluttered, 'It was greeeaat!'

18

The next day, Nat busied himself with his daily routines, extending his walks to two hours as the Berlin heatwave continued. He spent three consecutive days in his local outdoor swimming pool, the last afternoon swimming with Martina. He felt relaxed, laughed more than he had laughed in the whole of the previous year and felt nothing less for her despite knowing what he knew. The words "Nothing to do with me," inoculated him, relaxed him and allowed him to continue to enjoy his days with her as if nothing had happened. His feelings were growing and Martina's easy reciprocity was doing him the world of good. What he knew was what he knew, but it was nothing more irksome than a pebble inside an otherwise comfortable shoe. He overcame the emotional wobble at the outdoor pool when he saw her for the first time after the sordid revelation, and never looked back.

He would announce his imminent departure to Greece a week before the due date. Just as he had practised his ultra-brief speech announcing the death of Sam to anybody affected by it, he would practise precise and honest words for Martina. But this time, he wouldn't be talking to an answering machine. His words would go like this, 'I might not have told you this, but I had a plan to spend three years in three different countries: six months in Greece, three in Britain and three in Germany. I'm heading back to Greece in a week's time for the next cycle. By the way, I think I love you.' It was a clear, matter-of-fact call for a response; he thought it might appeal to her. On the other hand, she might take him for a ridiculous, wanky, pompous git and just burst out laughing. However he framed his announcement, she would have to react one way or the other. And then he would have clarity.

He clocked up more quality time with Martina, edged ever closer to her emotionally and the days moved forward harmoniously. He suppressed any thoughts of the photos and revelled in the soppy and unreal state of being in love. When she told him she was going to visit her son for a few days in Hamburg, his spirits took a momentary nosedive as it meant that valuable time together would be lost before he left Berlin. He was tempted to tell her about his plans there and then, but dithered and said nothing.

On the evening before she left, they had a pizza outside the place where they had eaten before their first night together. As Martina was on an ultra-early train to Hamburg the next day, the goodbye was restricted to a respectable kiss on the pavement. Nat watched her walking away and was disappointed that she didn't turn round for a final wave. He wondered why she hadn't. Her beautiful, dark brown hair disappeared slowly down the underground steps and he resigned himself to moving onto more banal matters, although it grieved him to call the music of Frank Zappa banal.

He would have to speed up the Zappa music survey and he threw himself into the next batch, which constituted his work in the first half of the eighties. Nat had seventeen albums to go; he would just make it before Greece. When Zappa was below par, Nat would walk longer distances to shake off the disappointment. On day twelve he covered twenty-two kilometres, taking in Mitte and Kreuzberg. And he was missing

Martina. He carried on listening and, as night fell, he had a dozen albums left. He was starting to count the days.

Day eleven. It was raining, He changed tactics. He had no reason to leave his apartment, nobody to see: he would write the remaining eleven Zappa reviews in one day. An extreme measure, but doable. Who has ever listened to eleven Frank Zappa albums back-to-back in one day? He might well be the first man ever to do so. He cut corners, made only sparse notes and made sure that the albums were always playing, whether he was washing the dishes, having a shit or staring out of the window. It was Zappa non-stop. There was always a next one and then the next one. Suddenly it was five p.m. Nat stuck a salami pizza in the oven and gave himself a forty-five-minute break.

He munched and reflected. He often thought of Martina when he was eating and wondered whether there was any Freudian link. Supermarket pizzas were not a patch on the real thing but filled the hunger gap in a modestly tasty way. Perhaps Bill had thought of Martina as a supermarket pizza. He was angry at letting such self-defeating, second-class thoughts rattle him. He lay on the couch, emptied his mind and almost nodded off. He felt a thirst coming on but stuck to mineral water, making himself wait for a cool beer later in the day. Back to work.

He listened and listened and his head was on the verge of exploding. He finally got to Zappa's last album, *The Yellow Shark* which was the live recordings of the last concerts he presided over in September 1992 just over a year before his passing and which was released almost exactly a month before he died on November the second, 1993. A difficult time, a difficult album and Nat was momentarily unable to express an opinion. He gave it three and promised to come back to it one day when he felt less tired, less sad and less eager for a drink. The Zappa job was done. If he had any desire to get it into any sort of publishable form, there was still a lot of (re)construction work ahead of him, but the groundwork had been completed.

It was eight-thirty p.m. and he was spitting feathers. He wanted the simplest pub in Berlin and it was right on his door-step, the perfect antidote for a day of Zappaesque complexity.

Almost two decades after reunification, there was little left to be seen of the German Democratic Republic with the naked eye. Old buildings had either disappeared or been renovated so thoroughly so as not to be recognisable as edifices of the previous regime. Apart from the odd Trabi stubbornly refusing to go away, the new East Germans had embraced everything the west had to offer. The hospitality business was a prime example of that. The pub which Nat was now approaching at an above-average speed had somehow slipped through the net.

The establishment in question was an East German Socialist invention which seemed to be based on the state's calculation that every block of high-rise flats required a building attached to it which offered basic food and drink to satiate the imme-diate needs of the working (and drinking) classes from that particular block. Such salons were functional, lacking charm and comfort and any sort of culinary variety. They normally closed at ten-thirty, in an attempt to prevent the workers from overdoing it. Then all they had to do was stagger to the lifts and be ready to drag themselves out of their beds of pain the next morning, get to their respective places of toil and make their contribution to the collective effort to create the Socialist paradise that the powers-that-be were always harping on about.

Few things had changed in these charmless spaces since the similarly charmless days of the GDR. The beer and food were better but more expensive, everything else was the vanilla option. The emphasis was still on appealing to people suffering from thirst and they were still the same down-to-earth punters; they just had slightly different reasons for drinking. The thirst-inducing supermarket pizza was Nat's reason this evening. But he also wanted to people-watch, to be with people without knowing any of them or feeling the need to speak to them. He knew already that they would all be East Germans, drinking and socialising the way they used to.

The waitress gave him the customary glare. He opted for the medium-sized beer rather than the large version for two reasons: it stayed fresher longer and it gave the impression that he was a moderate drinker (although he wondered who gave a fuck anyway). The place was two thirds-full and the noise level was rising. Two portions of sausage and chips arrived at the next table and the hungry guests tucked in, bolting their food and talking at the same time.

Half the room was laughing and joking and the other half seemed to be cursing their luck, everything washed down with the same Berliner Patzhenhoefer Pils that Nat was also easing down. There were no surprises in this place. Drink, laugh, grumble, order, drink, laugh, grumble, order. Being alone, Nat's rhythm had fewer beats: drink, think, order. If he had had a book with him he would have been more conspicuous although it might have fended off would-be conversation partners. He wasn't in the mood for conversation, an ever-increasing possibility as the beer flowed. The first orders of schnapps were also starting to do the rounds, turning the possibility into a probability.

He had already spotted a couple in the far corner of the room with whom he was on nodding terms from his daily ascents and descents in the lift; their communication had never got past, 'Have a nice evening,' and 'It's been very hot today, hasn't it?' but if he had to visit the gents, which was located near their table, he might be obliged to advance their relationship beyond the usual banalities; he was not anxious to do this. He could have one more Pils without the need to enter their sphere of conversational influence by visiting the gents. He ordered that last beer.

He wondered what he would do with the remaining ten days in Berlin. Halfway through his third and final beer of the day, he had the answer. With the Zappa project now behind him, he would cover as much of East Berlin as possible by public transport the next day (Day Ten) and he would do the same to West Berlin on Day Nine. Day Eight would be spent thinking, thinking, thinking. Martina returned on Day Seven when he believed that talking, talking, talking would be the main option.

Day Eleven had been sapping and he had just mustered enough strength to finish off the job of reviewing Zappa's fifty or so albums. Twelve brilliant, eighteen very good, five good, six below average, three poor and six the pits. Being in evaluation mode, the previous hour just spent in the Socialist drinking palace would probably sneak in somewhere between good and below average, just like the supermarket pizza. Before he could continue justifying or even continuing this ludicrous break-down, he was away to the fairies.

19

Day Ten was bathed in sunlight, boding well for his day on public transport, cruising across East Germany's former capital. He was leaving his flat shortly after eight o'clock after putting together a doable plan resembling a mini-military campaign which would allow him to glimpse parts of East Berlin's twelve pre-1989 districts and claim afterwards that he was 'there' on one single day in his life; a bit like an East-Berlin Ulysses, only a lot shorter and much easier to understand.

He would begin by taking overground trains north and east, offering him unimpeded views of the high-rise estates East European capital cities used to excel in. His local train rattled through Lichtenberg and Marzahn where uniform blocks of imperious concrete resembled his own tower back at Fischer Insel. Only the colour was different. The tower blocks in Hohenschönhausen, the next district, continued to dominate the view from the window of the train. He was desperate to see something green.

He knew that Grünau in the south-eastern corner of Berlin had the lion's share of forests and lakes and he asked a young woman sitting opposite how best to get there. She took a long time replying and for an instant he thought she might not have understood him. She looked wholesomely natural in her navy blue summer dress and sandals; a faint Berlin accent was wrapped in a soft, velvety tone. It was the highlight of the day so far for Nat. He thanked her for the help, she blushed slightly. He wondered where she was going. He always wondered where people were going. And today he wondered where he was going.

Getting from Ostkreuz to Grünau was easy. He got off, followed a river in an easterly direction and picked up a good pace. The pre-midday sun was not yet too fierce and he was glad to be stretching his legs. He presumed the river to be the Spree and kept his gaze on it as he walked and walked and walked. After an hour or so, he was itching for anything that might offer a little light refreshment and shade, but so far he could only see a path, a river and trees. Another half an hour of the same passed when he saw the Berlin version of a tavern and it all seemed too good to be true: seats, tables adorned with tablecloths and all in the soothing shade of overhanging trees.

He found an empty table and sank into a chair next to it. It was exactly 12.45. He closed his eyes, felt good and could almost feel the first beer already swilling down him. He kept his eyes closed and tried to empty his mind.

'Now, don't fall asleep on me.' He opened his eyes and required a few seconds to work out who the speaker was. Jack. From Leeds.

'Good to see you, yer Scouse bastard!' This was a Yorkshireman being friendly. Before sitting down to continue the banter battle, Jack almost broke Nat's hand with the vice-like grip of his handshake.

In an attempt to steer the conversation into more civilised directions, he asked Jack about his wife, although he was sure of the answer already. It might have been more diplomatic to let Jack get round to informing Nat of her passing in his own good time, but Nat felt a sudden Teutonic urge to achieve clarity as soon as possible.

'Well, you know that Helga was never in the best of health,

Nat. She's been gone almost five years now.' Nat mumbled his condolences and they both said nothing. Perhaps Jack was also feeling Teutonic urges in him and broke the silence.

'Your dad still going strong?'

'Afraid not.'

'What about his brother?'

'Went not longer after him.' They both sat there for a few seconds, staring at the tablecloth. 'Well, we better get a drink down us, hadn't we?' said Jack.

They ordered beers but a sad cloud had taken away any possibility of their chance meeting producing any great joy. They efficiently summarised what they had been doing for the previous ten years and slowly rekindled their usual infantile Lancashire-Yorkshire banter. Nat guessed that Jack had well passed the seventy mark and wondered where he planned to play out extra time. As if Jack had been reading his thoughts, he answered Nat's question by launching into an impassioned but coherent monologue about how he saw things at his stage of life.

'Britain's finished. You know that, don't you? I'm happy that Helga and I never had kids; if we had, everything I had would be going to them to help them survive the rat race over there. Ridiculous prices for accommodation, whether you rent or buy, student fees and homelessness, drugs and obesity, knife crime, domestic violence and staggering incompetence at the highest levels of government. And I won't even begin talking about the state of the education system. And just to make sure the country goes over the edge of the cliff, half of its population has now decided that leaving the European Union is a good idea. Well, as Dylan Thomas said about Wales: "If this is the land of my fathers, my fathers can keep it!"'

He pressed on: 'I got out just at the right time with my generous teacher's pension. I rented out my terraced house in London for twenty years at ridiculous rates, then sold right at the peak of the property boom. I made a small fortune. Thatcher made a nasty capitalist out of me, but wasn't that the whole point of the exercise? If you can't beat 'em, join the fuckers, that's what I say. Helga left me some money and I'm just playing out my final innings doing the sort of thing I'm doing today. Living on borrowed time and ill-gotten gains. I have the outdoor life in summer and I hate the place in winter. I move to Tunisia both sides of Christmas, at half the price of living in Berlin. I can walk on the beach every day, do my hour in the sea, eat and drink sensibly while I'm there and come back a relatively healthy old man. I take three months' worth of books with me, read them and leave them there with some charitable organisation and carry on a year later with a new batch. At this rate, my flat will be empty of books by the time of my demise, by which time I hope to have nothing left in the bank. I'll just leave the key in an envelope for the janitor, with whom I'm on first name terms. There'll be enough money in it for him to dispose of my last chattels and to treat himself and his wife to a crackin' holiday. The rest is going to Amnesty International, no fancy funeral and Jack Shepherd leaves the world a vaguely happy man, leaving nobody to clear up any of his shit after him. I've got it all worked out, you see, Nat.'

Indeed, indeed. Everything worked out. Nat wasn't so sure whether he hadn't just heard Jack describing his own fate and he wasn't sure whether he was supposed to be happy or sad about it. He refused to give it too much thought. The sun was shining, lunch was arriving and they had food to demolish.

They had both chosen the same dish, not quite Berlin's answer to lean cuisine, but he sensed that neither gave a shit. Two generations of Northerners tucked in without further ado and any further ramblings would have to wait – it was rude to talk while you were eating.

The down-to-earth food and cold beers revived spirits but their meeting never fully recovered from Jack's speech, which painted a grim picture of Britain. Nat liked Jack's matter-of-fact recounting of his pragmatic solutions to the problems of getting old and his opinion of Britain mirrored his own. But the fact that Jack had even been thinking through such scenarios meant that death was probably the main thing on his mind; why shouldn't it be when you've breached the biblically spooky three-score-years and ten mark and find yourself alone? While he pretended to concentrate on his food, Nat was also fast-forwarding to his own twilight years in Berlin, or wherever.

'Well, anyway, Nat, are you courting?' Jack was churning out English from a bygone age. He had already used the ancient "If you can't beat them, join them", he had spoken of a "crackin' holiday" and now he was scraping the bottom of post-war lexicon by asking whether Nat was "courting". And when did anybody in the twenty-first century ever use the word "chattels"?

'If you're asking me whether I'm sharing bodily fluids with a person of the opposite sex, then I am happy to give you an affirmative. Any further questions?'

'Randy Scouse git,' was the best Jack could offer at this stage, but Nat's sardonic response at least gave Jack a dose of his own medicine. Jack had no further questions. The mood music was improving and Nat suggested a second beer although he remembered that Jack had a bike ride home ahead of him. Nat didn't fancy the prospect of Jack ending tits up in some riverside ditch in the ever-increasing aggressive heat.

'Yes, one for the ditch, as the Russians say.'

Jack's ability to read Nat's mind was beginning to spook him slightly. The word ditch appeared in Nat's brain and two seconds later Jack was using it in some dubious Russian drinking saying.

Jack did have a further question regarding the lady.

'Well, is she marriage material?'

'Oh God, yes.'

Nat surprised himself with his answer. He probably said it as he was in a Northern bubble of no bullshitting. Therefore, he must have meant it.

'Good,' Jack replied, without any further comment.

The beers arrived. They raised their glasses. There was another lull in the conversation and they both needed time to think. They were again finding it difficult to recover from the sad weight of the things on their minds. Their meeting drew to a harmonious close as the sun reached its apogee and Jack paid the grumpy waitress and wouldn't accept anything from Nat.

'You deserve it for puttin' up with me.'

They shared the city train to Ostkreuz and Jack transferred north by bike to Marzahn, his new home patch since he'd lost his wife. He scribbled his address on the restaurant bill and smacked Nat with one final insult, as a Yorkshireman has to do when he's saying bye to a Scouse mate. It had been a "crackin'" lunch break.

Nat headed due west to Treptow, one of the East Berlin districts bordering Kreuzberg in West Berlin and just nestling south of the centre of old East Berlin. He made for Treptow Park, home of the Soviet Union's main memorial to the men who lost their lives taking Berlin in April 1945. The beautifully mowed grass verges flanked both sides of the central stone paths that connected two monumental statues representing Soviet soldiers holding a liberated German baby on one arm while firmly slicing through the snake of Nazi-Fascism under their feet with the sword in the other hand. Very impressive. Romantic almost.

The Red Army had broken the Wehrmacht's spine and when they finally made it to Berlin, liberating babies, however, was not on the top of their list of priorities; making babies more like it, seen by some as the just reward for almost four years of grim deprivation. The mortal remains of 70,000 Soviet soldiers were resting below the monumental creation. Nat sat on a bench below one of the giant soldiers and dozed.

He forced himself up and pushed himself into an easterly direction, towards the Spree and into central Eastern Berlin. After a quarter of an hour, he found the bridge crossing the river. He would brush against the south eastern border of Friedrichshain and the Western extremity of Lichtenberg. He turned left along the river, happy to be leaving the soulless high-rises of Lichtenberg, where the East German State Police had their headquarters and where dangerous nationalism was growing again.

The first signs of dehydration were troubling him and he felt a headache brewing. He grabbed two bottles of mineral water from a kiosk, downed one and placed the other one in his rucksack. Refreshed, he approached the Oberbaumbrücke. It was the bridge linking Friedrichshain in the East with Kreuzberg in the West; nobody under the age of thirty gave this fact a passing thought these days. Nat was old enough to appreciate the full significance of a beautifully-restored bridge linking two former worlds. Now it just linked two small, colourful, gritty districts of East and West Berlin.

He was now heading north-west through Friedrichshain. It was exactly six o' clock. At this rate, he would be home within an hour. Every café was at least half-full; all of them trendy, funky and teeming with people not even half his age. Most were good-looking, sexy even, all in animated conversation, all with their lives ahead of them.

The day was taking a melancholy turn and his heavy legs weren't helping his mood; in fact, he felt melancholy slowly turning into a sad bastard attack. Taking a seat in any of the cafes he was currently dragging himself past wouldn't be a good idea; he had forgotten to put any reading material in his ruck-sack and sitting alone, psychologically naked without a book, taking in the sight of men half his age fondling women half his age was asking for trouble. He kept on walking.

As he approached the six-lane avenue crossing from East to West, the usual shiver scuttled down his back, combined with the momentary loss of breath and realisation that he was, as always, only a minute and insignificant cog in the monumental history of central Europe. He stood at the crossroads: to his right was Frankfurter Allee, which would finally end 440 miles to the east in Königsberg, now part of North-Western Russia. Turning his head 180 degrees left, he saw Karl-Marx-Allee starting its 330-mile path to the cathedral city of Aachen on the far western border of Germany, the final resting place of King Charlemagne the Great.

Nat found renewed strength in the grand, magisterial open-ness the boulevard offered. Karl-Marx-Allee was a throwback to the Moscow-influenced socialist realism with its pompous residential architecture, which provided you with a basic, meat and potato roof over your head and a bathroom. Party connec-tions and unswerving loyalty to the state helped you into one of these much sought after dwellings.

Karl-Marx-Allee displayed relatively few signs of the class enemy having had any success transforming it into a capitalist shopping paradise: a few outlets selling periodicals and tobacco, a couple of downbeat Vietnamese supermarkets, a grand-look-ing bookshop that had survived the former regime and an equally large florist's. New additions were two steak houses and a Greek Taverna, both doing well as early evening busi-ness slowly materialised. A Czech restaurant, a leftover from pre-Wall days, offering sturdy Bohemian cuisine, seemed to be doing less well. Otherwise, the avenue consisted of uniform (but not aesthetically displeasing) high buildings, rising like huge wedding cakes, overlooking the wide, spacious avenue and pavements.

Nat trudged on past Strausberger Platz which formed a roundabout around an out-of-use fountain. The stretch of Karl-Marx-Allee leading there was less memorable than the preceding section: the only edifice of any note was the massive Café Mokba, the only place in former East Germany which offered anything approaching the sort of decadent high-life which was common or garden on the other side of the Berlin Wall in Cold War days.

Another one thousand yards to Alexanderplatz. He rested his weary legs once and finished his second bottle of water. He was now satisfied that he had warded off a potential headache. He was going to head back two hundred years, to a hostelry which was supposed to have once been frequented by Napoleon (he didn't believe it). The food was homemade and based on recipes from grandma's pre-war days and the beer was banged down on thick, sturdy wooden tables by chuckling waiters who found their own jokes irresistible when often they weren't - a typical Berlin failing - but all the guests were surrounded by solid marble and delicate ceramic artwork which had a calming influence. The forest tavern where he had lunched with Jack was an example of "We know what you like" GDR functionality; this place was different, popular before anybody even thought of Berlin being the capital of a Greater Germany, a socialist Germany, or any sort of united Germany.

He trudged and marched, sweating steadily. The day had turned into a drudge. But he had, at least, come to some important conclusions: being permanently alone and thinking too much will seriously do your head in; he needed a home and, more desperately, a toilet.

The temptation to find a suitable tree was ever-present during the last five hundred metres, but he was finally there, darted inside and weaved himself through the cramped dining area, cursed his luck when he saw a metal spiral staircase ascending to the gents and with one final feat of concentration and willpower, got himself across the finishing line. He swilled his face, tidied himself up and hoped to find a seat outdoors.

A small table on the edge of the outdoor proceedings was calling him, destined to be his final destination of the day before the refuge of his own safe house. He wasn't hungry, sank a small beer, almost fell asleep, paid his bill, didn't understand the joke the overweight waiter cracked and dragged himself through the darkness and the avenues surrounding Alexanderplatz to his own tower block. He was too tired to think, just managed to drag the sweat-drenched summer garments off his exhausted frame as he waddled into the bedroom, falling asleep in record time. It had just turned ten p.m.

20

Weather-wise, Day Nine was an exact copy of Day Ten and the sun once again streamed through the windowed doors of Nat's balcony. He had no excuses for abandoning his idea of "doing" the western part of the city. Nat had slept solidly for close to eight hours and after his shower, he felt as refreshed and sparkling as a man of his age had any right to feel. He briefly interviewed himself about the previous day's sojourn.

Apart from the chance meeting with Jack, the day had consisted of moving in an expansive circular, clockwise direction alone in the blazing heat, while processing Berlin and its people. It reminded him of the philosophic thought of an American philosopher he once read, who claimed that we enter the world alone, meet some nice people, some not-so-nice-people and then leave the world alone.

Yesterday's nice people were, presumably, the girl in the summery dress and Jack. Three other people briefly entered his life: the waitress and waiter at the two establishments providing him with sustenance and the Turkish fellow providing him with coffee and a roll at the start of the day. Little or no communication beyond the necessities of the transactions had taken place, a meagre return for a man out in the open all day. It frightened him to think that if he hadn't met Jack, he would have got through 97.5% of his waking hours without conversing with anybody.

This fact didn't surprise him – this was Germany, after all - but it still troubled him. Jack must spend countless days like that, he thought. Why hadn't Nat offered him his company for the rest of the day? He immediately shook off the short spasm of guilt by convincing himself that they had efficiently informed each other of the general state of play in their respective old mans' lives and their meeting had reached a natural lull which resulted in them going their own separate ways to ponder on whether further meetings were desirable. They probably weren't.

He didn't want to end up like Jack, but he might; it just so happened that Jack's wife's untimely death had written his twilight year pages for him. Women didn't always hang around till the final whistle; some found a better offer elsewhere, while others died on you. Nat had the first experience and Jack the second. And there they were, representatives of two generations of working-class Brits, on a sunny Berlin afternoon, waffling over their beers, summing up their past and present with pithy, sometimes primitive Northern truisms.

He wondered how he was going to shape the western sector city walk. The only resolution he could come up with was that it had to be different. Nat had been walking for a year: more walking than talking, more thinking than doing. Apart from writing, he had done very little. Yesterday was one walk too many: he had overdosed on walking, a healthy exercise habit which had become mentally unhealthy when taken to those extremes.

Berlin had impressive urban in-your-face grim beauty and history on every corner, but once you knew all the sights, you knew all the sights. If you left your house alone and didn't chance to meet somebody you knew on the way, you would stay on your own. And then you would start stewing in your own juice.

On yesterday's walk, he had plunged himself into the Red Army history of Berlin, so he would redress the balance today. He would start the day at The British Military Cemetery on the south western edge of Charlottenburg, a former British sector of Berlin. He could be there within half an hour.

In contrast to the Soviet memorial, this was a real cemetery: over three and a half thousand Commonwealth war dead lay beneath the same number of individually named, pure white gravestones on a lush green carpet of grass. All of them had died during the four-year RAF bombing campaign which flew over two hundred raids between the end of 1940 and the beginning of 1945. Not one British soldier was engaged in land battles in or anywhere near Berlin during the war; British casualties all fell from the skies while they were in the process of dropping over 45,000 tons of bombs on the German capital during those four years of Total War.

Nat strolled, scanning the first dozen or so of the Commonwealth gravestones; none of the men had reached their mid-twenties. It was still and peaceful and he seemed to be the only person there. Halfway down the meadow, he turned round and observed the memorial statue in the distance, a fraction of the size of the Soviet one in Treptow.

After half an hour, he morosely drifted towards the exit gate. It was already lunchtime but he felt little hunger. He was now on Heer Strasse, the final section of the monumental East-West Axis. If he was in a car at this time of the day, he could turn left and head south-west and be in Potsdam in about fifteen minutes; turning right, he would be at the Brandenburg Gate in about the same time. Being on foot, he could turn around, head due south through the Grunewald, one of West Berlin's densest forests, and keep walking for an indefinite time, probably for the rest of the afternoon. But he was anxious not to repeat the mammoth, forest-dominated exertions of the previous day and to stray too far from public transport connections.

So he turned right, heading towards Theodor-Heuss Platz which would be, if his guesswork was right, about forty minutes away on foot. The views along the route would be uninspiring: cars travelling in east-west directions on a wide, straight dual carriageway. The number of fellow pedestrians would be few, most of them walking their dogs, he supposed. To survive the mundaneness of the next forty minutes, he plugged in his headphones and pondered which album might be appropriate company.

An album you can march to, was his first thought, especially as he was on Heer Strasse, literal translation, "Army Road". He plumped for an album by Brian Eno, "Nerve Net". It was an album within which he had wallowed in a previous time passage of his life in a different, dark Berlin dominated by the last days of a merciless winter, made bearable, beautiful even, by the temporal sensual delights of erotic love which later sank into the calamitous meltdown of the bitterest of disappointments. He wondered how the music would sound now in the midday heat of Berlin in August, free of the emotional extremes of that time.

It sounded wrong, all wrong. Open-air, sunlit Berlin in sweaty heat was everything the city hadn't been all those years ago and Eno's otherworldly music struggled to make any emotional impact on him this time round; it was almost as if he was hearing it for the first time. Despite all the incongruities, the music was at least driving him forward, keeping him on the move, encouraging Nat to imitate some spacey, sci-fi march which enabled him to make steady progress due east and reach Theodor Heuss Platz within the forty minutes he thought it would take.

The usual voice in his head expressed the usual desire to have a drink, but he couldn't see a suitable drinking hole anywhere nearby; a bombastic steak house jutted out almost onto the roundabout, but the thought of sitting there alone, clutching a beer while refusing to treat himself to an over-priced steak, to the consternation of some snappy Berlin waitress, depressed him.

He wasn't far from the Olympic Stadium, that monumental feat of nineteen thirties Nazi architecture, the arena that impressed every visitor, despite the horrors it foreshadowed. A Berlin day on August 1st, 1936, Goebbels's biggest PR coup, a successful attempt to convince the world that it had nothing to fear. All anti-Jewish slogans, billboards and signs were removed during the sixteen-day duration of the games and nobody visiting from outside the Reich could have possibly doubted that the country was not in safe hands, judging by the adulation the natives were lavishing on their Fuehrer as he declared the games open. A local guide in the stadium once told Nat that the most frequently asked question from tourists visiting the stadium these days was, 'Where did Hitler sit?' He would always tell them and they immediately queued to be photographed sitting there. Oh, dear.

There was still the small problem of getting a drink. He quickly decided on a no-risk policy, descended the steep steps of the Theodor Heuss Platz underground station and hopped onto the next train heading east: in little more than ten minutes he would be in Kant Strasse and he knew exactly where he wanted to rest his weary bones: Kant Café, the location of his first meeting with Martina all those weeks ago. He saw the choice as a good omen for the next day when they would be meeting after her days in Hamburg.

It was fast approaching three p.m. A good time: the lunch-time people had gone and the early evening strollers had not yet drifted in. He had virtually the whole of the side terrace to choose from. He shuffled onto a back row seat in the corner, which allowed him a sweeping view up and down Kant Strasse. He had walked enough; a hunger was developing and he had – he hoped - a good book with him, appropriately called, "The Restaurant at the End of the Universe". Nat was planning to start ploughing through this not-to-be-taken seriously sci-fi cult classic during lunch to take his mind again off the fact that he was alone again. If he read extremely quickly he could even finish it before the day was out, thus eradicating the necessity of thinking about anything else. First he had to decide what to eat.

Nat never ceased to be amused, not to say confused, by the number of salad variations available on modern menus; he was sometimes tempted to say, 'I would like a small salad, please,' and see what they would come up with. He never did say it because he knew it would simply set in motion a diffi-cult communication challenge which overstressed serving staff would not appreciate. He plumped for Caesar's salad, although even this seemingly bog standard order prompted a further fine-tuning question from the waitress.

'Would you like it with or without chicken?' was her peculiar counter-question. For Nat, this seemed tantamount to asking, 'Would you like fish with your fish and chips?' Perhaps he was being bloody-minded; perhaps he was, once again, displaying his seemingly endless propensity for being a cantankerous old fart. He went for the 'with chicken, please' version, provocatively asking the waitress to choose a glass of white wine for him. He settled down to read his book. Nobody could get him now.

He motored comfortably through the book. He didn't want to do it but he forked the contents of the bowl into his mouth with his right hand, whilst reading at pace the book in his left hand. He had never done this before; he felt like an ill-mannered, precocious toad. Was this how men started to behave when they'd been living alone too long? Would he start picking his nose in public next? Scratching his crotch when sitting in the underground? He nipped his neurosis in the bud and concentrated on the book.

After the first ten pages he had given up trying to work out who all the characters were and to comprehend where they all found themselves; he assumed they were all cascading through the infinite cosmos to give the author the chance to be witty and nerdy across billions of light years of space. There was a good laugh on every page and Nat let himself be part of the silly science-fiction skulduggery. He ordered a second glass of wine; the waitress appeared genuinely pleased that her choice of wine had caused him to order another. He tried to ingratiate her further by thanking her again. She giggled nervously and Nat noticed a trace of pinkness in her cheeks, which lifted his spirits momentarily.

By page sixty-two, his second glass arrived. This time with a question. A question which threw him.

'On your own, this time?' was the waitress's impromptu

opening gambit. He had to steady himself; the last person he thought would be trying small talk with him was the blushing damsel from half an hour ago. He wasn't even sure what the question meant.

'Yes,' he stammered. 'But what do you mean by "this time"?'

'Well, you were on a blind date last time, weren't you?'

She means Martina, he thought. And "blind date" wasn't a bad way of describing the hour he had spent with Martina about two months previously.

He was starting to stammer. 'Well, yes, it was a *sort* of blind date. A blind date, yes. How did you know?'

'Women spot this sort of thing. Especially in this business. It's great fun guessing who our guests are and what they're up to.'

He had recovered his composure. 'And what were we up to, if I may ask?' He was feigning mild outrage.

'Well, I wasn't sure what was on your mind, but I know what was on hers.'

Before Nat was able to ask for further details, the waitress was busy picking up his empty salad bowl and gliding away. This time it was her turn to smirk. Nat liked her style: cheeky but cute and as bright as a button. He was left wrong-footed by the incisive intensity of her unexpected input.

The waitress had kicked off a mild wave of emotional good-feeling in Nat; the memory of that first date was taking over and inducing a warm glow inside him. He wanted to ask the waitress more questions about what she thought of him and Martina as an item but he looked around the café and noticed that it was slowly starting to fill up – little or no chance of getting her involved in any sort of real conversation. His one last chance would be when she brought him the bill. He wanted to squeeze out some more information from a non-committed, female observer. He thought hard and beckoned her over so he could pay.

'What do you think then?' he asked.

'About what?'

'Well, do you see us as a couple?'

'Somehow, yes.'

She smiled for the second time that day – well, in *his* presence at least. It was a different smile this time, one which had her once again in the driving seat. They said goodbye and although he felt vaguely miffed that a mere slip of a girl in an alternative West Berlin café was affecting him so much, he suddenly felt a weight rising from his shoulders. It was touching on a religious experience.

It was too early to go home but too late to start any experimental strolling which might kick off a lonely pub crawl, get him increasingly sadder and push the end of the day into a confusing, alcohol-drenched dead end. Two glasses of wine were the exact amount of alcohol for that time of day - almost six o'clock - and an unexpected surge of self-certainty was lightening his soul. The day was trying to tell him something and he wanted to stay awake and alert to take in the message.

He had a ridiculous idea about how to bring the day to a harmonious close: he would make for a place where nothing could go wrong, where he could get on top of things without anybody getting in his way.

Half an hour later he was standing at the foot of Germany's tallest construction, 368 metres high and the German Democratic Republic's pride and joy for almost exactly forty years: the East-Berlin TV tower. He joined the queue, paid his entrance fee and shot up 203 metres to the viewing platform. The cloudless blue sky permitted a clear view well beyond the city limits; he believed he could see Potsdam, for example, in the south west. He could even make out the massive building housing the SFB radio station on Theodor Heuss Platz, the place he had fled a few hours previously.

He turned his head due east and took in the flatlands stretching out towards Poland from whence the Soviets had surged forward from the east in the final weeks of World War Two. Like a child, he fell into mild raptures, marvelling at everything spread out beneath him, similar to how he had felt sitting on the number ten bus heading down Prescot Road in Liverpool a couple of months previously. He couldn't do anything but marvel and it was good.

'Closing in five minutes.' The ugly bastard doing the rounds had an equally ugly voice to match. It was five minutes to seven; they had to be out when the clock struck seven.

He wanted to stay high so he checked out the restaurant. Another unsightly TV Tower employee guarded the entrance and briefly explained the reason for his being there: it was a Ray Charles tribute evening and there was a ten-euro entrance fee. Nat forced himself to like the idea and half-heartedly handed over the required currency of the realm.

He climbed five metres worth of steps, only to find yet another unattractive being blocking his way; before he could even ask himself what had happened to all the beautiful people in the world, the disfigured creature neatly picked up a menu and asked Nat to follow him. Nat couldn't remember the last time that a waiter had accompanied him to his seat in a restaurant. In the tradition of true East European "don't mess with us, you're only the customer" policy, Nat was given to understand, with the help of a barely audible grunt, that he should sit down at the table where the menu had just been placed.

Despite the complete and utter lack of charm and warmth displayed by the staff since he had got out of the lift, he remained convinced that he had made the right decision. His seat was right next to the window and there was nobody within a three-metre radius of him. He stretched his legs, looked around him and was optimistic about how the day was going to reach its conclusion.

The tables were arranged in a semi-circle around the central column, where he assumed the kitchen was to be found. There must have been thirty or forty people eating, drinking or waiting to do so. The waiting staff were dressed for the occasion but seemed nervous, edgy and liable to explode at the slightest hint that the guests might want something deviating in any way from what they had on offer.

The restaurant at the top of the TV Tower exuded a certain retro-Clockwork Orange charm, the thing that East Germans still presumably yearned for with their unique blend of masochism and nostalgia and which West Germans found quirky and amusing. Nat didn't feel part of either camp and opened the menu with some trepidation.

Just as he expected: the full pre-end of the Berlin Wall eating experience. It was bog standard East German fare embellished by a couple of spicy Hungarian goulash creations, an unpronounceable Polish speciality and a bewildering range of Russian cold plates and soups. There was Czech beer on tap and Russian vodkas in abundance. Not bad.

And the waiter looked like a waiter. Black suit, white shirt, bow tie and bib apron; the garb and bulbous gut were moderately hampering his mobility as he approached Nat, but at least he looked the part. He would have been in his late fifties, and Nat assumed he had earned his spurs working in the higher echelons of the East German hospitality business in the pre-1989 years. Nat braced himself for detached formality and the absolute minimum of human interaction. He wasn't disappointed.

The wines were overpriced and he didn't recognise any of them, so he ordered a large Czech Pilsner and a Russian Vodka. His choice seemed to amuse the waiter; Nat detected the stifling of a smile and tried to understand what caused it. Perhaps he thought that his latest guest was on the piss. He might be right.

Nat was intrigued by the mysterious Polish dish so he asked the waiter for illuminating information on the contents; this was Nat's customary way of finding out who *he* was dealing with and whether the man in question knew his stuff. The description he rattled off with precision had just the right amount of detail: this particular central European culinary treat would appear to be thinly rolled-out oven-baked dough, filled with savoury fillings. It sounded like just the right meal for the occasion. The waiter shuffled off and Nat checked out his fellow diners.

Another question concerning Nat at this juncture was whether the guests were Ossies or Wessies. His initial glance suggested that it might be a fifty-fifty affair in that particular half-circle of the restaurant. At the next window along, a German businessman was trying, in ropey English, to describe Berlin's Greatest Hits to two English-speaking guests. He was probably the same age as the waiter, but he was, with absolute certainty, West German. He looked smarmy, full of himself, dazzling, dominating white teeth accentuating his phoney smile. He was very possibly a complete arsehole.

At the tables in the inner circle, a nuclear family were waiting for their food: husband, wife and two disinterested teenage kids. Nat's instincts told him that they might be East Germans as the look on the parents' faces expressed gratitude that they were treating themselves in a special place. Nat imagined that they had told their children about the history of the tower they were now sitting in, hoping, probably in vain, that they should be grateful for the chance to eat in a place they themselves were rarely able to before the Wall came tumbling down.

The drinks arrived and they looked promising: frothy beer and threatening vodka. He started on the vodka and found it to be good, but needed to down a goodly portion of beer to ease the trepidation that vodka always aroused in him. It was 7.45 p.m. and the restaurant was gently spinning him around, as all good revolving restaurants do and Nat felt that nothing could do him no wrong. The statement was from a record he had heard many years before and he winced at the incorrect grammar. He was darned if he could remember the name of the song in which the offending line appeared.

A black man entered his field of vision to the left and settled himself behind a grand piano. He was wearing shades and as he looked up; Nat gazed at him. They smiled at each other. Nat let out a cheer, the piano man giggled and the fellow diners stared at Nat. Was there a problem? Nat beckoned the waiter and ordered another vodka as something stirred within him.

The piano man looked like he could take care of himself. Nat felt fortified. Relaxed. Ebullient. In fact, he felt just the way the piano man looked and couldn't wait for him to start playing.

Just as Nat's food arrived, the piano man did start playing, and a bolt surged through him, just as it had done in Liverpool a few months previously when John Ashton raised the roof back in Liverpool, singing about San Francisco. The Polish culinary creation was nourishing his body, the guy's voice was doing the rest to his soul. Floating in a cocoon of just rightness, Nat planned to hang onto this for as long as humanely possible. North, South, East and West, the sky was blue and the sun was going down over Berlin and nothing could do him no wrong. The faulty language and the perfect emotions told him that somebody was playing tricks on him this high up and he was wondering whether he was ever going to remember the name of the song and whether he was ever going to come down from his current high.

The next song, "Don't Let the Sun Catch You Crying", was another emotional ambush and Nat was now on the run. He knew the song from another place, another time, and he desperately struggled to place its whereabouts. As always, he believed that one last beer would give him an answer so he beckoned the waiter. He also asked the waiter to ask the singer what he fancied to drink.

A little while later, more smiles from the piano man and this time a thumbs up to boot. The beer and the artist's double-something arrived and he proceeded to tear into Nat's soul again with a near-perfect rendering of "I Can't Stop Loving You" and this time, primeval Liverpool flashed all around him and he could smell the Sunday roast. The song ended, polite applause rippled around the sci-fi room and Nat knew that he had to speak to this man. At least say thank you. Or something. He wobbled towards the piano; the other guests watched anxiously.

'Hey, man, you're doing my head in!'

"Ray" looked startled.

'Wa?'

'You're digging up some ghosts tonight, I'm telling you. I can't enjoy my beautiful food *and* your beautiful music at the same time! I'm from Liverpool, and you're taking me right back!'

'Well, that serves you right, man!' he said with the widest of grins.

The union of souls had begun in earnest and the rest of the audience must have wondered what on earth was going on. Nat's disjointed banter continued.

'Let me tell you something, man,' he said. 'Ray Charles' version's not a patch on Gerry and the Pacemakers, so I thought I'd try it their way.'

Gerry and the fuckin' Pacemakers. Gerry and the fuckin' Pacemakers. Of course!

Nat's tongue was no longer connected to his brain: power over his speech output was now severely limited. This was probably just as well as he could see the waiter approaching in something resembling a towering rage. He would surely be wanting to curtail any further links between a highly-strung, intoxicated guest and their over-excited entertainer.

'Would you please take your seat again, sir, and let the performer continue with the evening's programme?'

'Yes. Yes. Of course.'

Nat returned to his seat and melted into the background again. Normal service was resumed and people stopped staring.

Nat finished his beer and stopped drinking. The waiter appeared this time without any invitation, Nat got the message and asked for the bill. Ray had supped a double malt whisky at the painful price of nineteen euros. He tipped the waiter generously to the tune of nine euros. It was nine minutes past nine. Number nine. Number nine. The Lennon number. Lennon. Fuckin' Lennon. The very same man who sang:

When I hold you in my arms, I know that nobody can do me no harm, on the Beatles' *White Album* (1968). John and Gerry had come back to haunt Nat two hundred metres above Berlin on a late summer's night, with a Ray Charles tribute singer from somewhere in the USA acting as a cosmic mediator.

'I'm glad you enjoyed the evening, sir' said the waiter, this time with a smirk. Perhaps he was just relieved that further excesses had been nipped in the bud and his half-pissed, peculiar guest was about to get off the premises.

Nat said nothing and shuffled away. The singer was pausing between numbers, giving him a chance to say his farewells. He firmly shook the player's hand and said in an embarrassingly fake, American accent,

'That was really something else, man.'

'Got all you Liverpool guys to thank for that, man. Say hi when you get back!' were his final words before he launched into "The Long and Winding Road". Nat knew that all these words were going to linger.

It had been spooky but Nat was still on a delicious high. He simply wanted to get home safely, digest the contents of the day, including his Polish specialities, which were now starting to seriously repeat on him, and seek the peace of the night.

21

Tonight was the night and Martina would be there in a few minutes. In the afternoon he thought long and hard about what he wanted to do now that the end of his first annual cycle was approaching. He only had a vague idea about what he wanted, so putting vagueness into words wasn't going to be easy. The only thing he knew with any degree of certainty was that the three years in three different countries' idea was dead in the water. And that he had been missing Martina. He secretly hoped that she would say something which would relieve him of the responsibility of having to say anything at all. He ran through a list of things *she* could say and the possible consequences resulting from these utterances. He came up with five things she might say and five responses he could give:

1. 'I've been thinking and I don't think we have a future.' (He always had Greece to look forward to, the book on Zappa will be a bestseller and maybe there's still life in the three-year/three cycle idea, after all.)

2. 'I'm pregnant.' (Turn the music room into a children's room and start a new life. The lottery money will just last until the child starts university. The working class principle of doing the right thing was still deep within him. His parents would be proud of him.)

3. 'What if I joined you in Greece for a while?' (Why not? Winter would certainly be survivable with Martina to

share body heat with. A lot depended on what "a while" meant, of course.)

4. 'I've missed you.' Out loud answer: 'Not as much as I've missed you!' (No further explanations necessary.)

5. 'We need to talk.' (Shit.)

The only thing Nat genuinely wanted to hear was number four, a statement which only required the briefest of walks to the bedroom, minus clothes. The others would either require thought, cause anguish, create uncertainty and necessitate immediate and serious planning.

Well, that was the near future *not* sorted out. He calmed himself, and suddenly remembered the words of a young French female student he once had the pleasure of teaching during his university years. It was a conversation course and he had decided to be a teeny-weeny bit provocative by asking her the loaded question:

'Viviane, what's the difference between men and women?'

Her answer was as simple as it was brilliant. Either she was experienced beyond her years or Nat had been very ignorant of some basic truths down his years.

'Men think about now and women think about tomorrow.'

Her answer perhaps neatly explained why Nat was hoping for Martina to come up with number four on his list of possible statements. It probably also explained why Nat, like millions of other men, had had an adult life's worth of misunderstandings with the opposite sex.

He needed something else to occupy his mind.

So he decided to look back on the last year and get philosophical. What, for example, had he learned in the last twelve months that *might* be considered life-changing? Truly revelatory? He struggled to compose a list. Perhaps the list could form the introduction to one of the million self-help books filling up bookshop shelves every year. He thought hard, very hard. He forced out some truths, truisms, promising insights and dodgy revelations and scribbled them onto a piece of paper.

1. The past would always be there and it doesn't do to hang around in its disturbing space capsule for too long. (The first part is banal and the second part is what he had been doing for most of the year. But a necessary evil when you're writing a book, he supposed.)

2. Art is the true aspiration and by creating it, one is elevated to higher levels, which frees us from the drudgery, grimness and crushing realities of mortal life. (Now that's more like it; we're getting somewhere.)

3. We're not alone, there is life beyond the beyond. (Sounds like the title of a not-to-be-trusted esoteric self-help guide for confused middle-aged people who, having nothing else to lose, are searching for a new religion. This would probably have to go.)

4. Being alone, and deciding to stay that way, turns you, in the long run, into a monstrous, self-obsessive crank who does embarrassing things in public and who is unable to maintain and develop relationships with anybody beyond his front door. (A painful truth which might have to stay as a warning to any man giving up on company.)

5. The man who lets his dick rule his head is doomed. (He might want to strike that one off the list as it fell into that annoying category of time-wasting called "stating the bleeding obvious".)

6. The occasional drink does you no harm; too many do. (As truisms go, they don't get much blander than that.)

7. A woman always has the last word anyway. And most words. And she usually always sets the course, mediating between fantasy and non-fiction. (That one came from the gut and he wanted to leave it in for posterity.)

8. Your next breath can always be your last breath. (Again, tediously obvious, but during the past year he had spent an ever-increasing amount of time either thinking about death, witnessing it or worrying about when he would be experiencing it himself.)

9. You experience good luck and bad luck in life. (A banality to finish on, but at least nobody could refute it.)

Little of the above was new to him (and nor would it be to anybody else who had been on the planet for a similar number of years), but the events of the last twelve months had reminded him of the fact that however banal the list looked now, in the cool light of day, the pithy maxims contained therein had got under his skin and were annoyingly true. It was also clear to him that living on your own magnified their significance, as sometimes there was little else to think about. How much time did a man with a wife and two kids and a full-time job have for such mental meanderings? And that could be one of the reasons why they lived longer than men who live on their own. Giving a child a lift to their football practice, for example, might be time-consuming but it didn't cause the same degree of inner anguish caused by a brain churning over the "big" questions of life on a day-to-day basis and/or mulling over them later at night, washed down with too much alcohol.

The question that never left him throughout was: Where the hell am I going to end my days? Where indeed? A Greek island, Liverpool or Berlin? Or Wales? With the passing of Sam, Liverpool *seemed* to be out of the running, yet with the chances of a season ticket for Anfield increasing every year, he could still imagine himself being tempted. His body told him Greece, but there was the nightmarish island winter to survive with its bleak loneliness. The Berlin winter was cruel for different reasons but the city always offered enough distractions to keep body and soul together, even in the bleakest winter months. And Berlin was the only place with accommodation that belonged to him and to which he had permanent access. Somehow, the place in Wales had lost its attraction, but it was still within shouting distance of Anfield. But then there was still the problem of dislodging his tenant at short notice if his season ticket emerged earlier than expected.

He looked around the room and liked what he saw; everything in its place and almost all visible objects containing memories, good bad and indifferent, going back thirty years. He had developed a de-cluttering culture that summer, and for the first time in many years, he could find anything he wanted, whenever he wanted it. Not an achievement to be sniffed at after a lifetime of frustrating, time-consuming searching. This was something on which he could build.

If she arrived on time, he could present his latest culinary creation to Martina piping hot, toss the salad and pour the well-cooled, light summer wine and take in all her news. Find out how they both felt at this precise moment in their history and whether their relationship was about to become history or whether it was to continue beyond next week when he was supposed to be leaving Berlin, with or without her. The cheese topping on his pasta bake was approaching its optimal gold-en-brown beauty. At least he felt confident about the food.

At two minutes to seven, the doorbell rang. In the four or so minutes it took Martina to ascend in the lift, he tossed the salad and put the final touches to the dinner table. Quietly confident, but shivering inwardly. The bell rang.

Nat was in trouble as soon as he opened the door: Martina was wearing a flowing white dress and her brown hair nestled deliciously over her bare shoulders. She sported a newly-at-tained, light tan. She was as close to a mature Kate Bush as a woman could get. Jesus, everything about her was pulsating, a close-to-perfect woman. Two images flooded his memory bank: the disturbing dream back in Greece of thwarted lust towards an unattainable woman in white and his first sighting of Maria when they exchanged a civilized handshake in the Cozy Corner. But this encounter was neither a frustrating dream nor a civi-lized handshake: their sizzling embrace at the door effectively deleted faded memories of Greek neuroses at one fell swoop. This was something here and now and the movement of her body underneath the linen dress oozed reality and excited him. She nonchalantly swayed past him and hooked her bag around the back of the chair.

'Something smells good,' she said, smiling.

Something looks good, he thought

Nat had a choice: hot sex now followed by post-coitus, luke-warm pasta or hot pasta now and presumably less intense sex later; or, if their conversations entered choppy waters, no sex at all. And possibly not even pasta. He decided, with a supreme act of willpower, on hot pasta now and went about retrieving it from the oven.

'Did I ever tell you that a man's sex appeal automatically goes through the roof when he cooks a meal for a woman?' she said as if she had been rehearsing it all day, further unsettling Nat's already unsteady grasp on things. She looked amazingly in control of the situation. Nat felt like a rat trapped in a cage. But he was at least a happy rat.

His over-zealous attempt to also appear in control in this state of overheated confusion forced him into committing the classic oven-opening mistake – he was almost knocked off his feet by the intense wave of heat blasting upwards out of the oven. The industrial language escaping from the kitchen even rattled Martina's composure and she raced in to find him steadying himself by the sink. At least the kitchen maladroitness had focussed his mind on the immediate stilling of their hunger rather than any other desires of the flesh sparked by Martina's scintillating entry.

They settled into their usual seats. And stared at each other. He felt like a seventeen-year-old, besotted imbecile. She jerked a steaming hot spoonful of lasagne onto her plate and looked as serene and happy as Nat had ever seen her.

She related her time in Hamburg. She had treated her son to a few days on the North Sea coast; hence the tan. The son had no problems worth talking about, was enjoying his studies, and making the most of life as a student.

'I was worried about him because he was taking a long time to settle in. But I hardly recognised him. He was in great form. I'm pretty sure he's got himself a girlfriend. He didn't tell me and I didn't ask. But he was different, in a positive way.'

This was about as much as Martina had ever said about her son, Sven, and Nat was relieved that she was talking about him with such positive vibes. No long and intricate stories about him not getting over the death of his father. Or grim tales of depression, drugs and suicide attempts. Nat rarely asked any questions about him and so far the policy had been the right one. But he was tempted to ask her whether her son knew of Nat's existence. So he asked.

'Oh, yes and he's fine with that. I was fearing he might be a tad jealous but he seemed pleased for me. And that's why I think he's got a girlfriend stashed away; if he didn't, it might be a different story.'

Nat definitely didn't fancy the "different story" idea. Neither did he particularly fancy meeting Sven. Well, certainly not at the moment. Something in him was suddenly rooting for Sven's relationship with his new-found love to be a roaring success. He knew he was being a selfish bastard but doubted whether he had the strength and patience at his age to be competing with a mixed-up son for Martina's attention.

'And what have you been up to?' was her next question, inviting him to say something interesting. He wasn't prepared for the question and stammered slightly, threw in a few 'errs', asked for a little time to think, but was at a loss to say anything that might sound meaningful and coherent. What the hell *had* he been up to for the past couple of weeks?

'Finishing my Zappa book project. Having the occasional walk. Thinking.'

He knew that the banality of walking and thinking would spark no response but as Martina was an East German of a certain age, he felt sure the Zappa project would.

'The Zappa project sounds interesting. Tell me more!'

The natural smile that accompanied this spontaneous spurt of genuine interest moved Nat, making him want her even more; Martina looked almost childlike, beautiful, and he wanted to hug her, capture the moment and show her that he loved her. So he did, after carefully negotiating himself round the table as elegantly as humanely possible and being mindful of a half-full glass of wine that she he had just placed perilously close to its edge.

They kissed for a goodly while, didn't spoil the moment by saying anything, and Nat returned to his seat. He briefly described the Zappa book and she seem fascinated. They continued eating and something which could be described as an awkward silence momentarily hung over them until Martina continued where she had left off.

'Well, you're going to show me that Zappa book someday, aren't you?'

'Oh yes,' was his reply.

Something had happened and Nat felt in control of nothing. Two people eating and drinking together and not needing to say anything, lest the magic of the moment become sullied, was beautiful, but also unnerving. But not being in control didn't perturb him. He felt no compulsion to be in control of anything. It sounded corny, fantastic, far-fetched and ridiculous, but he was in a place where *nothing could do me no harm,* just as Lennon felt when he sang "Happiness Is a Warm Gun", the song that had been swirling around his head twenty-four hours before, 550 feet above Berlin.

This state of affairs couldn't last, of course. Nothing lasts. And Martina's next utterance hit him like a freight train. He felt dizzy and cold sweat spread across most of his upper body parts. And that part of his body responsible for disposing of digested food parts were all set to lose control of vital functions until he grasped his knife and fork with the last strength at his disposal, thus diverting the ultimate embarrassing moment.

'There's something I haven't told you.' Six words liable to destabilise a partner hearing them. The sentence transported him back, in a few blurred seconds, to three pivotal moments of the last twelve months: when he was trying to get some truth out of Maria in Greece, ('Are you really Costa's sister?'); then to the moment when he corrected the doctor in the Liverpool hospital who informed him of Sam's passing ('She wasn't my mum, actually. She was my auntie.') And then he remembered once again studying the naked pictures Bill had given him of Martina. That was his rag-tag year summed up in three equally ragged turning points. Now he was on the receiving end of words which might change his life again. How he regretted not having gone for the lukewarm pasta option. Nevertheless, he beckoned Martina to proceed.

'You see, I have a sister. A couple of years younger than me, but very like me, appearance-wise.' This didn't sound too sinister, and he calmed himself.

'And while I was in Hamburg, I spent a couple of days with her.'

Nat wondered how that had anything to do with their own relationship and why she was making a big thing of the rather innocuous fact that she had a sister who looked very much like her. Perhaps there was still bad news to come. He braced himself again.

'She's getting over a fairly disastrous relationship with a married man. My sister never seems to have anything other than disastrous relationships, but this was a first for her, a married man. I listened to her, as usual, but couldn't offer much solace. I'm not sure why I'm telling you this, but I suppose you're bound to meet her one day. She normally turns up once a year in Berlin with renewed tales of woe.'

Nat wasn't sure what to say. 'I'm sorry your sister's love life is disastrous', 'I'm sorry to hear that', 'You're not your sister's keeper', all sounded awkward, lacking in real meaning, patronising even. Actually, he didn't give a barman's fart about her sister's romantic disasters, but he still submitted his own personal take on the sort of relationship her sister was just emerging from.

'I've never understood why women get involved with married men,' he said, hoping against hope that Martina would agree with him and that she was not about to tell him about Bill, reopening the memories of the grisly facts that had come to light when Bill's photos came into his possession. He waited nervously for her answer.

'Well, I'm with you there,' she said, 'but some women seem to look for trouble and I'm afraid that my sister is one of them. Although, as I said, I think it's the first time she's done the mistress thing.'

'The mistress thing.' Nat was finding it hard to take Martina talking about "the mistress thing". Hadn't she been one herself? He needed to get off the subject, desperate to change tack, otherwise the obsession he thought he had shaken off would be threatening to take hold again.

Martina continued. 'I suppose there is something else I should tell you.'

Shit. Nat definitely didn't like the sound of this and his stomach tightened for the third time in as many minutes.

'When you do meet my sister, be prepared to see virtually my double in front of you. People are always amazed by our likeness. Everyone's convinced we're twins.'

The news was anti-climactic, but Nat was relieved that no new, dark secret was about to destroy everything. In fact, as he digested the information, his brain started to follow a new line of thought which resulted in an interesting, not to say, promising question: what if the dark-haired woman in Bill's photos was Martina's sister and not Martina herself? Well, if that was the case, it was the best news he could have hoped for. Nat immediately decided that this was the case and euphoric feelings of relief were almost lifting him off his seat. Yes, Bill's mistress had been Martina's sister! He looked at her and felt that a final impediment had been removed from their potential future.

But that wasn't quite the final impediment, as he well knew. Another hurdle lay ahead: his impending removal to Greece. He couldn't think of anything witty or original about Martina having an identical sister and decided to get the Greek topic out into the open once and for all.

He took a few seconds to gather his thoughts, gave her an intensive look, which visibly rattled her, and spurted out the garbled summary of those thoughts in the form of an outrageous question.

'D'you fancy moving to Greece with me?'
'I'd like that, yes.' She smiled. 'When are we leaving?'

22

Accompanied by that smile, on that Berlin evening, a unified goal exploded into life in a defining moment and ushered in the best years of Nat Wilson's life. He left Berlin, as planned, ten days later and at the end of October Martina joined him in Greece, after tying up everything she was leaving behind in Berlin: her sister was taking over her flat. Nat and Martina intended, for the time being at least, to continue Nat's life-in-three countries adventure.

Martina's adaptability was exemplary and inspiring; she coped with the Anglo-Greek parts of the year as if everything before had just been a series of dress rehearsals for this, the real thing. Their love was powerful and easy, based on common sense expectations of each other's strengths and weaknesses and mutual blind trust. Life was as smooth as it ever had been for Nat. His scepticism gradually crumbled with time and his life was filled with hitherto unknown stability.

He finished his Zappa project, which sold a couple of thousand copies, covering his production costs and producing a modest profit. His novel complete, he had been trying to find an agent for a publishing deal, with no success. There was considerably more joy with what one German agent regarded as the ultimate, quality Hitch-Hikers' Guide to Berlin and Liverpool, two books that Nat completed after his third year. Many people agreed with the agent and both books sold exceptionally well. He offered three-day intensive tours in each city whenever he was resident there, which brought welcome funds.

Martina also added a few bob, doing a German version of the Liverpool City Tours.

The major difference between pre-Martina life and now was that Nat's obsession with the past ceased. *Now* really did mean *now* and the past and future remained concepts to be taken with a pinch of salt. These days, when he said, 'Give me one more day,' he *meant* it, because it was all he actually wanted. In hindsight, his novel-writing year in the three-countries' project was his half-hearted attempt to process the past and put it to bed and it had had some therapeutic value. But life now seemed like the real deal and was all the therapy he needed.

And all the people he met up with again were, he presumed, getting on with their lives as best they could. Ian, the MS victim going for broke in one last lustful wheelchair frenzy; the other Yorkshireman, Jack, with his matter-of-fact scheme for seeing out his last years by spending every last penny earned in a long working life; Scouse John, singing his heart out for a pint and artistic fulfilment; Holger flogging his dubious artwork to the naïve Berlin bourgeoisie whilst enjoying the company of admiring women almost half his age. Or Ekky back in Liverpool, slowing down after a life of fun, football and fornication in Liverpool, leaving a trail of women in his slipstream, yet loved and revered by the beautiful daughters he had helped to create in that slipstream. And then there was Scottish Bill, savaging himself over his extra-marital affairs in his self-made documentary film on the male mid-life crisis. And Maria, drifting somewhere in Southern Europe and the Balkans, seeking a new lifeline. And what about Kosta, the honest Greek broker, trying to keep everybody happy?

And then there were the dead. The loss of Sam severed

the final family ties in Liverpool and reduced him in one fell swoop to being a visitor without a home in his hometown. The memory of her death lingered and haunted him regularly: she waved him off from the doorstep as he hurried for his bus and by the time the pubs had closed in town, she was gone. Many had gone before her and the list grew longer. One day everybody would be gone. And Nat liked to believe that he was getting used to it.

The novel had turned out to be the story of that year with regular flashbacks from his past which made a futile attempt to explain his actions. As usual, there were more questions than answers. The routines he constantly set up for himself were simply there to prevent him from losing his way before Martina had entered the fray in the final phase of that year and taken his mind off the long list of people, living or dead, who had filled up Nat's life for half a century. She had gently stopped an experiment which, if it had started its second cycle with him battling away alone, might have ended in a gutter in Greece, Liverpool or Berlin.

He had learned a few useful things during that year but when Martina came along he no longer needed to meditate, philosophize with others, delve into countless works of great literature or have that final last drink to find the ever-elusive holy grail. There was a woman beside him who was unflinching in her loyalty and support, but who also put him right when he was in danger of losing control and talking shit. He thanked anybody "up there" who had decided that he would greatly benefit from the love of a good woman.

He thought back to Rüdiger's comments all those years ago; comments which seemed so lacking in weight that he had simply disregarded them at the time but which eschewed the corny but unavoidable truth that if you didn't get the lucky breaks in life, you didn't get the things you think you might deserve. As Nelson lay dying on the deck of HMS Victory at the Battle of Trafalgar, he is said to have muttered the word 'Fortuna'. Fortune good and bad, fate, the luck of the draw, the rub of the green, the list of ways to express how the cookie crumbles is a long one. Nat attributed his good fortune to being in the right place at the right time with the right woman. A rare occurrence. And he was as determined as a man could be to make it pay.

After their first six months in Greece, Nat's tenants in North Wales, with impeccable timing, handed in their notice on his house. Nat and Martina moved in and within twenty-one days and without spending a fortune, they had transformed it into a Spartan but pleasantly functional, cosy residence.

At the end of August, they were back in Berlin, their first cycle together coming to a close. On one of those August nights, Martina explained her own take on the whole caboodle since she dramatically fell in with Nat's plans almost exactly one year previously.

'When the Wall came down, many East Germans were like children in a sweet shop with a lot of money. Most of them blew it and never found peace of mind. Something told me to wait and it was the best thing I ever did. Or maybe *somebody* told me to wait. And then you came around and I did know what I wanted. Sounds ridiculously corny. B movie stuff. D'you believe in fate, Nat?'

Nat didn't know what to say, so he dredged out a weak, 'Not sure.'

'Everywhere I've been in the past year were places I've been before. Everything I've done in these places came naturally. I can't explain it and I don't want to. Am I making sense, Nat?'

He wanted to say 'Not really' but went for a deceitful 'Sure.'

'I didn't grieve when my husband died. A high-powered emergency chip was activated and I entered an extra-terrestrial world in which I was propelled forward by the word "survival", a word which orbited around my body and soul day and night. I think it's one of the reasons why my parents turned against me. Do you know the book "The Stranger" by Albert Camus? About the man who was ultimately condemned by society because he didn't cry at his mother's funeral? I felt just like him.'

Nat did know the book and nodded frantically. So, he was living with the female equivalent of the main character in one of the key works of French literature on the philosophical concept of the absurd. He wasn't at that moment sure whether this was a good or bad thing. He was waiting for Martina to spill the beans on how (or whether) Nat had been one of the reasons for her transformation from whatever to whatever. And then she did.

'Your ridiculous porridge buying act was surreal. And by the time I got to Kant Strasse, I knew that you were the one.'

And that was the only time that Martina showed any desire to philosophize about their relationship. At least Nat now knew he was "the one". He felt honoured even though he had always mocked the expression, finding it corny and fanciful. And life continued thereafter in a dream.

They married a year later in a Berlin registry office. Having invited no other guests, they asked an elderly couple who were passing by on the street to be witnesses and they kindly obliged.

The couple left immediately after the short ceremony with the Beatles' "Help" ringing in their ears: they had to pick up their grandchild from the local nursery. Before doing so, they swigged down a glass of Champagne, wished the newly-married couple all they wished themselves and spontaneously hugged them in the foyer of the Town Hall. Martina burst into tears, as the witnesses swept out of the main door, never to be seen again.

And so the years went by with Nat not believing his luck, always half-expecting a fatal banana skin, a snag, a sudden meltdown. Nothing of the like occurred and his fear eventually faded completely. Nat and Martina's routine was calming and stabilizing, rather than boring and stifling, and provided the joy and strength to cope with anything that got in their way. Decisions were taken almost telepathically and carried out with smooth efficiency.

They decided shortly after getting married to drop the Greek residence part of the cycle; it was a drag on resources in the form of additional rent to pay, there was no opportunity to make any money and the island winters were as bleak as ever. Their life became North Wales and Berlin.

Saying goodbye to Kosta was an embarrassing scene of two middle-aged men weeping and hugging. Kosta had been Nat's lucky omen, protector and Friday afternoon Ouzo drinking partner. The man who worried about him like a mother, and cared for him like a street-wise elder brother, always trying to fix something that didn't need to be fixed. Nat would always love him and Greece.

Nat and Maria thrived in two worlds: in the urban grit of Berlin and in the calm, pastoral, damp green of North Wales, which was sweetened and made bearable by regular infusions of Liverpool madness and anarchy. Still no sign of the long-awaited LFC season ticket, but the "you can't have everything" cliché urged him to remain grateful.

Martina died on the eve of their fifth wedding anniversary, just making her fiftieth birthday. It was a short, painful, unexpected illness, appearing like snow in July. And everything stopped still for Nat Wilson apart from the desperate desire to survive and carry on.

23

He prayed that he had inherited Martina's survival chip. His simplistic belief that fortune sometimes went your way and sometimes didn't wasn't helping him at all now. He didn't touch a drop of booze for two years, cried every day and didn't write one single word of value. Shopping lists were his ultimate literary achievement. He stayed in Berlin, never left the city boundaries, saw nobody he knew and only left the building for shopping and walks, managing an average of twenty thousand steps per day. He lost fifteen kilos and gained some strength from that as the physical burden of moving was at least eased. Nightly dreams of Martina deprived him of his sleep but, as the year wore on, strength returned in tiny, step-by-step portions.

He never ate out, had one main meal a day and recycled every single recipe he had ever collected or written down in the course of his life. He discovered that he had enough to see him through a quarter of the year, after which he started again. He didn't have the courage to try anything new. The robotic execution of each recipe provided stability and sufficient comfort to get him through another day.

Was life just a collection of memories, snapshots of pain and joy, light and dark?

There was emptiness and a sickening feeling in the depths of his soul as the realisation that the only thing he wanted and needed had gone away forever. The absence of booze reduced confusion and instability and helped to keep the very worst attacks of searing pain at bay. As the weeks passed, he presumed that the pain was gradually fading away, or perhaps he was just getting used to it. He did anything and everything which reduced thoughts of Martina, but when he woke in the night, the pain had a vice-like grip on him and further sleep evaded him. He would get up, engage in any physical exertion he could think of and when day broke he would get on with anything that the routines of the day demanded with an over-the-top obsession. Automation, linked with physical movement, blocked out thoughts, his most dangerous enemy, but still they lurked, just before dawn. In totalitarian regimes and in the world of Kafka, it was the secret police and mysterious men awaking you; in Nat's case, it was the scream, reminding him that he had lost the very earth below his feet.

For two years, Nat willed himself to get better, to stay alive. He played a game with himself called the "One per cent formula", based on the principle that he was feeling 1% better at the end of every passing week. At the end of the two years, he naively calculated, he would be feeling 100% better. It was a huge, ridiculous lie, an experiment of mind over matter which was doomed to failure. But at the end of the two years, the pain had at least become bearable, his strength restored to levels which allowed him to function once again and to pretend to the rest of the world that here was a man planning to re-enter the fray.

Of course, the reality was that he was nowhere near a 100% recovery; but he slowly began to believe that living was better than dying. He had shaken off the gnashing jaws of total misery and now had sufficient strength to move onto a terrain containing manageable portions of pain and the faint promise of resuming something approaching normal service, preferably in the company of the rest of the human race.

He thought about re-establishing contact with people he knew in Berlin and the usual suspects sprang to mind: Jack, the Yorkshire man (was he still alive?); Holger (still in business?); Bill (are you joking?). He realised that the way back to anybody he had ever known in Berlin was at best littered with unpleasant obstacles and at worst, blocked forever. He had now turned sixty and he had gone for broke, lost it all and had now fallen so far under the radar of all the men and women he had known in his earlier Berlin years that he expected a resounding and fully deserved, "Where the bloody hell have you been?" from anybody he dared to contact again.

Yes, indeed, where the bloody hell had he been? Well, he had been busy playing the cards he had been dealt. The best hand had appeared in the form of Martina, the other hands a surreal and gruesome mixture. He found himself confronted once again with the age-old, weary truism that life is full of ups and downs; further musing on the eternal injustice of life being unfair was futile.

He was fast running out of family; it was now reduced to a distant, estranged stepson and an unstable Martina look-alike sister-in-law. On the Liverpool front, things looked little better, hardly a year passing without news of another Liverpool family member "checking out" for the last time. His father, Bob and Sam had set in motion a depressing trend and the laws of nature ensured that the trend would only be going in one direction.

Music was, as usual, his make-believe world, and sustained him throughout. He made sure it was omnipresent whatever he was doing, making life bearable and even occasionally giving him the briefest reminders of a time when black wasn't the only colour in town.

Six months had dragged by. It was a late Friday morning and he had just spent twenty minutes of headphone intensity in the company of the Beatles' magnificent, farewell musical fanfare, "Abbey Road" and Paul had just taken leave from Nat at the end of the second side with his memorable line: *And in the end, the love you make is equal to the love you take*.

The sun streamed through the window, and for the first time in just over two years, a little voice in his head said: 'Fancy a drink?' Before he was able to decide to submit or resist, the doorbell rang. It was a registered delivery, not necessarily a bearer of good news and Nat's mood darkened as he waited for the lift to transport Mr Postman to him.

Nat opened the door, signed and wished the young man a good day. A British postmark, a standard-sized envelope, it didn't look too sinister. He nervously tore it open and for the first time in a couple of years, he had some good news. He had been assigned a season ticket in the Kenny Dalglish Stand, at Anfield Road, Liverpool Football Club, commencing in the forthcoming season.

Well, he thought.

'Hmmm,' he hummed.

"Yeeees!"

Then he sat down and wept. The moment sounded the muffled starting shot of the hesitant beginning of the easing of his debilitating burden. He breathed easier, and in his head clouds parted, a patch of blue sky opened up in his mind and soft rays of sunshine unobtrusively and gently made themselves at home somewhere deep within him. It had happened before in his life and it was happening now: events take over and if the inner voice coagulates with those events, the man moves forward, stumbling at first, but with an unshakeable belief that all will be well.

The brief letter from Liverpool Football Club stated that to secure the ticket, full payment for next season's Premier League fixtures had to be transferred within twenty-one working days. He grabbed the necessary papers and cards and headed to the bank at a brisk pace. Once at the desk, he spluttered out the nature of his business, managed to screw up two of the forms he was beckoned to fill in and just managed to get his shaky signature onto the third and vital document before the visibly irritated bank clerk became tempted to display that Berlin rush of snappy, controlled aggression. By 12.12 p.m. Central European Time, his fate was sealed and he was about to prove, once again, that Bill Shankly's belief that football was more important than life and death was accurate and true. It was time for a celebratory drink. It would be his first in two years, and he knew exactly where he was going to break the fast.

He headed for the former socialist drinking hole that was still stubbornly attached to his block of flats. The last time he was there the cool, summer evening temperatures had forced him inside to drink and stare at his fellow drinkers. That was another day, another snapshot from life.

As he eagerly anticipated renewing his acquaintance with beer, the prospect of watching every home league game LFC would play in his lifetime exhilarated him even more than his Lotto win. He wanted to say thank you for this reprieve. Plastic chairs were placed in something resembling a seating order and Nat took his seat before saying grace.

The waiter appeared with something on his mind, gruffly informing him that he was to move closer to the adjoining table. He didn't like the waiter's tone, nor his look, nor the ridiculous nature of what Nat saw as an order. He was, after all, the only guest on the makeshift terrace outside what was basically just a functional, charmless drinking establishment. In a second, he was thrust back to the time of the equally charmless German Democratic Republic when the paying customer had the rights of a black slave sailing west on a ship from Africa in the 18th century.

Nat referred the waiter to a taxidermist and a brief staring match kicked off which Nat was hell-bent on not losing. The spell was broken when Nat quietly gave his order for a beer. Both men then behaved as if Nat's insult had never been pronounced and the waiter shuffled off, returning with the only reason why Nat was sitting there at all: a large glass of cold, frothy *Pils*.

Surprisingly, the waiter did not slam down the glass as retaliation for Nat's previous insult. More surprisingly, Nat handed him a five euro note, requesting him to keep the change. Both men were showing generosity where outright aggression had threatened just a couple of minutes before; an unsteady harmony had been put in place and both men were relieved. Nat was poised for the task in hand and moved his hand slowly towards the beer glass, savouring the magical moment. He raised the glass, and expressed eternal gratitude to somebody, anybody, somewhere, anywhere for the beer now deliciously sliding down his gullet and permanent live access to the *beautiful game* for the rest of his life.

Nat was also grateful that he hadn't hit the waiter. It had been a close thing and would have been an embarrassing first, a blot on his violent-free record thus far in life. He wondered why he had come that close, why at that moment, in that situation. After a second gulp of beer, he put himself through a brief but intense (and amateurish) self-analysis and quickly realised that he was telling Berlin to fuck off, something he perhaps should have done many years before. His verbal outburst had produced a satisfactory result: an aggressor had been shown how far his aggression would get him and clarity had been attained.

The way people communicated in Berlin had always blemished his overall evaluation of the city. The fact remained that in everyday life you were regularly on the edge of a blowout with some snappy Berlin grump. Until now Nat had always turned the other cheek; he now felt that the strength needed to maintain that policy had just expired. It really was time to get out before he ended up behind bars or in the local A&E.

Martina had kept him within the Berlin mainstream by regularly re-heating the old chestnut that the Berliners' bark was worse than their bite; she was critical of some of the more extreme examples of their bloody-mindedness but she was able to understand better her fellow Berliners' mood swings than a man from a still green and pleasant land used to people smiling at you rather than scowling. As long as Martina was there, it was of little consequence to Nat anyway. Now that she was gone, the potential for blow-ups had drastically increased.

His reasons for staying in Berlin were becoming less numerous by the day and Nat's exit strategy was already taking shape. He was about to reduce his life-in-three countries experiment to life in two neighbouring countries: England and Wales. England, or to be more precise, Liverpool for life, Wales for seclusion. He wasn't yet thinking about the logistics or possible consequences. Like an amateur he was relying on feeling. The cottage in Wales was waiting for him, the bank transfer was starting its trip westward to Anfield Road at the very moment he was finishing the last drops of his beer and everything was going to be alright. They were the only facts he needed to work with on that particular June afternoon.

The decision not to have a second beer was a crucial one as the operation to get out of Berlin began at the very moment he had transferred the season ticket money. He did not have oceans of time. He had to sell his flat, prepare the cottage for his arrival and move. Have money, can do. Nat had money, could do and he had just over two months to get settled in North Wales to see Liverpool's opening Premier League game in mid-August. The next weeks would be devoted to this end; any other thoughts or activities would simply get in the way. Most importantly of all, he would have to do everything in his power in the forthcoming weeks to suppress the idea that maybe he was making a colossal mistake.

It was also time to sit down and have a serious new look at the maths, something he hadn't done since his Lotto win. In fact, his financial situation still gave cause for optimism and peace of mind: his two pensions were now providing extra security and although he had seriously dipped into his savings on numerous occasions over the years, they still represented a comfortable bolster. The sale of the flat, even based on pessimistic estimates, would shield him in old age.

He tried to suppress the chilling reality that one day he could become an immobile, babbling, demented old man, unable to carry out the simplest tasks of human survival. Care homes were expensive places. Well, if he had any money left by that time, they could have it and care for him. When the money ran out, the NHS could keep him alive until some faceless bureaucrat decided to pull a plug on Nat Wilson's turn.

Such thoughts presumably crossed every human being's mind as they got older and Nat was keen to put them to bed quickly before his momentum to start a new life floundered at birth: what would come later, would come later. His immediate concern was to set himself up for whatever final acts his particular show contained. If there were no people to look after him, money would have to. The idea didn't fill him with joy, but it was still better than having no money.

24

Within a month he had received a reasonable offer for his Berlin flat and the estate agent advised him to accept. He did, which obliged him to vacate the premises by the end of August. Tight but doable. He arranged for his books, record and clothes collection, along with any furniture needed in Wales to be removed by mid-July.

The only real contact he had made in his years with Marina in Wales was with the Joneses in number twenty-one: humble but still proud, salt of the earth types and perfect neighbours, definition thereof being "those you never see or hear, but who are always there when you need them". They happily agreed to oversee the Welsh end of the removal. The new owners in Berlin also made life easier for Nat by agreeing to take over anything Nat decided to leave behind.

Nat couldn't believe how smoothly things were going and was nervously waiting, in his customary neurotic fashion, for the big hitch. July came and went and there wasn't a hitch in sight. Nat had the first two weeks of August to say goodbye to Berlin but could find neither the energy nor the desire to do so. This was no longer the Nat bursting to rediscover Berlin and conquer all the demons he had been fighting there. He didn't have the fight in him anymore; he wasn't defeated because he no longer had an enemy.

He was quietly leaving the battlefield, peaceful and content in the knowledge that he had found his meaning of life: the love of a good woman. The fact that this had agonisingly slipped away was something that he had to accept or else perish. Anger had ceased to have meaning for him; softer words and concepts were now Nat Wilson's guiding lights.

The previous few weeks had shown that somebody, or something, had been rooting for him. The season ticket news, the ease of his move to Wales, and the dawning realisation that life did go on, made him feel as though he was in safe territory once more.

He sat on the balcony on the last day, making two beers last the whole afternoon, letting himself fall soft and gently into the memory of all the years he had spent there, and kept the positive switch on throughout, refusing to let sadness get the upper hand, forgiving himself for the mistakes he had made and forgiving all those who had done him wrong. He convinced himself that nobody had intentionally caused him ill-will, that he had experienced more victories than defeats and that even the inhabitants of this hotchpotch metropolis called Berlin meant well, despite the seemingly endless supply of negativity foaming from their overactive motor mouths. Martina's belief that this was the case helped him cling to this belief; he archived it as a truth and promised never to willingly renege on the idea that Berlin was a city more sinned against than sinning.

In this soothing mood of reconciliation and almost hippie-like innocence, he also saw the ten months immediately preceding Martina in a different light. She had returned suntanned and beautiful in a killer white dress, seductively enjoying his home-made pasta bake and deliciously sealing his fate. The disjointed thoughts he had assembled in his long-since forgotten first novel seemed an age away and had hardly set the literary world on fire – five hundred and forty-seven people had bought the book and he had received eleven emails from readers who were longing for the follow-up. To call it a modest success would have been kind, but he was grateful to all those who bought it. And especially to the eleven readers with a longing.

His take now on a new life in Wales was summed up in the question: 'What have I got to lose?' Night fell, he sipped down a final neat Scotch, kept calm, resisted every temptation to let nostalgia and sentimentality possess him and turned in for his last night in Berlin.

25

The first nine days in Wales ganged up on him, roughed him up, had him on the ropes and pummelled him to within an inch of KO. It rained every day from dawn to dusk. Life in the house without Martina was akin to being locked inside a haunted house. In the house itself, an invisible but vicious sadist called memory appeared from behind every door swinging a club at him whenever he moved. So he avoided movement. The Joneses had filled the fridge and pantry with enough supplies to prevent him from having to leave the cottage to buy anything and he fervently hoped that he would have enough to eat until the rain stopped. Staying indoors was painful but the lesser of the customary two evils and he stared out the frightening reality that he was alone.

But the final weeks in Berlin had given him a pollster to build on and ensure survival. And the vicious sadist faded into the background. And on 9 September it finally stopped raining. And Liverpool were playing in the next few days. But what was the use of a season ticket if you don't know how to get to Anfield? He didn't have the strength to organise the passage. He had already missed the first two games of the season and he was becoming fearful of inertia becoming a lifestyle. And then a miracle came a knocking.

The knock on the front door woke him out of a late afternoon slumber, the first sign of life outside the cottage since he had returned. He opened the door and saw a young man, in his late twenties perhaps. Neat, self-composed. He looked edgy but friendly.

'Sorry to bother you, Mr Wilson. My name is Paul Jones, my Aunt Blodwyn asked me to call round to see how you are.' He was well spoken, his words emerging clearly and in that familiar North Wales singsong brogue. Nat asked him in, offered him a cup of tea and they exchanged a few words about the awful weather. It took him a few minutes to work out who 'Blodwyn' was; he had never been on first name terms with Mrs Jones and now he was getting to know her distinctive Welsh first name and a member of her extended family into the bargain. He presumed that Paul was one of her many nephews. Nat asked him to call him Nat but instinctively felt that Paul might have problems with that. The young man exuded a deep sense of respect, a rare thing amongst the younger folk of today, Nat thought to himself. Anyway, Paul had another reason for visiting.

'Auntie Blod told me that you've recently obtained a season ticket for the Reds, Mr Wilson and I was wondering whether you'd like to join me and a couple of mates for the home games. We've had our tickets for a few years now. We go in two cars so there's plenty of room.'

Nat's belief in God returned to him the second Paul made this nervy announcement. A religious experience? Whatever it was, it was the perfect ready-made solution. He realised that it was no big surprise that there would be a hard core of supporters in this North-Eastern enclave of Wales, but for him to be living in the same village of blokes who regularly made the pilgrimage was verging on the miraculous. Nat thanked Paul with tears in his eyes, which momentarily threw Paul, but Nat pulled himself together and a friendship based on the common passion for a football team began. Paul and his mates would pick him up the following Saturday at noon.

Paul briefly described his three mates to Nat. All local lads in their thirties, all married. Paul wasn't. All of them were used to commuting to the Wirral, Wrexham and Chester to earn their daily crust. Paul was the exception again, content to help his father and elder brother on their small farm in the village. They also had enough room to offer bed and breakfast facilities to anybody passing through, like lost tourists or weary travellers taking a break between the long trek from London to Holyhead en route to Ireland. They even had the occasional LFC supporters as guests who had flown in from places all over Europe, unable to find affordable accommodation in Liverpool.

Nat bade him farewell, still unable to fully grasp just how lucky he had been.

'We'll be here at twelve on Saturday, Mr Wilson' Paul smiled, turned and walked down the path. He watched Paul turn right down the main track towards the village; Nat liked Paul and was charmed by those formal mannerisms and olde-worlde approach and found it touching that a younger man should be taking the trouble to take time for an older man.

He ventured out for the first time in ten days, unsteadily manoeuvring himself down the gravel path leading from the unkempt back garden. He was heading for the lake, a walk which would take him about twenty minutes. The weather was clearing up; the sun was still keeping a modest profile, but he sensed that it still might make a full breakout before the afternoon was out, the temperature steadily rising by the minute. He had the countryside to himself and he picked up the pace down the rough paths. The fields were sodden with the non-stop rain of the previous days but they were drying, the shades of the grass embellished by the numerous shafts of sunlight escaping through the ever-widening gaps in the clouds.

The weather seemed to have a grudge against this corner of Wales; a day without rain was a rare occurrence and Nat greedily grasped these minutes, fully aware of the fact that they may not be around for long. He was also painfully aware that he would need to get used to roaming the paths that he had regularly trodden with Martina. And this particular path navigated together during their time in Wales was indeed a regularly trodden one. He was facing his fear and surviving the path, the turn of the weather helping him. Nat had fallen into a black dog hole in the previous week, had started to slowly scramble out, then been lifted out by Paul's visit and was building on his recovery by breathing in the fragrances of the re-heated Welsh grass and gazing up at an increasingly blue sky. He was re-charging some emotional and physical strength before the rain inevitably started again.

He neared the edge of the lake; the sun bullied itself into the proceedings for the first time proper and Nat's spirits rose as he plonked himself onto the only bench available. He sat and sucked in the scene. He felt like the only man in the universe, but he didn't feel bad. His goals were modest and achievable and he just hoped he would be granted enough time to see them through. The only time he would need to look at his watch would be on match day when Paul and his mates arrived. Nat Wilson's ambitions now stretched to asking himself just two questions: How long have I got and what do I want to do with that time? The answer to the first question was guesswork but he already had the answer to the second one. And so he would plough on.

It was getting cool on the bench and visibility was deteriorating as dusk crept in; thankfully, the sun was still making its presence felt. But he knew that within an hour he would need a torch, the mere thought of which filled him with fear. So he sloped off. More balanced than at the start of the day. With something to look forward to. With the guarantee of company at least every second week.

He passed the cottage and decided to have one last drink in The Harp, a cosy, simple, decent boozer, a place where people stayed for an hour and went home. Which is exactly what Nat wanted to do. Sounded easy, but he also knew that he would have to find the courage to enter for the first time without Martina.

He looked around and recognized a few faces propping up the bar, playing darts or closely gathered in the corner, as if they were plotting something. The "corner people," as Martina and him used to call them (Die Eckmenschen were normally the Welsh speakers who generally kept to themselves). As he and Martina normally conversed in German, there remained forever a hard-core knot of two groups of people who nobody understood. Nobody cared, staying in their own worlds, be they worlds full of Welsh, local gossip, agricultural matters, German or any other spontaneous flotsam the clientele made use of as a means of communication.

They had never really made any friends in The Harp. He didn't expect that to change this time round. People said "Hello" and "Goodbye" and that was as far as the communication went. It was almost like being back in Germany; no hostility, rather muted indifference. Richard and Gwen, the married couple who ran the place, made a bit more effort, for obvious reasons. They seemed to be genuinely pleased to see him again. He gave them the news about Martina and they made the usual noises, which was followed by an awkward silence. He carefully transported his pint of Dragon's Brew to the table by the window and prepared himself for half an hour of low-key musing.

He found a *Daily Telegraph* on the seat beside him, overcame his deep-seated disinclination and started to flick through it. The last time he had had that rag in his hand was well over a decade ago at Liverpool John Lennon Airport. The ten years between then and now flashed through his cranium and briefly made him shudder; he quickly recovered and found one of the few parts of the paper not thickly coated with tedious Tory twaddle: the sports page. Today it was primarily devoted to the next day's Premier League games, including the visit to Anfield of newly-promoted Wolverhampton Wanderers. He still couldn't quite believe that he was going to be there. But he thanked God he was and swigged down his favourite Welsh Bitter.

He had scanned the paper and was halfway through his pint when his gaze drifted towards a youngish woman at the bar. As always, he was trying hard to avoid the dreaded male gaze, the one he had heard about so often in the past decade or so. But this time, nobody could point the finger because nobody seemed to be watching him, everybody busy with the people they had chosen to be with. The object of his gaze was busy talking in a vivacious fashion with Richard who was happily pulling pints next to Gwen behind the bar. Nat had a perfect side view.

It cast his mind back to the day he had watched Martina through the shop window all those years ago in Berlin; he was attracted in the same way and for the same reasons. She was natural, she oozed humility and he imagined that physical proximity to her would inspire and uplift. The spell was broken when Gwen quickly needed to attend to a punter returning an empty glass and asking for a refill. At that very moment, the woman turned towards Nat, creating the classic awkward moment he had been so desperate to avoid. She smiled, thank God. He smiled back and awkwardness smoothly transformed itself into an innocuous, innocent second of agreeable harmony.

Nat returned to the business of finishing his pint. For a split second, he considered doing something foolish, like passing the time of day with her. Bearing in mind the ungainly movements necessary to get close enough to be able to do that, Nat sensibly decided to stay where he was. His ageing limbs simply weren't able to produce quick, smooth, agile movements anymore. Never mind.

But he was doubly troubled by niggling feelings of desire and by the renewed realisation that sitting alone in a pub was a sad bastard occupation. It had been a long day, by no means a bad day, but he was looking forward to his bed, while achingly wondering where that woman was going to rest her head at the end of the day. He returned his glass and said goodnight. She responded and her smile briefly lingered in Nat's direction. He trudged home, had the smallest of night caps and effortlessly drifted off to sleep, comforted by the thought that tomorrow was match day. You knew where you were with football.

26

Match day. Nerves. Anticipation. Mild, but growing excitement during the hours before kick-off, intensified today by the fact that it was the first home match of a brand new season. In the Liverpool days of his youth, the bus got him to the ground within twenty minutes, and he was back in time for tea by six. Life was more complicated now and a certain apprehension gripped him as he waited for the lads to arrive.

His bell rang just after twelve and a welcoming party assembled around his door. Queuing up to shake his hand, they all expressed their pleasure at meeting him, introducing themselves, reassuring him, without actually putting it into words, that it was going to be a great day and that they would look after him. After the introductions, the lads stood there, looking like they were expecting some sort of team talk. Nat rose to the occasion, the teacher in him re-emerged and he started blathering the first things that came into his head, hoping that they would get his message, even though he wasn't even sure what his message was going to be.

'I can't tell you how grateful I am to you people, you know. I've had a bit of a bad time of things recently, then came the season ticket. Then came Paul with the news that you lot go to every home game! And you're willing to put up with an old dude like me every time!' There were embarrassed laughs. 'Talk about a lucky break! And I'm not even Welsh!' This was met with heartier laughs. 'Anyway, I'm paying for anything that goes down your gullets in the form of food and drink on these match days. Got that? OK, let's get to Anfield!' It was over the top and corny, but Nat meant it.

The boys let out a goose-pimple rousing cheer and Nat knew immediately that he had struck a chord. Dramatic, emotional stuff indeed. But football was nothing if not dramatic and emotional. A deep sense of gratitude gripped him as they set off.

They talked about football and little else in the car as they cruised North East Wales, up South Wirral and through the Queensway Tunnel into Liverpool. It was all predictions, fears and hopes for the new season. Personal matters were hardly covered, the sole focus was the match and the desire for three points.

By one forty-five and in the bowels of the stadium, Nat was at the head of the queue at the pie stand, passing back all manner of pies, pasties and plastic beakers of tea to "his" lads. Eventually, they all had to split to take up their seats, but Nat found new mates in his section of the stand. It had been a long time and he had to adapt quickly. After the stillness of Wales and the detached way of Berlin life, Nat found himself in the middle of infectious noise, surreal humour and total solidarity; everybody was loud, effervescent, ridiculous. The Liverpool tribe had an endless supply of natural enthusiasm, and it was beautiful and uplifting. And Nat was never going to be alone for every second weekend of the football season for the rest of his life.

When the game kicked off, tears rolled down his cheeks, as he knew they would. The game flashed by in a blur. Liverpool ran out 3-1 winners after a dour fight against lively, well-organised Wolves. Reunited outside the ground, all smiles and roars, they finally made it out of the traffic jams and were in town by six-thirty. Nat knew a take-away fish and chip shop, near one of his favourite town pubs, and after they had dined on busy Ranelagh St, struggling with steaming fish and chips and plastic cutlery, Nat suggested a pint. Approval was unanimous, and minutes later Nat was passing frothy pints of real ale into the back room and orange juice for the two drivers. He went for a Guinness. The post-mortem could begin and everybody proffered their verdict.

The locals joined in the banter, as the Scousers eased the Welsh contingent out of their polite shells. They downed a second pint and they were edging towards eight o'clock; Nat was slowly feeling the pinch. The day had been perfect and he felt that it was time to head for the Welsh hills before an alcoholic haze dulled and sullied the beauty of it all. The boys were ready and whilst depositing their empty glasses at the bar, they bade the landlady farewell as if they were taking leave of the queen. They all instinctively knew at that moment that fish 'n' chips, followed by two pints in her pub were the future, set in stone.

Dusk had fallen but there was still sufficient light to take in the gentle green landscape of the Wirral with its modest, almost countrified streets of Merseyside suburbia. As they crossed the border, the River Dee and the hills of Snowdonia were gradually fading out of sight. They would be home by nine.

The journey home that he had made countless times in the back of his parents' car as a child was, of course, always in the opposite direction. They were always sad to leave, returning to dusty Liverpool after the vibrant air and lush greenness of North Wales, rolling hills replaced by concrete as overcrowded, built-up, decaying urbanity welcomed them back. Their spirits only lifted when they were settled back in their cosy two-up, two-down terraced house in the only town they had ever lived in. But Wales was never more than an hour's drive away and it was a comforting thought - a limited but precious lifeline to country life. For Nat, the remaining survivor of that unremarkable Liverpool family, the comforting thought now was that Liverpool was only ever an hour's drive away in the opposite direction.

After half an hour of excitable chatter, silence slowly took over and filled the car, everybody processing anything they felt the need to process. If Liverpool routinely got those three vital points, it would always be the most beautiful routine any of them could hope for. And if they didn't, it was only a game, a lie which kept them all going until the next time they headed to Anfield. Above all, they wanted Liverpool to win for Mr Wilson. And Mr Wilson wanted the same for them. Co-dependency of the most precious kind.

27

The routine rhythm of life Nat had signed himself up to during the last year before Martina appeared had been an integral part of his original "three-years-in-three-countries" experiment. He had survived that year by giving his life a routine he believed everybody needed, based on Woody Allen's suggestion that ninety percent of life was just "turning up". These Welsh twilight days had taught him what "just turning up" really meant because there was little else to do there other than turn up. Life consisted of sleeping, walking, cooking, reading, writing and treating himself to an occasional drink in The Harp. North Wales offered rugged greenery, roaming hills and endless space, but little chance of anything else. The briefest speeding up of his heartbeat, compelled by the most innocent exchange of looks with the thirties-plus girl at the bar of The Harp reminded him of something beyond the routine, but he was no longer sure what that something was or whether he wanted it.

Music remained the constant solace, which stirred his soul when everything else was dulling and blunting it. He had streamlined his CD collection down to just under four hundred, finally deciding on what constituted the real greats, the "life wouldn't be worth living without" masterpieces. The rest he sold to a second-hand record shop in Liverpool for a song. He kept all the Beatles for all the usual sentimental reasons and all the Zappa's albums to remind him of the time he met Martina and the modest, but sweet success of the book he wrote about them. He then spent the best part of a month deciding what the remaining 350 or so should be and he could now reach out and grab a CD with his eyes closed and be guaranteed to find something to cut through any mental or emotional malaise currently afflicting him.

On some days, with little else to do, he would spend half a day filing away on pages of a short story, taking a short break when the rain stopped to stretch his legs and clear his mind, returning after half an hour to plough on until he made a breakthrough, transforming less than inspirational shit into something he thought might be regarded as literature; or at least entertaining. Yes, he was still trying to create literature, even though he was still far from sure whether he actually knew what it was. He always trusted his instinct to tell him whether it was or it wasn't. Attempting to create something of lasting beauty in his writing lifted him to a different level of consciousness; he felt the same way listening to music masterpieces or watching a beautiful Reds' goal at the end of a perfect move.

These were the highs, the moments beyond the turning up. *Beauty is truth, truth beauty, - that is all/ Ye know on earth, and all ye need to know.* The John Keats' assertion that puzzled him as a schoolchild had now come back to enlighten him just as his English teacher had assured him and his schoolmates it would. But Keats didn't talk about "turning up". People grasped and accepted that necessity automatically: routine.

In a reassuring comfort hovering somewhere between beauty and routine, he had been devoting himself to activities which calmly inspired him and kept him ticking over spiritually and intellectually as he climbed the Mount Everest works of literature he had been carefully putting off reading for thirty years or more when time restraints, i.e. work, ruled the day. He got stuck into the six mammoth volumes of Winston Churchill's "The Second World War", "The History of the Decline and Fall of the Roman Empire" by Edward Gibbon, the complete works of Heinrich Böll, Thomas Mann, Franz Kafka, Ernest Hemingway, Charles Dickens and William Shakespeare and everybody's favourite reading challenge, "Ulysses", by James Joyce.

He ceased watching live football on TV, preferring to listen to Liverpool's away games live on the radio, just like his dad used to in the decades before him. In this way, he was groping back to the time before the eighties when the only live football matches you saw as a football fan were the ones you went through the turnstiles to see. Nat Wilson, therefore, had created his own peculiar retro world. Life was like continual sixties pop hits on the radio: nothing you would really want to switch off; it was calming, mollifying even, and he was in sole control of the on-off switch.

He had been in Wales for more than six months now; spring was tuning up and the beginning of the end of the football season was rearing its ugly head. He didn't want to contemplate life without the regular sojourn to Anfield. He was becoming anxious.

And the loss of Martina also meant that life had partly returned to the past tense as he chronologically waded through every memory his mind could re-live. He wrote these memories down, without any heed to style, form or structure. He convinced himself that by reassembling every memory he had ever had, he would have a good idea, before his moment of passing, what his life had been about, which would, he hoped, allow him to be able to say whether he had done more good than bad. If the whole content of your life really did flash through your mind at the exact moment of your death, Nat would be ready: he had already produced the written version to avoid any nasty surprises.

He also realised that he was delivering this final summary to somebody, somewhere. Were all the acts of love, attempts at communication, relationships long and short, laughter and tears, moments of sadness and joy and colossal mistakes and wrong turnings all for nothing? Please, God, no.

Yes, he thought, *I am asking some higher force for a final school report.* Even though he knew that a reply would not be forthcoming, the thought still calmed and pacified him and it was a good companion for the many hours he spent alone in the cottage or wandering along the local paths within his daily five-mile radius. As feedback from higher forces had so far been non-existent in his life, he was willing to provide his own feedback. Self-evaluation on a cosmic scale, so to speak.

He hated to admit it, but he was working out his chances of gaining access to whatever the endless number of religions might offer in the way of eternal life. W.C Fields, on his hospital death bed, was visited by a friend, who was astounded to find Fields, a lifelong atheist and bon viveur, reading the bible. When asked what on earth he was doing, Fields replied, 'I'm looking for a loophole.' Nat had a nasty feeling he was also loophole searching as he had to confess that, unfortunately, his life sometimes went quite well, as a result of others missing out. And, taking was always easier than giving, especially in his younger years, when the needs of other human beings were conveniently overlooked in the heat of the battle for fun and pleasure. This clinical bookkeeping at the end of an unruly life mildly repulsed him. Why hadn't he just been a good boy all his life? Or turned to Catholicism and regularly gone to confession, which, presumably, permitted continual bad behaviour as long as you said sorry afterwards?

He was reminded of his teacher training days when the person observing your lesson normally opened the post-mortem with the tricky question: 'Well, how do you think the lesson went?' This time God was asking, 'Well, Nat, how do you think you lived your life?' He wouldn't be able to find a satisfactory answer beyond the gloriously tepid, 'Well, I did my best.' Followed by the equally meek and guilty adjunct, 'But I suppose I could have done better.'

So if he just about qualified for some sort of agreeable afterlife, he was hoping for all those higher forms of human achievement such as beautiful music, literature and art. Routine matters like cleaning your teeth, doing the washing up and talking about the weather would, presumably, not be included. But what about the pleasures of the flesh? If there were any available, he would like to enter in a perpetual state of vigorous adulthood. Any post-mortal state resembling the bookends at either end of life would be better than nothing, but also a savage disappointment.

He realised that he was primitively mixing up the physical and the spiritual and hated himself for doing so. The physical ended, presumably, when you gasped your last breath; art, literature and music might be swirling around for eternity, but the physical presence of women, for example, would be sadly missing for eternity and, therefore, his post-mortal state would be irrelevant. Similar to a dream: you can see but you can't touch.

300

But he still felt compelled to draw a picture of a place he wanted to be in when the time came. And it was really rather simple: he wanted to be back together with all the people he had ever loved in his life. If he knew *that* was possible, he would happily go tomorrow, as any sensible human being would. But he didn't know. Aye, there's the rub. And neither did the rest of humanity. It was the fate troubling everybody; the fate that we all deserve, perhaps; the entrance fee, the price of life. And so he pressed on.

At this later stage in life, it was just a question of hanging onto the belief that all would be well because that's all you have left. Being alone now in his Welsh cottage amplified this truism and depressed him but focussed his mind in equal measure. He just hoped that he had given enough love, done more right than wrong. It all sounded embarrassingly hippie-like or like something you might hear coming from any God-fearing pulpit.

It was the wretched age thing again. As a young man, these things never preoccupied you; as an old man, it was almost the only thing on your mind. Things bounced off you when you were a younger man when you had the fight in you and you were surrounded by people rooting for you. But as middle-age sped towards old age, parts of the body previously unknown to you started to cause trouble and death paid ever more frequent visits, indiscriminately taking out your backup staff like parents, relatives, friends and lovers along the way. And you sadly concluded that resistance was useless. And the hope of being able to seriously change anything became ever more futile as the years fly by.

All these unsettling journeys into previously unchartered and scary waters were unnerving and were regularly processed in an uninterrupted series of recurring dreams as March got underway. The scream dream season was back and all the usual suspects were coming and going, bearing mostly bad tidings: parents, family and women were the main culprits, continually churning up a slippery mess of loss, sadness and helplessness. None of them seemed particularly impressed by Nat's efforts so far and a mood of gentle recrimination hovered and gyrated during the blurred and feverish nocturnal meanderings.

Nat was just relieved that the dreams were not too scary; however, they still had disturbing Kafkaesque elements which darkened his mood by reminding him of the futility of kidding yourself that you were always in the driving seat. That you were always the hammer and never the anvil. That Beethoven's fateful fifth symphony chords wouldn't come banging on your front door one day. The dreams only served to underline the gloomy conclusion that at the end of the day you were in the hands of fate and your ability to change anything was frighteningly limited.

On one particularly peaceful morning, with promising shafts of spring sunlight gradually emerging over and across the River Dee, Nat fearfully opened his eyes after another night of dreaming and made a decision. He couldn't stop dreams from happening but he could stop being obsessed, disturbed, influenced and fascinated by them. He did believe people who claimed they received life-changing messages and guidance in them; it had just never happened to *him*. Not once in over half a century. Paul McCartney has sworn on numerous occasions that the melody to "Yesterday" came to him in a dream and his mother asked him to "Let it Be" under similar nocturnal circumstances, and we all know where that led him. Good for him.

A flickering memory of a distant dream, however, suddenly stirred within him. There was a message in a particularly torturous dream in Greece, about a decade previously, featuring a woman in a white dress and the missive was an unequivocal one: happiness on Planet Earth was going to prove elusive for Nat Wilson. Well, that turned out to be true, he thought. One dream message in fifty years. So be it. And he concluded, therefore, that the "white dress dream" was the exception proving the rule; otherwise, dreams were just there, a troubling mess of nonsense, painfully squeezed out of the depths of our subconscious, signifying little.

So he vowed, with immediate effect, to kick start the waking hours the moment he opened his eyes every day without wasting one single thought on the useless confusion he left behind in dreamy slumber and to grab anything the upcoming waking hours had to offer.

The rising Welsh sun also needed coaxing and nurturing over the river to warm his spirits. It might well be a great day, at least weather-wise, and he felt profound gratitude that he was being allowed once again to make something of the gift called "today". The words "give us this day" once again softly echoed around his head and he experienced, on the tenth day of April, a liberating feeling of clarity, a nemesis, a lancing of the painful abscess that had threatened to take over, and he felt stronger, abler, free of the customary pain and debilitating doubt. He wasn't able to explain what had happened during those ten days of conversations with himself about God and the world and everything in between, but it had removed a lot of emotional debris. And after ten days of rain, a day of sunshine seemed to be in the making.

There was, however, one last lingering memory of something somebody said which he had been dragging around with him for many years. The statement in question was made by a colleague from a previous time passage: 'Life only happens just before you die.' It always made perfect sense to him and he felt this could be the perfect time to whip it out and get it into the early morning sunshine. Before it started raining again.

28

The routine tasks of the day then slowly pushed themselves back to the top of the agenda: he was about to get himself a new ironing board, something he had been promising himself for longer than he could remember. His joy was all the greater because he was about to get one free of charge. The hastily written supermarket notice board had advertised one from somebody claiming that it had been "used only once".

Nat had spent some time wondering why anybody would use an ironing board only once and then advertise it as an object to be taken away free of charge. Never mind. All he had to do was make his way to Glascoed Way, number four. "First come, first served" seemed to be the message. He was determined to be first and he hurried down the main street, confident that he could get there before anybody else.

He was there within five minutes. The flower arrangements on both sides of the path suggested that a woman inhabited the house. Indeed, a woman opened the door and Nat recognized her immediately. It was the girl from The Harp.

He smiled awkwardly. 'Hello, I've come about the advert for the ironing board.'

The statement had a rather ridiculous ring to it and he felt mildly disappointed that, after more than sixty years of a varied, interesting and full life, he was saying, 'I've come about the ironing board' on the porch of a Welsh dwelling in the backwaters of North East of Wales. Had he not hoped for more by this juncture? Or is there not more to life than this? Did he really need a second-hand ironing board? Couldn't he just pay thirty quid online and get it delivered to his door? The look of the woman answered such niggling questions and he was happy to be just there at that moment in time; being anywhere else would have been an error. Then he realized that he hadn't even introduced himself. But he didn't have to.

'Mr Wilson!' she said

Everybody else in the village called him that, so why shouldn't she? Nevertheless, he was determined to leave the house on first-name terms, if nothing else.

'Could you do me a favour?' he snapped. 'Could you please call me Nat?'

She offered no resistance. The sudden outburst had won her over.

'That's fine, Nat. I'm Marie.'

He instantly regretted his comment, which had sounded more like an order than an invitation. But he didn't apologize and she asked him in. He wondered why he was entering this house at all but he knew that he had to. In his mind, the ironing board had now become something of a side issue.

Her living room was bright, fresh and tidy. She offered him tea and a seat on the sofa. As he waited for the tea, he saw a half-opened door which seemed to be leading to a bedroom. He was slowly losing his composure and redoubled his efforts to remain business-like and civilized. He was aware that a woman had let a strange man off the street into her living room. Strange man, trusting woman. He was relieved when she returned so that he could start accumulating bonus points on the trust front: *Don't be afraid, I am only interested in your ironing board*, he thought.

After an hour's easy conversation with Marie, the statement

was no longer true; but the age difference, life's events and the customary ravages of time kept any unmentionable ideas he might have seem futile and ludicrous.

Marie's story related a fairly trouble-free life in rural North Wales where she had trained as a nurse in nearby Mold; the painful body blows came in the form of her father's early death when she was six, and a disastrous early twenties' love affair. Her mother's recent diagnosis of Motor Neurone Disease rounded off the three horrific blips. The doctors doubted whether her mother would make Christmas. Marie seemed calm, without a trace of self-pity, but she also looked tender and vulnerable.

The mother lived upstairs, carers attended her around the clock. Marie herself slept downstairs, in a narrow room on the far side of the kitchen. Nat offered her a truncated, matter-of-fact version of his own life, much like the one he had offered to Martina all those years ago in Café Kant. This time he decided to go for an even leaner option focussing, purely accidentally, on three blips of his own, all involving the loss of three women. He tried to finish on a high, with a slightly over-the-top, rambling laudation on finding his spiritual home in the hills of North Wales and the group of Welsh lads who shared his devotion to the cause of Liverpool Football Club.

Marie looked decidedly unconvinced but forced a smile. Nat wasn't sure whether he had hit the right spots and tried a new tack which he regretted the moment the words left his mouth.

'I miss the company of a good woman.' As a conversation stopper, it had few rivals.

Just when Nat thought he had blown everything, Marie gently blushed, coyly smiled and salvaged the situation by simply looking at him with a mixture of compassion and, he hoped, understanding. He just hoped it wasn't pity. Nat returned the smile and they both drifted into a semi-conscious world where words failed to express anything on peoples' minds. His awkward admission had at least established the true state of his affairs. Marie's state of affairs was as yet unclear to him; he hoped for something but wasn't quite sure what a man of his age could or should be hoping for from a woman considerably younger than him.

'Why don't we get out to the coast in my car sometime? The sea air will do you the world of good. You look a bit pale, if you don't mind me saying so.' Her Welsh twang sounded smooth and enticing.

No, I don't mind you saying so, he thought. *I don't mind you saying so, especially like that. And you're right.*

Nat had become dependent on a bunch of local lads to get him to Anfield every second week, and he was about to become similarly dependent on a local lass offering a regular supply of sea air and her company to boot. He wasn't worried and felt no fear, only endless trust in good people who had emerged to help him through his twilight years. They had emerged from the undergrowth of the River Dee or out of the clouded Welsh skies at just the right time and the only words that came to mind were, 'Thank you.'

'Yes, I fancy that.' He tried not to sound too over-enthusiastic.

A change of carer shift was about to take place and Marie would have to let the next one out and the next one in. It was time for Nat to go. He slid the ironing board under his arm, wanted to plant a kiss on Marie's cheek, thought better of it, and sauntered out of her front door, successfully manoeuvring the ironing board past the potted plants. He turned round when he reached the bottom of the path and she stood there waving. He clumsily raised his left arm and waved back as best he could, fearing he would drop his new possession. The renewed spring in his step as he reached his garden path had appeared from somewhere and he believed it was taking him somewhere new.

29

The trips to the coast started a few days after the ironing board transaction. Marie always brought a large flask of tea with accompanying sandwiches. Nat supplied the salt and vinegar crisps and was allowed to choose the destinations, ranging from his childhood favourites, Prestatyn, twee, pretty and unpretentious; Rhyl, garish, noisy and rough, then onto historical sites further along the coast like Conway and Carnarvon where they would scamper across the ruins of Edward's castles like excitable kids. Sometimes they were forced to sit in the car as the rain pelted down. She always parked the car facing the sea; sometimes the rain stole the view.

Every dry moment of their coastal afternoons was spent walking on the beach. On a particularly hot day in June, Marie dropped her rucksack on the sand in front of Nat, stripped off down to a jet-black bikini, muttered something in Welsh and headed to the sea where she picked up speed and dived in, reappearing twenty minutes later. Nat's eyes never left her for the duration and continued as Marie dried herself off with a huge bath towel she had dragged out of her rucksack. The black of the bikini had made him a contented prisoner. Yes, the black did it. But he couldn't remember why. She spread the towel out below her, leaving Nat enough space to lie down too if he so wished.

He so wished, got down on his back as elegantly as a man of his age could and stared rigidly into the blue sky, desperately hoping that Marie would do the same. He knew what she was going to say next and she did.

'Penny for your thoughts, Nat.'

'Nice bikini.'

She giggled, moved closer and kissed him softly on the right cheek. They had kissed many times before on purely friendly terms when saying hello and goodbye, but the significant presence of a tongue briefly but tantalisingly darting across a generous section of his cheek transmitted a new, invigorating message.

As he lay there, transfixed, the only words shooting through his head was the Hendrix line: *Excuse me, while I kiss the sky*.

But he knew Marie was lying next to him on a beach in Llandudno and he was defenceless as she slammed the door of his cage and locked him in. As one wise man once said, "Sooner or later, sex makes a fool of all of us." Nat just hadn't been sure that it was going to happen so late in life.

In a desperate attempt to appear in control and to prevent further descent into emotional self-destruct, he asked what she had said in Welsh before she took her dip.

'Something like, "well, here goes",' she replied.

Here goes. Exactly, here goes.

They lay there silent for about ten minutes, saying nothing, the sun drying Marie and exacerbating Nat's mental and emotional hurdy-gurdy. He carefully moved his hand towards hers and squeezed it gently; they remained thus until the sun disappeared behind the clouds. It never reappeared that day. Marie stood up, dried herself off one final time and slipped her clothes back on. No words were spoken and they left the beach hand in hand. Something had changed and they didn't want to ruin it with the paucity of words. The conversation during the half-hour drive along the coast road gently related the beauty of the day and little else. Everything was left strictly unresolved, lest the spell be broken.

A good night kiss of new intensity at the garden gate was all that followed and the wondrous day was over. Their meetings continued almost daily in the early summer days that followed except when particularly stubborn and endless downpours kept them housebound. On the sunny days, their closeness increased naturally and gradually as they explored new coves and sheltered bays, snatching longer kisses when they thought nobody else was in sight.

The innocent goodnight kiss at the garden gate routine continued, but Nat was in no real hurry to upgrade it to a higher level of erotica. He assumed that the upgrade would one day take place, but was anxious about the consequences of such a development and in no hurry to break the spell of innocent, tender affection. He was even more anxious about the age difference. In the year of Marie's birth, Nat had made more wrong turnings in life than a drunk driver. He had had good times, too, but he was plagued by the distinct feeling of underachievement, and bad decision- making, brought on either by a lack of maturity and knowledge (innocent, M'lud) and a surfeit of irresponsibility and recklessness (guilty, M'lud). Since he had started his ill-conceived "three-years-in-three countries" experiment he had at least achieved some degree of self-enlightenment, which was rounded off by the purple patch with Martina, cut short by cruel fate. The exodus to Wales and the return to his hometown and football fanaticism did not seem like a bad deal at his stage of life. And now Marie at the garden gate.

30

Saturday had come around again and Paul had bad news that he had to share with Mr Wilson: today's trip to Anfield by car was off. Both drivers were out of action, one with a debilitating dose of the flu, the other on an emergency call out for his company. They were stranded. It was only eight o'clock and if Mr Wilson could somehow get to Chester by nine-thirty, and catch the connecting train at nine forty-five he could be there comfortably for the early kick-off at twelve-thirty against Spurs.

Mr Wilson seemed to be quite friendly with Marie. Maybe she could take him in her car; a taxi would be expensive, but another possibility. Getting back would be less of a problem, as Rhys could pick him up from Chester after the game as long as his emergency call-out didn't last the whole day.

Paul just hoped that Mr Wilson was up; he would hate to have to drag him out of bed but Paul was sure that he would forgive him this inconvenience. He felt equally sure that he would never forgive him for a home match missed. He rang the bell. Nothing. The second time, nothing. After the third buzz, he heard movement. Then he heard a singularly unearthly scream and his blood turned cold. It was the scream of a woman. That same woman, a woman he knew, but difficult to recognize in her naked and bedraggled state, tore open the door and continued the scream at the same volume in the form of a simple instruction:

'Get an ambulance! Fast!'

The ambulance wasn't fast enough. Nat Wilson was declared dead on arrival at Mold Community Hospital at 8.54 a.m. Cause of death: a massive heart attack. He was sixty-four.

Liverpool suffered an early season setback with a 2-0 home defeat against Spurs later that afternoon. The Liverpool Echo noted in their report of the same evening: 'The Reds seemed oddly out of sorts and there was a dreary feeling hanging in the air suggesting that they were never going to score a goal in this match, let alone win it.'

Looking East, heading West

It was her beloved walk, her only walk. The one she took with almost religious fanaticism. It covered the sole stretch of Wales' North Eastern coast. She parked her tiny Korean car in the last Welsh enclave squeezed into the South-Western corner of the Wirral and then followed the River Dee northwards. On the other side of the river was the western coast of the Wirral Peninsular. At the beginning of her walk, the Dee was a short stretch of water, little more than a mile across. As she progressed north, the expanse of water separating the two countries widened until it became increasingly difficult to make out anything on the English side of the river other than the odd church steeple.

In summer, Anne wore flowing dresses and sandals, her body invigorated and refreshed by the stiff breezes rolling off the river. On unusually hot days, she wore a black bikini underneath; there was little chance of the male gaze on most stretches of the route if she did decide to shed her dress for a few minutes along the way. As the year moved into the final quarter, she simply added more layers and donned sturdier footwear. The changing light of the seasons, the intermittent rain and wind and the constant fresh sea air were her lifeblood on these sojourns; she wasn't quite sure why she ever started them but she knew that she could never stop.

As the nights drew in, she started her walks progressively earlier, ensuring that she was back at her car by dusk. In December and January, for example, she started her outward journey by twelve-thirty at the latest. She generally gave herself just over three hours for the whole operation. She took a twenty-minute break for a sarnie and tea after about ninety minutes, hugged a tree and then headed south. On one particularly long walk in June, she spotted the Irish Sea in the middle distance: she had been trudging north for over three hours. She had no fear of getting lost, as the coast never left her side. And she would always survive thanks to the food and drink supplies in her rucksack. The walk was the sacred part of all her weeks, representing beautiful routine.

Anne had just turned twenty and was a fully trained nurse working in a hospital in nearby Mold. She lived in a house left to her by her mother who had died six years previously after a short illness. She was an only child. The strong village community protected Anne and she wanted for nothing, social services having not much more than a perfunctory presence in the crucial years between fourteen and eighteen. The locals were simply always there. She also had inherently strong survival mechanisms, developed skills to keep body and soul together and pulled through with an admirable display of independence and fortitude. But she also knew that without the people of the village, things would have been far more precarious.

Her gaze was invariably to her right as she marched north-wards up the coast. She was Welsh and she felt strangely comforted by the river separating her from the English. Still, she felt drawn towards the green pleasantness stretching out over the water. Her father had been English, a man who had died before he or even her mother even knew of Anne's existence. He was from Liverpool – the city beyond the river on the eastern side of the Wirral. Anne had never been taken there by her mother or encouraged to explore anything beyond the confines of that corner of Wales.

As puberty took hold, a couple of years before her mother's demise, she started to ask questions about her father. Her mother kept short shrift, mildly evasive, without being out and out dismissive.

'The books he read and wrote and the music he loved are all in the attic if you want to have a look sometime. And there are two cases of photo albums and football and music souvenirs in the corner. I had a good look at the photos a few years ago. From his childhood to his Berlin days, where he lived before he moved here. There are hundreds of pictures of people and places I don't know, but I couldn't bring myself to throw them away. I hardly recognised him in most of them. I'm just sad that I have no photos of him here in Wales. His football mates might have one of him, though. Ask Paul. If anybody knows, he will.

'We had a short love affair. He was a good man. And then suddenly he was gone.' Her mother neatly summed up their short time together without too much emotion but her face could never fully hide the painful sadness. On the only occasion she ever saw her mother have too much to drink, she believed she heard her mumble the words, 'He died in my arms.' But she wasn't sure. She always hoped that she hadn't heard it.

Anne had never touched her father's cases but knew she would have to one day. She wanted to see if she had any resemblance with him: curiosity had grown as she grew. She thought today might be the day. But recognizing her father in the photos would be pure guesswork; her mother had never shown her one single photo. It would probably make sense to see whether Paul had something first; at least she would then have something to work on.

She rarely got much out of her mother on the subject of her father. Before she died, she gave Anne a bank account number with an address scrawled next to it and told her to visit a notary public at that address as soon as she turned eighteen. She did and become financially comfortable overnight. She knew it was largely her father's money. She had noticed, however, that if she ever needed to cover any educational costs, money had always been available. She realized that she knew little and knew that she had to begin the odyssey to find out who she was, where she was going and how she was ever going to get to wherever she wanted to go.

A gull screeched as it soared over her head, zooming east. As she dared to edge ever closer to the coast, braving the early autumn breeze, she momentarily shivered and felt something like a bolt travelling up her spine. A word she had never before uttered eased out of her lips: Dad. Soft tears welled up in her eyes as she looked east. Somebody, somewhere, was looking west and she didn't feel so alone. Somebody, somewhere, east or west was taking care of business and, for the time being, she was pinning all her hopes on that remaining the case. That had been the case for the past twenty years and she would keep the faith, with or without a mum and dad. She thanked God for short love affairs and long walks: routine matters.

THE END